# REBORN

## CAPTAIN DARING, BOOK THREE

## BLAZE WARD

**Reborn**
**Captain Daring Book 3**
Blaze Ward
Copyright © 2022 Blaze Ward
All rights reserved
Published by Knotted Road Press
www.KnottedRoadPress.com

ISBN: 978-1-64470-294-9

Cover art:
ID 532907938 © prometeus DepositPhotos.com

Cover and interior design copyright © 2022 Knotted Road Press

**Reviews**
It's true. Reviews help. Even a short one, such as, "Loved it!" So please consider reviewing this book (and all of the ones you've read) on your favorite retailer site.

**Never miss a release!**
If you'd like to be notified of new releases, sign up for my newsletter.

http://www.blazeward.com/newsletter/

**Buy More!**
Did you know that you can buy directly from my website?

https://www.blazeward.com/shop/

# ALSO BY BLAZE WARD

**Captain Daring**

*Revoked*

*Returned*

*Reborn*

**Hunter Bureau**

*Mirrors*

*Latency*

*Pleasure Model*

*Inhuman*

**First Centurion Kosnett**

*Encounter at Vilahana*

*Consensus at Aditi*

*Hegemony at Dalou*

*Princes at Ewin*

*Empire at Gloran*

*Domain at Yaumgan*

**The Jessica Keller Chronicles**

*Auberon*

*Queen of the Pirates*

*Last of the Immortals*

*Goddess of War*

*Flight of the Blackbird*

*The Red Admiral*

*St. Legier*

*Winterhome*

*Petron*

**CS-405**

*Queen Anne's Revenge*

*Packmule*

*Persephone*

**Additional Alexandria Station Stories**

*The Story Road*

*Siren*

*Two Bottles of Wine With A War God*

**The Science Officer Series Season One**

*The Science Officer*

*The Mind Field*

*The Gilded Cage*

*The Pleasure Dome*

*The Doomsday Vault*

*The Last Flagship*

*The Hammerfield Gambit*

*The Hammerfield Payoff*

*The Bryce Connection*

**The Science Officer Series Season Two**

*Alien Seas*

*Buried Among the Stars*

*Captain Navarre*

**The Lazarus Alliance**

*Escape*

*Return*

*Rebellion*

*Revolution*

*Liberation*

*Retribution*

*Alliance*

**Shadow of the Dominion**

*Longshot Hypothesis*

*Hard Bargain*

*Outermost*

*Dominion-427*

*Phoenix*

*Princess Rualoh*

**The Handsome Rob Gigs**

*Can't Shoot Straight Gang*

*Can't Shoot Straight Gang Returns*

*Hunting Handsome Rob*

*Handsome Rob, Assassin*

# CHAPTER 1

Joie Dearing studied her image in the mirror. It was the middle of the night, but she hadn't really been able to sleep. Or get back under after waking from her first sleep.

Too wound up. Too something.

She hadn't undergone her first surgery, so she still represented a cybernetic Human. One arm, one eye, one ear replaced after that truck bomb in Egypt. Bullet-proof cloth under the skin of her torso. Argenite alloy reinforcing a lot of her bones.

She wasn't all that worried about Yormevs and his alien Heecha scientists being able to take her apart and put her back together. They'd been planning for something along those lines for more than a year, but hadn't found the person they'd wanted to do it on until she came along.

She would be whole again. Human, at least briefly. All the electronic and metal parts would be removed. Organic parts quick-grown to replace them.

And then the fun began. Or whatever you wanted to call it.

Her foe was a US Army General who had taken all the genetic engineering research Technology Research Command had done and upgraded himself and at least a handful of others into what Joie had just started calling Advanced Model Humans. AMH, because the military was all about the three-letter acronym for things. The TLA, as it were.

Not fertile, so not a new species.

Not yet.

That was coming, but the Heecha had made it clear that the other aliens, the Danorak, had meddled too much in a world that was supposed to be off limits. Before Humans became a serious threat to the rest of the galaxy, somebody would drop a Carrington Event on the Earth.

Blow up every satellite in orbit at once. Collapse the power grids worldwide. Disrupt and poison every computer network in existence, because they'd already penetrated all of them to see what the dangerous monkeys on Earth were up to.

Was she enough to stop that? Even with her friends, there were less than a dozen of them. Against the full might of a US Government that might not be certain what TRC was up to, but had certainly supported wars everywhere. Troops everywhere. Assassinations and revolutions everywhere.

Hegemonic power gone bad. Rank and sour. Willing to tear the rest of the world down rather than allow others to have an opinion that challenged the grim Yankee way of thinking.

Multiplied now by angry aliens bringing their own conflicts and issues down here to Earth.

Joie took a deep breath and turned on the light. She had slept in panties and a T-shirt, with the temperature in her cabin set just right.

Texican skin. It had been Mexico before the white slaver colonists arrived in the early nineteenth century. After 1848, it became the United States, but the southwestern corner of the US had a lot of people living there already who weren't white as the Eastern Seaboard would later classify things in law.

Long black hair, straight to her shoulder blades and usually kept in a pony tail or a braid, since she had two hands now to do that. Dark eyes. Dark skin. Tall at one hundred and eighty centimeters. Impossibly heavy today because of the Argenite alloy. Athletic and muscular, but nobody would ever guess she weighed ninety-two kilograms most days.

That would go away, but she'd have the muscles built up. Better, her fucking fake boobs would go away and she'd be back to what she'd been when she'd just been a soldier. Before some—male—idiot in command had decided that the best way to make her an agent involved inserting a couple of half-grapefruits.

Not that she had strong opinions on the topic or anything.

She'd missed being Human, but they had turned her into Captain Daring and sent her out again and again to save the world. Their idea of the world. Which involved killing a lot of people because she'd been ordered to.

Joie would have to explain that eventually and hope that there really was a loving and forgiving God out there somewhere.

Then again, maybe they all deserved to be in hell.

Joie flexed her hands into fists in the dimness of her room then released them. That helped a little, but not much. Maybe what she needed was just to go do forms for a while. She'd stayed extremely late in the dojo with Sifu Wĕn—Teacher Wĕn—more than once, even sleeping on the couch.

She got up. Found baggy pants and put them on, skipping socks and shoes as she made her way out the hatch and into the rest of the Heecha ship. And it was a ship.

Starship. Traveling in space in ways she hadn't asked and they hadn't volunteered.

Joie already knew too much. If she was successful, she would be accepting voluntary exile from Earth for the rest of her life, so that nobody could ever figure out what had happened.

Or how to replicate everything.

She just had to find everybody who knew the truth first, and remove them as well. Technically, instead of metaphorically.

Exiled to the stars. All of them together.

The hallways always felt wrong, but the Heecha were taller and thinner than Humans in their real form, though they could easily disguise themselves enough to walk in Seattle or Manhattan. The hallways made her unconscious mind slightly queasy.

At least they were empty, because this wing of the ship had been designated for only Humans and a few Heecha who were helping her in her new mission.

Joie walked to a particular hatch and let it slide open in front of her. She wasn't surprised to find Sifu Wěn lotus in the middle of the dojo floor.

Nobody really knew the truth about the Sifu. Only that a lot of former soldiers had trained with the fifty-something woman and all swore that she was the deadliest person any of them had ever met. Considering what most of them had, as a rule, done in their military careers, that was high praise.

And a little frightening.

Sifu grinned as Joie stepped to the edge of the mat.

Joie folded herself into a similar lotus and focused on her breathing.

"I have given much thought to the nature of change," Sifu Wěn said abruptly, before Joie even spoke. "About the compression of learning in times of great stress."

Joie nodded, silent.

"You came to me as broken in spirit as in mind," Sifu continued. "I had thought at the time to create a form called Wounded Crane, but that would never do because that would have suggested that you were lesser than others. Instead, you were merely as good as any I had ever trained. That was before you got better."

"Better?" Joie asked, unable to contain the word.

"I have seen Carter Faulkener move," Sifu Wěn nodded. "Interviewed the man earlier today to understand how you beat him the first time. You came to me broken by Taylor Kehoe, though he was only following orders he now questions. Still, his sin was great and his penance ongoing."

Joie caught her breath at the harsh vehemence in Sifu's tones now.

"You could beat Faulkener today, Joie Daring," the woman said. "So I have been giving thought to your new foes. The ones you mark as Advanced models. Asked myself how I would build such a thing, were it in my power."

Joie's eyes sparkled. Nobody knew all the various martial arts Sifu had studied, but there were hints that it might encompass every one practiced today. There were only so many ways to move. Each martial form simply assembled them in different orders and gave them different names, but all came from a single source called Humanity.

General Bouchard might not be Human anymore.

"Have you reconsidered?" Joie asked hopefully.

Sifu had been offered the same sort of upgrade that Joie was going to undertake, and declined, claiming that she was an old woman, set in her ways, despite the fact that both Carter Faulkener and Ernesta Hernandez were in their fifties and sixties. For now.

All three of them would be reverted to somewhere close to twenty-five when it was done. Peak Human performance, upgraded to face Bouchard and his troopers.

"I have given it much thought, but I suspect that your foes will fall into certain traps of behavior that are not readily evident until they face someone prepared to offset and neutralize them," Sifu said in much more serious tone.

Joie blinked. Sifu thought she was Bouchard's physical equal on the dojo floor?

"How?" Joie asked.

"I am an old woman, Joie," Sifu grinned. "I don't have time to deal with young punks hyped up on their battling power. Or whatever silly shit they call it. If you cannot hit me, you cannot hurt me, so I must endeavor to not be in the way of your fist or foot. And then throw you into a post or in front of a bus driving by."

Joie's mouth had fallen open. She managed to close it before any flies took up residence, but it was probably a near thing.

"I will need to see how good you are when you are upgraded," Sifu nodded. "Then we will know if I can still compete with your foes, or if it will become necessary for me to join you in exile."

"Just like that?" Joie asked.

"I've seen more of this planet than almost anybody, Joie," Sifu replied, deadly serious. "Those fuckers don't get to mess up every-thing. Destroy everything. Not if I can stop them. Now, what do *you* need?"

Joie rose and considered her needs. She'd walked in here prepared to do forms for an hour or more until she got tired again. Or relaxed enough to actually sleep.

That was unnecessary now. Instead, she rose and bowed at the waist in deep respect for all the things Sifu Wěn had given her.

"I needed to remember that I had friends," Joie said simply.

# CHAPTER 2

Valmy Youri Bouchard. General, United States Army. Commanding General, Technology Research Command.

That title, that responsibility, had allowed him to commandeer an aircraft out of Washington, DC, and fly it halfway across the planet with a small team of operatives who knew most of the truth about himself and his plans.

Most.

Nobody but him knew all of it, but the volunteers he had assembled had all passed every possible test of loyalty he had been able to devise and refine over the years.

Now, he was standing in a hotel room in Hanoi. The premises would have been sealed off, had that been necessary, but he'd already seen everything he needed to see. And told the Vietnamese government more than they needed to know, but not enough to compromise his team.

Either the team on the ground already or the one he'd brought with him.

It had been enough to show the Russian and Chinese representatives the decapitated head of Carter Faulkener in a bucket of ice to convince them. That had ratcheted down tensions tremendously over the last few days.

Even the Russians were willing to behave if you killed someone they wanted dead. They didn't get to keep the head. Even dead, *Mithras* had too many secrets he could give up. It had been packed on dry ice and sent back to the States for analysis.

But Valmy had a bigger problem. One that would get out eventually, no matter what bribes and threats he offered to everyone involved. So he was in a room that had belonged to Kehoe. The door frame had been damaged when Garrison Konicek had kicked the door in after nobody could find Kehoe. Or Sergeant Stone. Or Daring and her old boyfriend Graydon.

Gone. Poof, like some magic trick.

Worse, Konicek and Chelsea Vanlaere had been left behind by whatever had happened. And something had happened, because Kehoe's room had been locked and chained from the inside, even with him gone.

Valmy sat on an uncomfortable queen-sized bed and listened as Konicek completed his briefing.

Nothing had changed in the twelve hours that Valmy had been in flight. Or the hour drive to the hotel.

Valmy got up and paced. Konicek and Vanlaere both moved out of his way, the former moving to the bed and the latter putting her butt against a wall.

There was a desk. It still had a computer bag next to it, with a charger in the pocket and other detritus of life on the road. Things Kehoe would have taken with him, given a choice in the matter. Similarly, Stone or someone had left an unfired semi-automatic pistol in the room safe.

Suitcases were here and in rooms belonging to the four that had disappeared, along with all their clothes save what they had been wearing. Phones left behind in two cases, but not four.

Taken out of their beds? Bed. Graydon's room had shown no sign of sleeping, while Daring's had two bodies worth of mussiness.

Valmy turned at the end of a pace and considered.

"Gather up everything," he ordered. "Even stuff that maybe

belongs to the hotel. We'll pay a fine. Whatever. No evidence left behind."

"Sir?" Konicek blurted.

"This room, this hotel," he said. "Too exposed. Too compromised. We will evacuate the premises and get to the airport as soon as possible."

"What if they come back, sir?" Vanlaere asked.

"It's been days, Lieutenant." he turned to her. "They won't be. Whoever took them means business. We need to get back to where we have access to our own team and resources. And quickly."

"I thought the Russians were mollified, sir," Konicek spoke up. "They've seen Faulkener's head."

"And by now they know that the team responsible for it has vanished without a trace," he replied. "That will make them nervous, but for other reasons."

"Because we don't know, General?" Vanlaere asked.

"Oh, I have a few ideas," he smiled. "But this is not the place to brief you about what's really going on."

"We have other enemies we don't know about?"

"*You* don't know about, Vanlaere," he corrected her. "Time to fix that."

# CHAPTER 3

Ernesta studied herself in the mirror. Sixty-one years old. Gray hair. Crow's feet and laugh lines. Dressed in comfortable jeans and a loose sweater because they kept it too cold on this ship.

Medium height. Medium build. Just right to disappear into a crowd when she'd been younger and doing things that the Mexican government had frowned upon.

Well, officially. For a few bribes, the right men had generally turned a blind eye, leaving her mostly to deal with the foolish Americans and their ignorant arrogance about culture and their prudish demands that the rest of the world believe the same things they did.

She was older now. A grandmother many times over, with one son who was a doctor and a second who was one of her Regional Managers in the family business. At least for now.

Ernesta Hernandez might never return to Guadalajara. Nor to the life of luxurious crime she had known. Folks would have to step up and handle things, but she'd been training everyone for this day for years, even before she knew it was coming.

And it was coming.

Tomorrow, a stranger would greet her in the mirror. A younger woman. One looking enough like Joie Daring to pass as a sister, or at least a cousin. To be twenty-five again? Even without being able to have any more children, what could she do, knowing everything she did now?

Except that it would be somewhere else. A new adventure, quite literally on another planet, if the stories from Yormevs were even remotely true.

What would it be like, leaving Earth for good? More interesting, what would Mitch say? He'd been looking at her with eyes normally reserved for Joie, but those two seemed to have moved beyond having been lovers and turning into old friends.

Did Ernesta want a much younger lover, even as he would suddenly be the older?

Decisions, decisions. At the same time, Joie needed her. Needed Ernesta's mind. Her experience. Her sneakiness.

Because while Joie had spent more than fifteen years in the US Army, Ernesta had spent more than fifty dancing dangerous games with them. And winning. Even Carter couldn't say that, though he'd been a terrorist renegade off and on for twenty-some years.

What would Ernesta do with another fifty years of living?

What could she do?

That question was even more interesting than the thought of being young and having a hardbody again, like she'd done in the era of crop-tops and hiphuggers.

A knock at the door and she turned away from the old woman who'd greeted her this morning. Answering it, she found Yormevs, standing next to Joie. Ernesta hugged both of them.

Joie needed it and Yormevs wasn't fast enough to elude her. Apparently, Heecha didn't hug.

Foolish. She'd have to cure them of that as well.

"You ready?" Joie asked.

Ernesta couldn't help the little giggle that escaped her mouth. The excitement of it all.

"Still think you should go first," Ernesta replied. "We're here because of you."

"You'll be easiest to do," Joie countered. "Just reset you forty years. Carter and I have parts that have to be calculated and replaced first."

Ernesta turned to the tall alien man.

"So will Carter still live for the centuries that the original treatments promised?" she asked. "Or does that get reverted as well?"

The man had thin lips. He looked Siberian or somewhere North Central Asian to her. Maybe Mongolian. Sharp, wide eyes in a green so dark as to be almost black. Black hair, thick and wavy, brushed back and maybe held in place with some product that didn't give it a greasy look.

Almost down to his shoulders in length, like he was a painter or something. Not a single gray hair, but the face promised you that he was in his fifties. And the black seemed natural, fading through a variety of browns and bronzes, rather than that uniform soot color guys normally got with dye.

Dressed in slacks and a tunic that buttoned up the left side, like a Belgian chef or a 1930s pulp hero adventurer. Everything was brown. Not milk chocolate, but brighter than the really good 90% stuff. Bronze, if you could do that in cloth. Assuming it was cloth.

Yormevs's face went through several emotions as she watched, before settling in a place she figured was ambiguous.

"We cannot be sure until we commit the act," he finally said. "Those Danorak fools might have made him immortal accidentally. Or the Humans he was working for. Doubtful, considering the primitive state of their genetic engineering, but stranger things have happened."

Ernesta nodded. Not that she'd want to live forever. At least alone. Outliving all of her friends would suck. At the same time, it might come down to her, Joie, and Carter, if the rest lived normal lifetimes and died.

"What are you up to?" Joie asked.

"Thinking about immortality," Ernesta answered.

Joie grabbed her arm and linked elbows before she could continue, dragging her into the hallway and towards the medical lab where it would all happen shortly.

"And?" Joie asked.

"How many Humans leave Earth forever if we are successful?" Ernesta asked. "A score? Maybe two?"

"That depends on Bouchard and his people," Joie turned serious.

"They might be so wedded to evil that they don't end up surviving long enough to ask that question."

"We just kill them all?" Ernesta gasped. "Where's the Joie I know?"

"Worried about the other eight billion folks at risk if this goes wrong and Yormevs's people decide to crash Earth hard."

Joie nodded to the tall alien who was following them silently. Ernesta caught the man's nod.

They were playing for extremely high stakes today. Like, all Human civilization being wiped out.

"And you can't just kidnap them all with your beam thing?" Ernesta asked.

Joie wasn't that much into science fiction, but Ernesta was. Had read all the weird shit in the library as a kid, then moved on to clear out every used bookstore she could find, tearing apart the ancient classics and the modern schlock. Still did when she had time.

"We do not know everyone who has the knowledge of the transformation," he replied.

Same answer as before, but she'd held out hope.

"And not everything will be written down in a computer system that you have already penetrated," Ernesta nodded. "Thus, you need Human agents who can walk around the surface easily."

"And understand Humans, Ernesta," he replied. "Your kind are utterly insane by our standards, which is why you were supposed to be left alone for several more centuries. The hope was that you would grow up."

She laughed. Couldn't help it. Humans might, but that would be measured in centuries. Meanwhile, Bandi and his friends had been force-feeding alien technology, driving Humans to levels far beyond where they were supposed to be.

"So what was that about immortality?" Joie asked, circling all the way back.

"If you and I are going to outlive everyone except Carter, is it worth it?" Ernesta turned to her newly-adopted sister.

"Should we ask Mitch if he wants the treatment?" Joie asked saucily. "Is that what you're about?"

"Carter would need someone, too," Ernesta countered. "Maybe this Amy person you've talked about."

"She has a thing for lumberjacks with beards," Joie laughed. "Blond and muscles just makes it worse."

"He's not a bad-looking dude, Joie," Ernesta allowed. "Just a nutcase terrorist who turns into a complete goofball when he relaxes. Any good in bed?"

"Never asked, never found out," Joie replied. "Too busy killing him twice. Even if he survived both. But maybe Amy would be interested, once we sort everything else out. Gotta survive and save the world first."

Ernesta wanted to say something sarcastic and salty, but they had arrived.

Joie turned and took her into a medical laboratory.

Big, coffin-like device in the middle of the large room. Several Heecha standing around, without the makeup and things Yormevs did to look more Human. The skin was too green for pink Humans. The eyes too big.

"Strip," Joie ordered, when Ernesta just froze, struck dumb and numb.

Automatically, Ernesta pulled her sweater over her head, then quickly stood there nude. Not naked. Merely unclothed.

None of the aliens looked at her like a naked woman. Just a farm animal going to the vet, maybe.

Joie held her hand and they approached the device.

"You'll be fine," Joie murmured in her ear after a quick kiss on her cheek.

They opened the coffin and one of the aliens gestured her inside.

The metal was cold on her bottom and back. There were lights on inside, which was good as the top closed.

Otherwise, it might be a foretaste of hell.

# CHAPTER 4

Valmy would have liked to keep certain secrets until the current generation of politicians was all dead and gone, but someone had forced his hand. Didn't know who, but the *what* had always been in the back of his head.

Konicek and Vanlaere had rounded up everything. Cleaned every room down to the point of stealing the sheets and the towels. He had a budget for shit like this. This time didn't even involve buckets of blood first.

Everyone else was on a second aircraft, a transport hauling detritus of the mission. Faulkener's head was already halfway across the Pacific. He had Konicek and Vanlaere in the business jet he had brought.

Vietnam's coast was receding, had he wished to look out a window and see blue.

He turned to the others.

"Project Herakles," Valmy began, drawing eyes to him. "Carter Faulkener was the first so-called supersoldier. Genetic engineering plus Argenite alloy implants designed to make him the perfect weapon. Problem, they stood out. Stand out. Of the six that were initially created, only two remain active today. Three are now dead and one retired."

He watched the two soldiers with him.

Army Captain Garrison Konicek. Codename: *Hei-Di* after a Chinese myth. ABC. American Born Chinese, back several generations. A little tall and broad, but far stronger than he looked. Sharp and loyal.

Army Lieutenant Chelsea Vanlaere. Codename: *Coatlicue* after the Aztecs. Hispanic female with curves and muscles. Like Konicek, far stronger than she looked.

"Project Cybernaut," Valmy continued. "Joie Daring was the first with upgraded, combat-level cyberware. Plus exceptional natural ability. Many of those, because we have such a range of wounded warriors who gladly volunteer to return to duty if we can repair them. And we generally can, these days."

Both nodded when he paused. All known history. Deeply understood.

"Project Carpenter was something else," Valmy informed them. "On the books, we continue to produce our cybernauts for various missions. However, we have started creating new versions of Herakles soldiers. You two, plus several others. Not many, as yet, as we work out the final details of the genetic engineering. Stronger, faster, tougher. Improved to include a healing factor that is almost regenerative in nature. Bullet wounds that go straight through can be healed in minutes. Burns and fragmentation slower, but still faster than most people would believe possible."

Both nodded. All of this was part of the recruitment process, because the changes, while invisible, would be so radical that they had to assent. Operating body temperatures so high that a normal doctor would freak out. Utterly sterile right now, because Valmy had specifically ordered those parts cut out until he knew how everything would work.

The other Carpenter soldiers would live about twice as long as humans. Maybe two hundred years if they were lucky, but possibly only one hundred and fifty. Still, more.

Only Valmy was planning to live longer. If he had to adopt heirs in a few centuries, he had the time to find them and groom them.

None of the current crop would work. They were all soldiers. Not kings or queens.

"Now, the part of the story that does not leave this aircraft," Valmy finally got to the dangerous bits.

Konicek and Vanlaere both perked up. Leaned forward, eyes and beings focused on him.

"Human technology is not responsible for all this development," he said simply. "For much of the last two hundred years, there has been a certain group of aliens assisting us secretly. Driving the state of the art higher and higher, faster than we could have done it."

Both were absorbing, so he nodded and drew a breath.

"World War Two would have probably looked much like the first one," Valmy continued. "Primitive tanks and canvas aircraft. Men with rifles and gas masks against mustard gas and other poisons."

"But for aliens?" Vanlaere asked.

She was the sharper of the two. Konicek was fast and smart, but Vanlaere was still better.

Valmy nodded.

"The Russians captured our main alien after the war," he said. "That man worked for them until the Soviet Union collapsed in the 1990s, then he fled home, only returning in the 2050s to start again, this time with us, because the Russians and Chinese were declining powers."

"We have honest-to-God aliens working with Technology Research Command?" Konicek asked, a little shocked.

Valmy nodded. Again, Vanlaere was the smarter of the two, which was why he had assigned her to Daring's team on the inside.

"So what do you think happened to Daring and Kehoe?" Vanlaere asked now.

"Our alien has always said he was working secretly," Valmy replied. "That other aliens would not approve of his work, because we were not supposed to be so advanced and technologically sophisticated. If anything, we are today more than a century ahead of where the big aliens think we should be, and that's accelerating. Global computer networks and smart phones should be new things we're just starting to explore, rather than where we are."

"And they aren't paying attention?" Vanlaere asked in a disbelieving tone.

"We've been at pains to make it look like Human innovation, Lieutenant," he smiled. "They can't argue with us in that case."

"And Daring?"

"I have long expected that our pet alien has enemies that want to stop what he's doing," Valmy said. "They can't attack directly, because that would set off too many alarms, but I have a theory that someone located Daring and Kehoe when they took down Faulkener."

"Why did they ignore us, sir?" Konicek asked. "We were with that team when it disappeared."

"Kehoe and Stone would have been in the same room, and could be hit as a single target," Valmy said. "Same with Daring and Graydon. Hernandez was already dead at that point. You two are Project Carpenter, but whoever it was might not have understood how dangerous you are. I assume that they wanted Daring and Kehoe for what those two know. In that scenario, neither of you really have nearly as much value."

Both nodded. He didn't mention that the aliens might have known exactly how dangerous a Phase III supersoldier was, and chose to avoid that problem. Daring was good. Doubly so to have taken down Faulkener a second time, even if Hernandez died in the struggle. Daring had been wounded and possibly disabled, so she might have been easy to take, except that the rooms showed no signs of struggle.

"What about Romana Pham, General?" Vanlaere asked.

"What about her?"

"Daring and Hernandez were investigating Pham's disappearance when this Faulkener case intruded," Vanlaere said. "She disappeared in a similar manner, right out of one of our bases. No clues. No evidence. Just gone."

Valmy nodded. Then cursed.

He'd been so focused on destroying Faulkener for good this time that he'd overlooked that point.

Had those other aliens captured Pham at some stage? Were they going after all of his agents? Pham was still Human, because sometimes you need to send in someone that can pass any manner of scan without raising any mental or medical alarms.

But she'd vanished right out of a barracks, in the middle of the night.

Just like Daring and Kehoe.

How many enemies did Valmy have across the universe right now?

# CHAPTER 5

Taylor Kehoe felt a decade younger. Granted, he was only forty-three now, but the stress of the last year had worn on him harder than he'd realized. Unconsciously, had he been expecting General Bouchard to betray and then burn him for that long?

Apparently.

And now all that shit was gone, because he'd betrayed that son of a bitch Frog Bouchard first.

Taylor was in the mess hall this morning. Waiting. Graydon and Daring were in with the aliens who were working on Hernandez. Taylor was basically babysitting Faulkener, just for something to do.

"Do you really have to eat that much?" Taylor finally griped.

The man had a hubcap it seemed. Couple of kilos of meat, eggs, potatoes, gravy, cheese, and several biscuits. Apparently, the aliens understood takeout and had just dealt with Carter's metabolism that way. Some joint out of DC that took online orders, served breakfast all day, and didn't ask a lot of questions at pickup.

"Last meal for the condemned, don't you know," Faulkener replied around a mouthful of food.

"What are you going to do when they slow your body back down?" Taylor asked.

"Then I have to learn to eat like you people," Faulkener laughed and swigged some coffee.

The things they had done to make Carter Faulkener into *Mithras* had taken him from average to nearly two meters tall. Heavier than any football player still employed, but that was a combination of denser muscles and alloy-lined bones.

And they were going to make the man Human again. If they could. Assuming everything went well with Hernandez.

Joie Daring would be third, because Kehoe had put his foot down and told them that if they fucked up somewhere, Faulkener got to be the dead one. Even Faulkener hadn't argued too much on that one, but he was almost a new man since the aliens had captured him.

The other set of aliens, after the batch he'd met in La Plata, Argentina, back when all this started.

How many damned sets of aliens were there, anyway?

"What was that?" Faulkener asked. "You were muttering."

"Bandi didn't know what happened to Romana Pham," Taylor replied. "Nor do the Heecha around here."

"So who has her?" the man asked, putting his fork down and turning serious.

"Better question is how many sides this boardgame has, pal," Taylor said. "You've got the ones that want to upgrade Humans to build the perfect army to conquer the galaxy. You've got this group trying to help us to stop them. And Pham disappeared, maybe the same way you and Joie did. I feel like we're missing someone."

"Ask Cōng," Faulkener replied.

"Sifu Wěn?" Taylor asked. "Why her?"

"Dangerous woman," the giant nodded, diving back into his food. "Goes places a lot of folks, even men, wouldn't be welcome. Smarter than she looks. Looked her up once. That was why I went to the coffee shop to bother Joie. Didn't appreciate at the time that the store manager might be just as dangerous."

"Watanabe is one hundred and fifty-eight centimeters tall, Faulkener," Taylor snapped. "Weighs maybe fifty kilos. Soaking wet."

"And got right up into my face, or my chest anyway, and threatened to throw my ass out of her store if I misbehaved," he replied.

"And lemme tell you, at that moment I believed her. Rabid Chihuahua, that one. But go ask Sifu how she'd do it. The rest of us are all soldiers, and we're wrong, or we'd have figured it out by now."

Taylor hated it when that pretty boy lunkhead said smart things. Reminded you that he'd been the first person selected for Project Herakles, back about when Taylor was born.

Big, dumb, and blond, except when he wasn't.

And he was right.

Taylor stood up and surveyed the mountain of food still in front of Faulkener.

"You need a lifeguard for that?" Taylor asked.

"You haven't got the legs for it, Kehoe," the man replied around a whole half biscuit crammed into his pie hole.

Taylor laughed and set out to ask the newest member of his team what she thought.

His team?

Yeah, he supposed so. Joie's team, but she wanted him running it, like he'd always run her in the field. Mitch doing analysis. Joie, Carter, and Ernesta in the field.

That left Wěn Cōng Mǎ. Fifty-something. Cantonese by culture. American Born Chinese by accent.

Deadly enough that she made Carter Faulkener, one of the most notorious terrorists and assassins in the world, nervous.

What did she know, indeed?

# CHAPTER 6

Cōng sat in the new dojo she had consecrated, meditating on a lifetime of sins and silliness that had brought her thus. Friends who had once been merely students had asked her to take on a special case in the woman born Josefina Dearing.

The secret government superagent generally called *Captain Daring*.

Wounded Crane had been remade as Angry Elephant, because one flexible limb that did things from up close and central.

Except that Joie wasn't going to need it much longer. Assuming everything went well.

Cōng considered recording a whole series of videos and probably several books she would have to produce, just so this new form didn't fade away again later. Someone, somewhere, would need it.

One-armed people living in the modern age still couldn't usually afford a replacement arm so exceptional that it was a proper replacement. At least not for punching some yahoo in the gob.

Soon, though.

Until then, Angry Elephant.

The hatch to her space opened and Cōng slit one eye open to see who intruded this time. Joie was waiting on Ernesta, and that would take time for the recovery. The others tended to keep their distance, to the point that the aliens were more likely to come visit.

Except that none of them understood violence in a manner that the average Human took for granted. And Cōng was surrounded by above-average Humans on that score.

Kehoe.

*The Other Asshole,* to hear Joie describe him in the past, distinct from *That Tall Asshole* of Carter Faulkener.

Except that even a man like Kehoe had been able to admit he'd been wrong. To own it. To learn. To even throw himself wholeheartedly into undoing some of the evil that he'd unleashed on an innocent-enough world.

Cōng opened both her eyes and studied the man as he approached. Watched him step up to the line the aliens had painted for her. Nodded with pleasant surprise when he removed his shoes and bowed to her before stepping across that line.

Joie was limber enough to sit lotus. Kehoe knelt instead. The aliens had done something to the floor in here to soften it in falls. Better than steel, though you still had to know how to fall to avoid injury.

Kehoe was facing her square, but had moved off her own line to her right, like a student in the middle of the pack careful about his place in the hierarchy.

Cōng approved.

"What brings you?" she asked, letting her Southern California accent dominate the tones.

"I need someone smarter than me," the man said, utterly surprising her. "We are all soldiers, as Carter points out, and our training and logic has failed."

He was being polite. Admitting fault and seeking assistance to correct himself, like a good student.

Impressive.

Fucker might actually turn into a useful Human being one of these days.

Cōng let her face ask the question rather than speak. She'd always been told she had expressive eyebrows.

And her name—Cōng Mǎ—meant *Clever Horse.* Wěn meant *Steady.*

People who didn't raise horses never appreciated how sneaky they could be.

"The Danorak have been helping Technology Research Command for more than fifty years," Kehoe continued. "Secretly, on both fronts. The Heecha captured Joie and Carter, and then she brought the rest of us along."

He didn't have to say who *she* was. Joie was central to all equations here.

Kehoe fell silent and grimaced.

"What happened to Romana Pham?" he asked. "Or more specifically, who has her?"

Cōng nodded. She'd given much thought to that topic since Joie had approached her most recently.

And Kehoe was right that the others were soldiers. People used to charging at a problem, because that was what soldiers did.

Many of the arts Cōng had studied in her life were like that as well. Identify your enemy. Get up into his space and do excessive damage to him as quickly as possible.

Not all of them, however.

Sometimes, your best solution was to avoid the first punch then run away.

"Who does not have her?" Cōng asked, falling back on a retired philosophy professor she'd met in a park in Breckenridge, Colorado, about thirty years ago.

Bald and bearded. Had looked a lot like Socrates.

"We do not," Kehoe said, referring, she presumed, to the Heecha. "TRC does not."

"What other enemies do the Danorak have?" Cōng suggested.

"Potentially, the rest of galactic civilization," Kehoe said. "We do not know anything about them save that as a culture they have proscribed contact with Humanity for roughly four more centuries."

"And they will be greatly surprised when they come," Cōng laughed. "What did the former you plan to do with such an advanced army?"

He was good at lying with his eyes, but only when he wanted to do so. Right now, Kehoe was being honest, as a student of philosophical inquiry should be.

"We always figured that the Danorak intended to have an army of advanced Humans," Kehoe replied. "That they would wish to use us to conquer the galaxy for them."

"And how would that have worked out?" Cōng pressed, rather enjoying herself in the role of grouchy, old fart in the park.

"Badly, for them," Kehoe laughed harshly. Like a bag of glass being hit with a hammer. "Our contingency plans called for TRC operatives to capture their diplomats, steal their tech and their ships, and be able to dictate terms."

"Then I see two options, assuming that the Heecha wish to keep Humans both safe and contained as they had said," Cōng nodded sagely, wondering how she would look with a beard. "First, someone else wishes to abscond with the Danorak's army they were building."

"And second, Sifu?" he asked, even granting her the title of Teacher.

"Maybe they are collecting their own small army of expert warriors today, against whoever the Heecha have been arguing with over coming in and smashing everything."

"How so?" Kehoe asked, brow furrowed.

"Romana was still an unmodified Human, was she not?" Cōng asked him.

"Yes," Kehoe agreed.

"I would not want someone like Carter Faulkener," Cōng said. "Or even Joie Daring. Or those new models that you had more recently."

"Why not?"

"They are all the things that the aliens would see bad in Humans, Kehoe," Cōng noted. "Advanced, technological creatures. Romana, however, might be able to train more soldiers, while understanding all of the things that the rest of you have been up to. She was, according to Joie, exceptionally dangerous with nothing more than training."

"Indeed," he nodded. "Probably the best female agent I had in that category. Bouchard probably would have sought to recruit her for his other project, except that she was still too loyal to Joie and knew about everything we had done to that woman. So in a way, I suppose that saved her."

"And does not yet make Romana Pham your enemy, Taylor Kehoe," Cōng smiled. "Though I would suggest you let Joie or Mitch talk to her first."

She liked the little cringe that overcame him at that thought. Romana Pham would still think he was part of Bouchard's organization, especially if she'd been out of the loop for most of a year.

Kehoe fell silent.

"Can we win?" he asked.

"Humanity itself can survive a crash of the nature that the Heecha suggest," Cōng replied. "I've been in places where they would just shrug when all the electronic toys everyone had taken for granted failed one day. They would go back to the old ways."

"You're describing the more primitive parts of the planet," he pointed out.

Cōng nodded.

"Most of North America, Europe, and East Asia are fucked if we screw up," she said. "Joie thinks casualties north of five billion in the first year. I put it at seven billion after a decade, at which point it probably stabilizes, because folks will be able to mine dead cities for metal instead of having to dig it up. Most places would fall to high Iron Age tech and stay there for a generation or three. Carter and Bouchard would live that long. Would Bouchard be willing to live as warlord of the ruins?"

"He'd take Bandi's ship and a cadre of fanatics and probably turn pirate," Kehoe said. "Go capture alien scientists and steal as much of their tech as possible to bring it home to rebuild."

"If I was an enemy watching this, I might want my own Human armies to stop him," Cōng pointed out. "And maybe build my own space navy to enforce the sorts of blockade that obviously haven't been sufficient before now. Is that Romana Pham?"

"It might be, Sifu," he said. "Thank you."

She watched him rock back into a squat and stand, nodding deeply to her before he left the mat and grabbed his shoes.

Cōng considered all the paths open in front of her. Being young again might be interesting, if only because that gave her so much longer to travel around and learn things.

On the other hand, she might have to be turned into another one like Joie and Ernesta, if only to save the rest of the world from what might be coming.

# CHAPTER 7

Joie opened her eyes in darkness.

She had gone to sleep broken. Lying there in the shadows, she had awakened whole.

Light intruded rudely, causing her to squint. Pressure changed as the machine opened itself to spit her up, like a whale regurgitating a prophet.

Was she?

Joie didn't know.

Sifu Wěn was the philosopher. Joie had been content being a soldier, both before and after the tragedy that made her over into what she had been yesterday.

But today was new.

The lid retracted and she saw worried faces.

Mitch. Kehoe. Sifu Wěn. Carter in his newer, younger form.

Ernesta, looking like a younger sister Joie had never known.

Even the Heecha scientist, Yormevs Coeurle, was there. His smile was almost as good as the others. Almost as big.

Ernesta's strong hand reached out and helped Joie sit up.

Joie had caught it automatically in her right hand. Her new hand. The thing that Yormevs had grown for her in this box.

She had gone to sleep broken, and awakened whole.

Even her tits were smaller. Back like they'd been. Who she'd been.

Everyone here had seen her nude going in, so she had no self-consciousness that they saw her now.

The sides lowered and Joie turned, putting bare feet on the cool metal deck.

Ernesta surprised Joie by sitting next to her, hips touching and one arm around her shoulders.

Mitch handed her a bundle of clothes, but Joie left it in her lap for now, as her equilibrium was thrown off. Ernesta had been through this. Joie felt calm strength flowing from her.

Enough to face the whole world. And all the aliens.

As well as the assholes maneuvering for advantage in some grand war of conquest they all had planned.

Only she could stop it.

What idiot had put her in charge of saving the galaxy?

Kehoe, she supposed, but he'd been following orders when he'd burned her two years ago. Bouchard had been convinced that she'd done a deal with *Mithras* rather than killing the man.

Even a sexist pig like Bouchard had apparently not been able to wrap his head around the fact that Joie had simply been better.

And now…

She just had to be better than Bouchard.

And whoever else out there was doing things in the shadows.

"Ready?" Ernesta asked.

Joie nodded and dumped the clothing in the woman's lap, keeping a T-shirt and pulling it on. Even something so simple as not having to stretch and tug it over those stupid fake boobs was fantastic.

Ernesta rose, holding out a hand in case Joie fell over. Pants next.

Shower at some point, but after watching Ernesta and Carter come out of this machine, Joie knew that she wouldn't sleep again for twelve hours. She needed food soon, but not until her body got a chance to reset itself.

Lots of it, though that would taper off as her system got over the shock of new parts and integrated them. Even Carter was eating like a jock instead of a horse now.

She finally got herself upright and was staring at Kehoe from barely fifty centimeters away.

Kehoe.

That same asshole who had burned her. The same one who had started all this by knocking on her door with his cybernetic bodyguard sidekick.

They locked eyes, and Joie could see worry there. Concern for her. Not as a soldier, but as a friend.

As the woman who had been right, time and again, in spite of everything Kehoe had thought he knew about the universe.

How the fuck did she pull off this next trick?

"You can do this, Dearing," he said quietly.

Joie couldn't remember the last time he had called her by her real last name. Everybody shortened it to *Daring*.

Still, he was trying. Learning. Even Sifu had nice things to say about the man, weird as *that* was.

Ernesta linked arms with her and helped keep Joie steady as the mob headed down the corridor to the conference room. Alien doctors had already confirmed everything they wanted to know about her surgery, before they'd opened up that coffin.

Helped that they'd reset Ernesta to a younger model first. Then shrank Carter and removed the metal bits.

They'd grown her a new eye. And a new eardrum.

And a new arm. That worked.

She found herself unconsciously marveling at it as everyone got seated. She was whole again.

And more than whole.

That squint that let her activate the menu on her eye didn't work anymore, but she could see temperature gradients in the way things were bolder in her sight. No better way to describe what was basically a new sense nobody else had besides the three of them.

Mitch stood up and all eyes turned to him. Silence became entirely complete.

"I have had several days to meander through the complete database system that TRC maintains," he said as an appetizer. "As suspected, very few of the interesting bits have been written down.

One presumes that *need to know* goes well beyond the original meaning, and only a handful of people know the truth. And most of those are kept using air-gapped systems."

"We have not attempted to penetrate such facilities," Yormevs said next. "We are not Human enough to easily vanish, and any failure on our part would have alerted people to the threat. That is, in fact, why we felt that we needed Joie Daring and her friends. Even as weird as that request has turned."

He was smiling when he said that. Others laughed. Joie understood.

They had needed a trained warrior. To which they had added two defectors, a terrorist trying to redeem himself, a patterns analyst, a Mexican Crime Lord, and a Cantonese-American killer.

Truly, weird.

And yet, all of them friends. Even the former enemies.

Dangerous times require dangerous choices, and all of humanity hung in the balance to hear the Heecha talk.

"So I assume that our first mission will include surprise," Mitch continued. "And that all subsequent ones will not, because we will alert TRC to the fact that transporters actually work and folks can come and go without opening doors. Analysis suggests that removing your Danorak friends from the equation first brings the most benefit, because Bandi and the others have been mice in the cupboards for fifty years now, in addition to all the things they did for the Nazis and the Soviet Union in their time."

"It buys us time," Kehoe clarified. "TRC still has folks doing things. I've been compartmentalized to the point that I only know a fraction, but that fraction suggests that the loss of the aliens only slows our technological progress down. It does not stop us, let alone cause any manner of regression."

"It does give us the ability to control the gameboard," Joie said. "That was why I asked Mitch to investigate it. If we can take Bandi and the others into custody, we might be able to convince them to leave for good. They have a starship somewhere, but even the Heecha can't find it."

"One presumes that it has been put into a deep hibernation mode,"

Yormevs said. "We have looked, because without that, both Humans and Danorak are trapped until they can build a new one. And that cannot be done easily in secrecy."

"Do the Danorak have possession of it?" Sifu Wĕn asked. "Or has TRC taken possession of it like they did many of the other things?"

"We cannot know until we ask," Mitch said. "We cannot ask until we can contact them without TRC minders supervising the conversation. We cannot just grab them like Yormevs did with Carter and Joie the first time, because we do not know what sensors or defenses they have in place to prevent that. Honestly, I don't even know where they are, having abandoned their previous lab in La Plata."

"I do," Ernesta beamed. "After we visited, I invested in real estate in the vicinity. That let me tap into the network of folks who deal with such things, and ask innocent questions about people moving around. The locals were more than happy to talk, particularly when I hinted that I might buy more buildings."

Joie grinned as Mitch's face went blank. The man knew Ernesta Hernandez was smart. And a powerful figure. Joie didn't figure it had ever crossed his mind how much she was worth.

Lots. Much of it successfully laundered over the decades and available to invest in real estate.

"Still in La Plata?" Joie asked.

"Down about six blocks and over one," Ernesta nodded. "Still just inside the delivery zone of that one sushi place Carter liked so much, but facing onto the residential neighborhood instead, where you have far fewer tourists moving around. Makes surveillance easier. Makes our approach harder."

"Oh, but it doesn't," Joie laughed. "They'll never see us coming."

# CHAPTER 8

Bandi Algom, known to the Humans as Sal McKenzie, had first come to this silly planet in 1928 CE on the local calendar system. Just over one hundred and seventy-five local years ago, when Humans as a rule had lived for about sixty in those days and maybe eighty today.

But he kept a low profile in Argentina and nobody appreciated that he didn't age if he only kept secretaries around for a few years before replacing them.

He preferred not socializing. Not doing much with the locals, beyond using incredibly primitive tools and computer languages to create things so common off-planet. Much more of a challenge, and his bosses had used that as a lure initially.

These days, the crimes he had committed while being here would keep him in prison somewhere for the rest of his life.

Nobody had warned him about the costs. The Humans called it a Faustian bargain.

So he sat in his office, just off the main lab, and thought about that man Faust, as well as the scientist von Frankenstein. Both literary characters, but Humans understood who they were. The deals that they had made.

The evil they had wrought.

The costs that had only become apparent when it was too late.

At least he had Joie Daring on his conscience as well. One bit of good, for all the stupidity he had undertaken.

A knock at his door caused him to look up from the printout he had been ignoring.

"I've been standing here for two minutes, wondering if you'd died," Sora said coldly.

Bandi grimaced and waved her to the chair across the desk.

"Wool-gathering, as the locals call it," he responded, taking a moment to study the woman.

There were a lot of German immigrants and their descendants in Argentina. A few related to folks Bandi had known in the before time.

When he'd been working for the Nazis. Before the Soviets rounded him and others up and put them to work in camps and factories in Siberia.

Sora Ijynth. Known to Humans as Camilla. Hausfrau frumpy, to use the old German vernacular he had first learned to come to this hell-hole. Dirty blond that didn't stand out much. None of them did. You needed people who could be disguised to appear as intensely average around here.

Not that people pried. Lots of family secrets nobody wanted aired meant that people kept things at a politely distant social level, most of the time.

"Anything good?" Sora asked.

She and Hanni Cara—Franco, as they called him—had been with him for forty years now.

Those two still had the fire of true belief, but Bandi had questions. Doubts.

"Trying to figure out what the next step is," he told her.

"Still arguing with yourself over Daring's belief that the Americans are making more genetic supersoldiers?" Sora asked.

"Cybernetics is reaching a plateau where it should be so common that everyone can replace or upgrade parts in another decade," Bandi replied. "Then what?"

"What do you mean?"

"They're Humans, Sora," he said sourly. "Tribalistic at the best of times. Technology Research Command has spent decades looking for ways to push the envelope with their agents. Project Herakles was probably a mistake to start with, but we had Faulkener and the others, and it was easy enough to prove our worth. Cybernaut should have been our starting point."

"They can't make any more of the Herakles model without our help," Sora snapped.

"Are you certain of that?" Bandi countered. "Do you have anything to base that on besides native Danorak arrogance?"

She opened her mouth to snarl at him. Sora was good at that. One of the reasons he had never considered even fooling around with the woman, Human form or Danorak.

Beauty, as the Humans said, was skin deep, while ugly went to the bone. And today, he found Sora's soul an ugly, spiteful place.

Maybe he needed a vacation.

Sora, wonder of wonders, shut her mouth before saying something she might not regret later. She was usually predictable about that, too.

"You think she's right," Sora said. "Daring."

"I think that the scanalyzer we left with Bouchard in Washington, DC. is sufficient for them to conduct all manner of tests on animals and confirm when things work," Bandi replied. "I think that *Mithras* and the others were successful enough that, in the thirty years since, smart Human scientists could reverse engineer what we'd done. Bouchard is the one that concerns me."

"Why him?" Sora asked, even climbing down off her high horse of superiority to be polite for once. "He's been most helpful for nearly a decade."

"That decade," Bandi said. "We live so long that we don't notice that sort of stretch. Humans do. The US Army is supposed to rotate commanding officers on a regular basis. As short as two years. As long as four. More than that is exceptionally rare."

"As he has said, not many people know what TRC is up to well enough to replace him," Sora said. Then her face fell. "Shit."

Bandi nodded.

"Does anybody know what he's up to?" he asked. "We've been

happily inventing things for him and his predecessors, moving the state of Human technology along far more rapidly than any off-world predictions. But not so fast that people back home would notice. Why?"

"So we had an army of Humans technologically sophisticated enough to let the Party conquer the rest of organized space." It was Sora's turn to grimace. "All we had to do was arm them and march them into ships."

"You don't think we couldn't do that now?" he asked. "Gather up a million or so? Give them uniforms and rifles and land someplace, killing everyone who wanted to argue with the Party?"

"Can a million Humans even hold a planet?" Sora sniped.

"Fear, Sora," he said. "If the other species are afraid of being next, how many will rise up and argue? Especially after somebody executes the first thousand who do?"

"Then why wait four more centuries?" she asked. "Nothing out there is developing fast enough to matter. We were just trying to accomplish as much as we could before the scheduled Date of Contact."

"We probably could have loaded a million Germans up in 1939," Bandi noted. "Or ten million Soviets in 1968. Hit one of the Core worlds instead of Hungary. Why wait so long?"

"Are we going to be able to control the Humans when we get there?" she asked in a terrified whisper.

Bandi nodded in concern.

"What happens if the Party is expecting a million normal Humans?" he queried. "And instead, are facing a billion? Say with advanced models in command? People more dangerous than Captain Daring or *Mithras*, because they've been genetically engineered to the limits of an ever-expanding Human genome with several more centuries to do it?"

"Shit," she whispered a second time. "Have we unleashed an apocalypse on the galaxy?"

Bandi grimaced at her.

"And you wondered if I had died while sitting here, Sora," he said. "Instead, I was contemplating if we've been sold a pig in a poke, to use the Human allegory. We accepted Bouchard's stories, however evasive, because we wanted to get Humans to a point where they were dangerous enough to be a threat. But we forgot one key point."

"What's that?" she asked.

"That's at an individual level," Bandi said. "And four more centuries were supposed to be long enough for Humans to develop and become nicer neighbors. What if we've given them time to engineer a whole new species of predators, just before the Party decides to provide them with starships?"

"What do we do?" she whispered. "Do we confront Bouchard?"

"I can think of far less painful ways to commit suicide, thank you," Bandi replied tartly. "Joie might be someone we could ask, but she's come back into the fold with Kehoe and the others to locate Romana Pham."

"They still can't find her?" Sora asked. "Did some serial killer soldier rape the woman, kill her, then bury her body in the middle of an army base?"

"They don't do that anymore, Sora," Bandi said. "At least, I think the Army has gotten better about removing those people before they commit rape and murder of other soldiers. It's not like the old days."

"Then how could she disappear?"

"That was the reason Kehoe had us reactivate Daring," Bandi reminded her. "So that the best agent they ever had could seek out the woman."

Sora fell silent. Bandi had nothing useful to say, so he sat and watched her.

"Are we alone down here?" she finally asked.

Sora didn't mean the two of them. She meant other species. Folks not part of the Party. Outsiders.

Aliens.

Threats.

Bandi's shrug was a Human mannerism, but he'd been studying them and living among them for more than two hundred years.

"What do we do?" Sora asked.

"I have considered contacting our superiors with my qualms," he said. "The annual report we file will catch them entirely off-guard to begin with, since there had been no warning about Joie Daring. When we add Romana Pham and the fact that our cover here was nearly blown, they might do anything."

"What should they do?" she asked.

"I begin to wonder if we should ask to be evacuated from the planet, Sora," Bandi said soberly. "If things have taken on a malevolent turn that threatens to get out of our control. Assuming we had any."

"Well, in that case—…"

A beep interrupted her. The telephone.

The phone on his desk was for local communications. Wires that were part of a network.

It also contained an alarm. Said alarm had started beeping madly, the first time since he had caused it to be installed as part of the move to the new building.

Sora's look was utter panic. Bandi found himself a little more phlegmatic, but he'd been preparing himself for the other shoe to drop, as the Humans liked to say.

Just not today.

# CHAPTER 9

Ernesta was young again. Slender. Sexy. Hardbody. Folks on the streets of La Plata eyed her walking by. A few whistled.

It put her mind back in those days, though by the time she was twenty-five, she'd already borne two of her three children and graduated into middle management.

No, she felt more like when she'd been nineteen and just promoted from simply runner to enforcer working for her grandfather, who had been in charge in those days.

Carter and Joie looked more like themselves, if you forgot how tall the man had been. He was actually a shade shorter than Joie now. She'd been teasing him about that mercilessly.

But Ernesta was a complete stranger. And a deadly one, once Joie's teacher had started moving faster and faster while sparring. Ernesta had never learned much in the way of unarmed fighting, but she was so fast now that she could simply duck or sidestep a punch.

Though she preferred to use a combat semi-automatic pistol loaded with some funky ammunition that Yormevs had engineered for her. Punch through ballistic cloth like soldiers wore or Joie had been lined with, then fragment and cause massive damage.

It made her more confident. And she had Joie and Carter hiding nearby in a van.

La Plata was a wonderful place. Compact and designed for walking about in ways that reminded Ernesta of Europe rather than the Americas. Lots of people on the streets, as the day had been just right in terms of cool and dry. Enough for a jacket to cover a pistol on her hip, but not cold enough to zip it up.

And glorious sun.

So she walked.

Bandi's office and lab had moved. And apparently it had been a close decision at the time, but whoever was in charge had chosen not to take space in a building Ernesta had bought. That would have been better.

Instead, Ernesta had to scout the new place. She'd only been in the city once with Joie, staying barely more than a day before returning to Mexico.

Maps only got you so far. Even 3D walk-through displays. Nobody ever included the sounds of the city. The brush of people moving by you in crowds.

The smell of street vendors cooking beef over an open flame and then wrapping it in a flatbread.

Her stomach wanted to rumble, but Ernesta had a mission.

Nobody would recognize her. Not even her own kids, more than likely. After all, she'd lost five kilograms, moved several more around, and all of her hair was black again.

And the cute boys were checking her out as she walked. That was its own bonus, over and above the way Mitch's eyes followed her around the room. Any room.

Residential street. A block off the main boulevard where so many folks were. Most of them were tourists, however, with more of the locals over here where they could walk without bumping constantly.

Ernesta had an electronic tour guide in one hand anyway, just to look a little lost and give her an excuse to stop not quite across the street from her target and study things.

After all, she started doing this sort of thing forty-five years ago, and some of those skills never went away.

White stone facings, over brick or concrete shells. Usually six to ten stories tall on this street. Ground floor retail in more than half, cute little shops catering to locals. Somebody was making chocolates nearby from the smell.

Ernesta tucked herself into a spot on the wall where people could get around her. Studied her book like she was reading something important about the architecture.

Really, she was reading people. Sniffing for falseness in the way they moved. Stood. Spoke.

The Mexican Federal Police had no sense of humor on many things, but they also had never been able to hire competent actors to try to set up stings and ambushes. Too cheap to pay for talent, unlike Ernesta and her organization.

Nobody stood out immediately. The hour was just after lunch, when folks might take a long break before wandering back to work. Or wives might meet their husband, one of them coming from home and the other from an office.

Or maybe sneaking home for a quickie. Ernesta hadn't taken into account how much regenerating her hormones to her twenties was going to make her horny. That body, this mind. Dangerous combination.

A face in the crowd stood out. Ernesta recognized the woman, but averted her eyes quickly before drawing attention to herself. The other woman was deadly. Fast. Cunning.

More importantly, trained in ways Ernesta was not.

But her presence here altered equations. According to notes Mitch had compiled, Lt. Freya Malik, aka *Pakhet*, was supposed to be in Central Asia, available for missions on short notice.

Obviously, Bouchard had pulled her out. And it made sense to send her here, as she was one of only a few people that knew about Bandi and his front company, Elliott Engineered Integrated Logistics.

Plus, *Pakhet* knew Joie and Carter on sight. Or would. Neither had changed that much.

Ernesta, on the other hand…

She watched the Afro-Carib woman move purposefully through

the crowd, eyes restive but not noticing the young woman she'd walked by. Must not like girls.

*Pakhet* entered the building directly across from Bandi's new lab and vanished.

Ernesta counted to twenty, put her book away, and kept walking.

At least they knew what they would be facing.

And who.

# CHAPTER 10

Carter was somebody else. Somebody short, which was all sorts of insanely weird, after towering above almost everybody like some demented god of war for thirty years.

Ares, made flesh.

Now, he was just a dude. Who could still lift up a motorbike and throw it a respectable distance.

He'd even stopped shaving, letting his beard come in just chestnut enough to be visible. Blond hair on top was thick and long enough to be an artist, but not a hippie.

*Got some standards around here, ya know.*

La Plata had been a great place to hide out two years ago. Fantastic restaurants covering the whole damned spectrum. Live music from street punk to full orchestras if he didn't mind a taxi ride.

He did miss the place, but he was here on a mission. Backup muscle for the ladies, then they would disappear again.

Ernesta slipped into the back of the van and closed the door, not quite looming over him but full of herself in ways that got his attention.

Maybe the smell of awesome, whatever that was. She had it going on.

And had turned into a complete and utter babe. Or had been one before. He'd never worked with her organization or had to attack it, so he'd only known the woman when she'd been matronly.

And deadly.

She sat next to Joie, across from Carter. Kehoe was on his side. Mitch and Sifu Wĕn had stayed at the hotel.

"Saw somebody just now," Ernesta said with a glorious grin. "Our old friend *Pakhet*."

Carter couldn't help the profanity that slipped out. Fortunately, both women across from him routinely used worse.

"Problems?" Joie asked. "You know her better than I do."

"She's you," he replied. Paused. Grimaced. "Old you. Cybernaut you. Blowtorch-in-her-fucking-hand you. Utterly loyal to TRC, so she'd probably shoot me or Kehoe in the face as soon as she saw us. I'm not blowtorch-resistant these days."

Joie laughed.

"I'd ask who are you and what aliens replaced you, but I already know that answer," she said with a twinkle in her eyes that was contagious.

She was right.

New person. Shorter. Lighter. Didn't have to eat constantly. Wasn't blowtorch resistant anymore.

Still meaner than a rabid boar, though.

He laughed with her.

"So how do we take her?" Ernesta asked. "I presume that you cannot just walk up and say hello, considering that Bouchard or someone had to put her here specifically to keep us from contacting Bandi."

"I'd send you, if you had more training," Joie said. "Or Sifu, but I want to keep her a surprise for later."

Carter watched Joie get a devious gleam in her eyes.

He liked it already.

"You ever free-climb?" she asked him.

"That's for skinny kids with death wishes," Carter replied. "However, gimme a rope and I can freefall assault drop out of a chopper better than just about anybody you know."

Joie nodded. Then turned to Kehoe.

"You have the scanner thing Yormevs gave you?" she asked.

Carter watched the man pull a thing about the size of a small pill bottle out of a blazer pocket and put it in Joie's hand.

Carter would be lying if he told anyone that he'd been paying close attention to those parts of the briefings. Joie wanted him here for muscle and crazy. The others were tactical experts.

Man's got to know his place in the grand scheme of things.

Carter blew shit up.

"Ernesta, you'll lead," Joie said. "Three of us will penetrate the building, but you'll be out front. This scanner will give you a direction, but don't get too close. I need to know what floor and what window Carter will come crashing through."

Oh, yeah, playing to his strengths. And his silliness. This would be more fun than that warehouse job in Hanoi for Uncle.

If only because he'd gotten right proper tired of *Pakhet*'s snide superiority when Kehoe had kept him on a short leash. Short enough that he could bark at the woman, but not bite.

Until today.

ZOOM!!!!!!

"No fire alarms, Carter," Joie said succinctly.

"You're no fun at all, Daring," he replied.

"She has a Mark II, Carter," Joie reminded him. "An XM24E4 *Sunbolt* Cyberarm rifle. Blowtorch to the face. You just told me you don't tan well with those."

"I distinctly remember you shooting me in an armored chest piece with such a weapon, Joie," he grinned. "Blasted my silly ass into the far wall hard enough that I left a dent. *Then* you got out the damned pepper spray."

At least it had been Joie who'd kicked his ass. Man could live with that. Even an Ares Wargod wannabe like him.

Athena had chosen Joie Daring as her avatar, obviously. Maybe Zeus and Odin, too. And a half-dozen others.

Many laughs. He'd spent decades doing that lone wolf thing. Made a lot of money, but spent most of it paying bribes to other folks, though he still had a nice retirement stashed.

And best of all, he got to be one of the good guys now.

At least until the gods woke up and demanded to know what the hell he was doing.

*Burn that bridge when we get there.*

"So, Ernesta leads," Joie continued. "Up to the roof. By then, we'll know what and where *Pakhet* is, and can surprise her. I'd like to take her alive and unharmed, just because, like me, she thought what she was doing was right. Not her fault folks were lying to the woman. Questions?"

"I'm coming in the window as a distraction?" Carter asked, eyes big with excitement.

"Try not to get blowtorched in the process," Joie nodded.

"Even in La Plata, folks are going to notice me standing on somebody's fire escape. Or walking down it," he said dryly.

"I just need her neutralized, Carter," Joie nodded. "Then we cross over and talk to Bandi."

"More than one watcher?" Ernesta asked.

"Assuredly," Joie said. "But probably not even someone that *Pakhet* would know, though they would have been briefed about her. Us hitting the building will raise alarms, but she's one of the few who could provide positive ID later. I intend to change into the tightest shirt I can, just because Bouchard will key in on my chest when asking people. That will throw him off. As will any description that suggests Carter Faulkener, whom he specifically knows to be dead and decapitated in Hanoi. And you're just some *chika* we picked up to fill out a team, because you're dead, too. At least until someone comes along and changes all those reports and interrogations that Kehoe filed."

She paused and Carter felt the seriousness of the woman. Excellent team leader, but she'd been an officer and he'd been happier as a sergeant, at least until he'd gone into business for himself.

She smiled and it was good.

"Let's do this," Captain Daring said.

And Carter was happy to follow her lead.

# CHAPTER 11

Joie trailed Ernesta into the building, holding hands with Carter like they were on a date or something. Not her type. All jock and no brains.

No, much more Amy's type, but her old manager at the coffee shop had a lumberjack fetish, and blond muscleboy Carter still filled that role exceptionally well. Joie let her backbrain ponder things as Ernesta went into the stairwell first, Yormevs's scanner in one hand pointed up and left looking for pings.

She had about a ten meter head start, then they were up and in. Ernesta above them, not moving particularly quiet, because again, nobody would recognize her. And Argentina was so cosmopolitan that nobody would really stick out, so you could have a tall, dark woman of Ethiopian background walking around.

Joie and Ernesta both had oversized purses stuffed with gear for this. The would probably need it.

Eight stories tall.

They caught up with Ernesta at the top and studied the stairwell that accessed the roof itself. Pictures had confirmed that it was flat and designed for American-style barbecues.

"She's on Four," Ernesta said simply.

"My turn," Carter said, reaching into a pocket and pulling out tools.

All of them knew how to pick a mechanical lock like this, but he had practically demanded that job. Joie and Ernesta kept watch on the door nearby and the stairs down.

"Open," he said a few moments later.

Joie wasn't sure she could have opened the door as fast with the actual key in hand.

Then they were up on the roof.

This was the one risk. That someone might have come up here in the last few minutes since they'd looked from a tiny flying drone, but they were alone.

Carter stationed himself against the door. He might no longer weigh more than one hundred and fifty kilograms, but he was still big and strong.

And armed. *Pakhet* might not be willing to surrender, not that Joie could blame the woman.

She just needed that agent neutralized long enough to get to Bandi and see what defenses he had in place, having been surprised the last time.

Even Danorak might get a little paranoid. And she had no idea what kinds of tech he might be able to call upon at this point.

Joie stood still and watched Ernesta trace the entire roof with her scanner pointed down until she stopped.

"Directly below me," Ernesta said.

Joie studied the blueprints in her head, counting meters from two corners. That should be a kitchen in Apartment D. 4-D in this case.

She motioned Carter closer.

"If she remains in her kitchen, she'll see and hear you coming down from above," Joie said. "I can't imagine those things are quiet when someone uses them."

"Abseil?" he asked with that particular gleam in his eyes that said *Mithras* was going to get crazy.

Crazier.

This was *Pakhet*. Probably *craziest*.

And it might be necessary.

Joie looked around.

"Where can you tie off a rope?" she asked.

Carter moved to a bollard. On the streets, they were used to keep cars from driving up onto sidewalks or through front doors. Twenty centimeter cylinder about a meter tall. She had no idea why one was on the roof, except that the door might swing that far and stop.

"I'm in business," he grinned.

Joie shook her head and hoped that he didn't get himself blow-torched. She walked to a spot on the edge of the roof and pulled a piece of simple chalk from her bag, marking where the kitchen window should be. He could lower himself on a rope next to the fire escape and not make noise, but not for long until someone screamed bloody murder or demanded to know what the hell he thought he was up to.

Cops wouldn't take long to get here in this neighborhood if that happened.

She handed the man her bag and watched him pull rope and a climbing harness out. She grabbed a thing Yormevs had given her at the last minute. Beam pistol. Should stun a Human unconscious pretty effectively, except that he'd never had a reason to shoot anyone, and no time to test it.

Better planning next time. Assuming a next time.

Carter had a similar one. As did Ernesta.

"You'll knock," Joie instructed Ernesta. "We want her by the door, in spite of that waking her up from whatever she was doing. I'll be out of sight against the wall. You'll need to duck quickly if she reacts badly."

"Trust me," Ernesta said seriously.

Again, Sifu might have been better, but *Pakhet* might know the woman on sight.

They would only get one shot at this.

"Let's go," Joie said, taking the lead and getting quickly down to the fourth floor. She paced off the door she wanted, then carefully and silently pushed her butt up against the wall next to it, out of sight until she moved.

Joie nodded to Ernesta and took a deep breath.

# CHAPTER 12

Ernesta was back in Guadalajara in the middle of the last century, doing things that she could tell her father but never her priest. He would forgive, though at the same time might still be too tempted by some of the rewards posted. Better not to place temptation in front of that old man.

He was only Christ's representative. The man was still Human. Had been. Dead for decades now.

Joie was set. Ernesta had her purse slung across her back, visible but not within immediate reach.

Not a threat.

The only thing she had in her hands was a piece of paper with an address written on it.

She was not a threat. She was a tourist who had gotten lost and entered the wrong building looking for tea.

Whoops.

She pasted a friendly smile on her face and knocked.

They had contingency plans, but everything from this moment was subject to random chance, so Joie and Carter were counting on her.

Ernesta waited. The fisheye peephole darkened. Nothing.

The woman inside wasn't expecting anything. More than once,

Ernesta had killed someone by waiting for them to look through such a thing, opening fire as soon as they did.

It worked on amateurs.

Ernesta assumed a professional.

Nothing.

She knocked again. Politely. Stubbornly.

The peephole got dark again. This time, *Pakhet* would be looking through it.

Ernesta waited. Patient. Polite.

Smiled even. Maybe rocked back and forth a little like someone a little bored.

Not a threat. Honest.

Hands inside turned a bolt. Then a second one. Ernesta saw both places where keys could go into locks. She assumed a chain or something inside, plus a foot braced just right to keep someone from kicking the door inward when the resident opened it.

Someone Human.

Whoops.

The door opened inward just exactly enough for an eyeball to become visible.

She'd never met the woman in the flesh. Just gotten descriptions from Joie and pictures from Kehoe and Mitch.

As tall as Joie. Lean, just like her. Masai background, to look at her. The folks from the Rift Valley that routinely won marathons and basketball tournaments.

Dark skin. Rich and almost black. Short hair buzzed just long enough to show off her curls. One pretty cheekbone.

Ernesta had a role to play.

"Yes?" *Pakhet* asked in Spanish with a pretty good accent.

Ernesta answered in the same tongue.

"I'm looking for Consuela?" she asked, confusion furrowing her brow now.

Like she'd been expecting a short blond hausfrau instead of a tall Masai warrior.

"You have the wrong address," *Pakhet* replied.

"4-D?" Ernesta answered. "One six four four?"

The woman relaxed, at least the bits Ernesta could see.

"This is one six five four," she said. "You're one building off."

"Oh," Ernesta exclaimed. "I'm so sorry. Thank you. Sorry about that."

"It's okay."

The door started to close. *Pakhet* was blind for about a half-second, not prepared and without the bolts shot that would keep someone out.

Ernesta charged, slamming her full weight into the panel. Her upgraded muscles. The things that Yormevs had done to her because Joie needed a friend right now.

*Pakhet* was caught off guard. She'd moved her foot to step back. Taken her weight off the door itself to close it. Not looking.

And Ernesta had been upgraded.

She didn't need to get inside with the woman. Ernesta knew she was the least dangerous person here, at least in close combat. She might teach the kids a few things with a rifle, were that necessary. Hadn't been for a while, but that wasn't the same as never.

She was the distraction. The disruption. Her weight staggered *Pakhet* backwards, even as the door rebounded and bounced Ernesta back into the hallway, both of them off balance.

*Good thing I brought a friend.*

# CHAPTER 13

Joie had gone into the Zone. There was no better way to describe it.

Time was moving like cold molasses around her.

She listened as Ernesta sold Freya Malik a pig in a poke. Watched the woman slam herself into the door enough to rock the other agent backwards.

Joie *moved*.

She'd danced with Sifu Wěn to get a feel for what this new body could do, but hadn't really *appreciated* it.

Adrenaline was a spiteful, terrible overlord.

Joie was in motion as soon as Ernesta charged, stepping out and pivoting, again like dancers.

Ernesta rebounded from the solidity of Freya and that door. Joie charged. Freya wasn't braced this time. The door knocked the woman on her ass.

They were all experts at close combat. You had to be in order to have this kind of a job. Constant training, even without teachers like Sifu Wěn.

Freya was already rolling backwards as her bottom touched tile. Joie had to move with her.

Freya had a cannon she could use. Joie needed the woman alive. Unharmed, even.

She pounced.

From the kitchen came the sound of a giant cannonball named Carter coming through a window. Not glass shattering, so Freya must have left it open. Less noise.

Carter still landed with a mighty thump.

Freya was back in a crouch. Joie threw a punch. Not intended to hit the woman, but to make her block it. With the cyberarm that had a blowtorch.

To not give this woman time to think.

A second punch followed the first. A third.

None connected, but Joie also wasn't pushing as hard as she could.

Freya might not survive that kind of punch.

And Freya was good. Solid. Dangerous.

Merely Human, though, despite all the cyberware, and that was the difference.

Carter stomped into the room and Freya made the mistake of glancing his way, suddenly surrounded and still down where she had no maneuverability.

Joie threw herself atop the woman, tackling her until they were flat on the floor, Freya's legs around her like lovers.

Joie let herself be punched once. Freya's off hand. The organic one.

She needed control of the blowtorch.

Twisting, she forced Freya's right hand inward, until the palm was pointed at the woman's face.

"I would like you to surrender to me," Joie said through gritted teeth, even as she tried to wrestle an angry puma into submission. "Or I can manually fire the *Sunbolt* and leave your corpse here to cool while I go about my business."

There was an external trigger built in. An assumption that the controlling cyberware might have been too damaged, so you could open a small slot with your left hand and find a firing stud.

Like Joie had just done.

"Daring?" *Pakhet* whispered in shocked awe. "What?"

"If you want to play nice, I'll pop your arm off for now and explain," Joie said. "I can do that. Didn't want to out of the blue, because we need to talk. What's it going to be?"

"Apartment is secure," Carter said, so he'd checked the other rooms.

Someone else here would have been bad. Another cybernaut would have been ugly.

Messy.

Potentially catastrophic.

"Okay," Freya said, looking at three people around her.

Carter probably had a weapon pointed at her. He was like that.

"Ernesta?" Joie asked.

There was a chirp and a click. Freya's arm detached, just like Joie's had, back on that day. No smoke or sizzling from other parts being destroyed.

Joie wasn't an asshole, like Kehoe had been before he got lost on the road to Damascus.

Joie leaned back with the arm. Freya let go with her legs.

Joie stood and stepped back as the other woman got up. Carter was all smiles, like a hungry shark. Ernesta was calm, certain death.

Freya took a hint and moved to the kitchen counter, climbing up onto one of the two bar stools and watching them.

Joie tossed the spare arm onto the couch nearby and squared up to the woman.

Carter had left the screen in the middle of the floor, broken badly from where he'd gone through it in a hurry.

"What are you, Daring?" Freya asked. "That's a real arm. And you were never that strong."

"This is *Mithras*, Freya," Joie answered, gesturing at Carter.

"Bullshit," the woman barked angrily. "He's too small."

"Oh, but I am, buttercup," Carter said in that voice of his that was always a little too cute in situations like this. "They fixed me. Like they did Joie."

"They?" Freya asked.

"This is La Plata, Freya," Joie said. "You remember the last time the three of us were here."

She ignored Ernesta for now. That woman had been there as well, but better to keep one extra surprise handy for later.

"Bandi and the other aliens," Freya nodded.

"There are a lot more aliens out there," Joie said. "Some of them recruited us to help."

"Is that why you vanished from Hanoi?" she asked.

"And how," Joie agreed. "Bad things are coming down because of what Bandi has done. And Bouchard. Our new friends want us to stop them before the rest of the aliens decide that we're too dangerous to survive."

Freya's eyes got big. Nervous.

"So you're here to kill Bandi this time?" Freya asked.

"No," Joie shook her head. "The others could have done that easily enough without my help. Maybe just blown up the building. Or something. I need to talk to him. Maybe disappear him, but this is Argentina, and that's a cultural thing the locals will understand. Stop him from making it worse."

"Worse?" Freya asked.

"Those other aliens have threatened to wipe out all satellites, Freya," Joie replied. "Crash all computer networks. Disrupt power systems. Everywhere. All at once."

"Fuck," Freya whispered. "Do they know what that means?"

"That's how nervous they are, agent," Joie said. "And what they've threatened to do if somebody doesn't stop TRC and the Danorak."

She watched the woman think. Hispanics or Anglos would have flushed with color about now, but Freya was already so dark that she might have turned into pure midnight.

Freya turned to Carter.

"You're supposed to be dead," she said simply.

"And I intend to be this time," he said. "There are incredibly few folks that know I'm not, so I have a new lease on life. Not about to let the aliens or those shitheads in DC muck that up. Understand me?"

"So why are you here?" Freya asked.

"You didn't know the truth," Joie said simply. "Kehoe's with me. He's broken with Bouchard. Defected, I suppose. And you are one of the most dangerous people I know. Certainly in this town. I needed to neutralize you so I could walk across the street and make Bandi disappear."

"What are you doing with me?" Freya asked.

"Stealing your arm so that you can't do anything to stop us," Joie said. "Tying you up here so you can't call Bouchard for a while. I don't need long. Then you are free to go about your life."

"You're really going to save the world?" the woman asked.

"If I can," Joie nodded. "We might be too late, but I've got to try."

"What happened to you?" Freya asked. "You have two arms."

"That was the deal for me helping the other aliens," Joie replied. "They fixed me. They fixed Carter here. That lets us hide in plain sight. At least until Bouchard gets a good description from you."

"Kehoe is on your side?" she asked.

"He is," Joie said. "Would you like to talk to him?"

Again, the woman's flinch was almost enough to knock her backwards off the stool.

"Could I?"

Joie reached into her back pocket, pulled out a thing that looked like a smart phone, and dialed.

# CHAPTER 14

Taylor was surprised by the phone ringing. Doubly so that it was Daring. And not. Almost nobody had this number, since he'd given up his old one.

Nobody he wanted to talk to from that old life anyway.

"Kehoe," he said as he answered, glancing at Mitch, seated across from him, eyes also surprised.

"You're on speaker," Joie said. "Got someone who wants to talk to you."

"Kehoe?" *Pakhet* asked in a full equally full of wonder and dread.

"Affirmative, Agent *Pakhet*," he replied. "What's the story?"

"Aliens saving the world?" she pressed. "Other aliens going to destroy it?"

"Kid, you have no idea," he laughed harshly. "Bouchard left my ass out to dry. I assume he meant to burn me with the Russians, the Chinese, and the Senate. Got out while the getting was good."

"Daring and Mithras have been—"

"Changed," he offered. "Repaired and upgraded for the new mission. Can't offer you the same deal today, but it might be something I can negotiate with my new bosses after we finish this mission. Still got your old phone number?"

In this business, he never put things on speed dial. Too easy to lose his phone or have it hacked. So he had memorized about five hundred numbers with some complicated mnemonics.

One of the reasons he'd done so well at TRC.

"I do, but I'll have to burn Daring with Bouchard and whoever else after this," *Pakhet* said. "Tell them that *Mithras* is still alive and turned into…whatever the hell he is."

"You offering to be taken into custody, *Pakhet*?" Taylor asked. "Removed entirely from the game board for a while as we get things sorted out?"

Long pause, but he was expecting that. Daring must have seen something in the woman to make her call in the first place.

Taylor wasn't sure he could turn *Pakhet*. Not immediately, anyway.

Being aboard an alien starship might do the trick.

"Yes, Kehoe," she finally said in a weak, soft voice entirely at odds with who the woman normally was.

But this was a day for miracles, so to speak. Even the most stubborn woman would have to rethink many of her assumptions about the universe and her place in it after learning some of the truth. Seeing Daring and Faulkener. Understanding how much risk there really was.

And *Pakhet* had always been sharp.

Daring and the others just had a head start.

"Daring, talk to the bosses and see if they're interested," Taylor said. "*Pakhet* is almost as good as you."

"Will do," Daring said, then cut the line.

Taylor turned to Mitch. They were in the middle of a mission, and things kept getting weirder and weirder around here.

And they still hadn't figured out who had Romana Pham.

Or what had happened to her.

# CHAPTER 15

Joie hung up on Kehoe and pressed a special comm button on the touchscreen. The devices all looked like smartphones, but didn't work on any local cellular network. Way too easy for AI systems to recognize her voice and triangulate strike teams down on her.

Or jets with bombs.

"Hello, Joie," Yormevs answered immediately.

He was…somewhere. On that ship, wherever it was. According to him, not on Earth, but she didn't understand how they could talk like this if he was hiding on the dark side of the moon or something. Three light-seconds lag each way.

But Humans couldn't travel at FTL, either.

"I have a friendly prisoner here, Yormevs," she said. "We captured Freya Malik and would like you to take her into custody for now. She surrendered and I have her arm, but you'll need to grab it as well."

"Interesting," the alien said. "Is she potentially another friend?"

"That's Kehoe's call when we get back," Joie said.

"Understood, Joie," Yormevs replied. "I have her coordinates, and that of the arm you are holding. Stand by."

Joie had never seen someone else be removed by the device. Only the flash of white light that embraced her and then released her.

It swirled up from Freya's feet, quickly engulfing the woman and then fading her out of existence, even as Joie was nearly blind from looking at it.

The arm vanished at the same time.

She blinked to clear her eyes, turning to her cohorts in crime.

"Someone will have seen that," she said.

"Or seen me breaking into the joint," Carter added helpfully.

"Let's move, then," Ernesta replied, heading to the door.

Joie presumed another watcher. Possibly automated systems in Freya's apartment. Nothing she had said would surprise many. It would just refine things for Bouchard, but Joie already expected a confrontation with the man at some point.

In the old days, a high noon shootout like an old cowboy movie, perhaps. This town wasn't big enough for the two of them.

Except that it was this planet instead.

And killing him wouldn't do any good.

Well, it would, but not in the right way. Some folks were just evil, but she'd never met the man personally to know. Only seen the results of his work.

And hers.

Things he'd ordered.

And it wasn't necessary to kill him, if she could somehow remove the man and all his immediate allies from Earth. Those that knew how it was done.

The tools could be corrupted. Mitch had assured her that he had access to the right databases. Carter knew a woman who could get them the right sort of juvenile delinquent to mess with them.

It wasn't enough to just crash those systems. There would be backups off-line that could be restored once folks knew that something had happened.

The backup tapes needed to be corrupted as well. That would require a subtle expertise that wasn't beyond the aliens, but something they didn't understand.

None of them spray-painted graffiti on walls for fun. At least not the Heecha or Danorak.

So she raced down the stairs behind Ernesta, Carter trailing quietly behind.

They got to the ground floor entrance without hassle. Possibly without witnesses, but Joie was too experienced at this sort of thing to believe that for a moment.

"Straight across through traffic, or at the corner like polite people?" Ernesta asked when they emerged into sunlight.

The afternoon crowds were starting to build. Folks coming from lunch. Or a siesta. Tourists lost like Ernesta's cover story. Vehicle traffic wasn't all that bad.

"Cross," Joie decided quickly. "Assume alarms behind us."

Ernesta nodded and started to jog. Joie trailed. Carter dropped back a little, so it wouldn't look like a bums rush.

Across the street and into a lobby. This building was all commercial. Offices and places like Elliott Engineered Integrated Logistics that did research, but rarely played with anything larger than a soldering iron, however advanced it might be.

Ernesta didn't bother with anything but the front stairwell. They knew where the target was. It still would have been funnier had Bandi moved into a building with Ernesta Hernandez as his landlord, however distant and obscured the relationship.

She followed.

Up and out on the third floor. Bandi and his friends had this whole level to themselves, so Ernesta walked into a lobby with a woman behind a desk.

Joie even recognized her from before.

Genevieve.

She wondered if anyone had told the woman anything approximating the truth about the last time the three of them had broken in. Might be necessary.

And it might have sent her screaming for the hills.

Genevieve looked right at Joie, and her eyes got HUGE.

The receptionist stabbed madly for a button on her desk and Carter shot her, but not before she found it.

Stunned her. Genevieve flopped over out of her chair and fell bonelessly onto the floor, but the damage was done.

"Carter, you guard the front, but we won't be going out that way," Joie said.

She kept moving. The door behind Genevieve was locked. Keycard or something.

Joie stepped back and planted her heel into the wood, just above the handle.

Upgraded muscles.

The strike plate wasn't up to the task, and the door wasn't solid. It shattered under the assault.

Joie charged through, looking for her alien friends.

# CHAPTER 16

Bandi reached into a desk drawer. Hanni had been the one who suggested that they all have weapons handy, having been surprised by Daring last time. Arguing with the man hadn't been worth the effort.

So he pulled out a pistol. Small. Compact. Well beyond anything that Humans imagined possible in anything save for their strangest science fiction.

Sora had gone gray. And frozen in her chair. Not surprising. She was a scientist, same as him, but had never had to work with Nazis or Communists to get things done.

The Americans and their allies were pussycats by comparison.

Bandi stepped to the door, looking towards the front.

The space was a large lab, with all of their offices around this side, storage on the back and across the way, and a small kitchen behind Genevieve's reception area.

He missed the other building, where they had two stories and more space, but this was good enough for now.

On his right, Hanni had emerged from his office. The man looked nervous, holding an identical pistol in hands that appeared to shake.

Bandi didn't appreciate being between Hanni and whatever

problem might have caused Genevieve to sound an alarm. Too many Nazi officers had gotten themselves shot in the back accidentally.

Sure, accidental.

"Hanni, come here," Bandi ordered the younger scientist.

If nothing else, that got the man from behind him.

Hanni had never seen a war from the inside, hot or cold. He complied, eyes a little too big and gray around his gills where his color wasn't right.

Something hit the door to the front hard enough to shatter the lock.

Bandi leaned into his doorframe and tried to steady his hand as the door opened and something came through.

Someone.

Couldn't be good. Not with that kind of entrance.

He fired.

And they ducked.

WHAT?!?

"Bandi, hang on for a moment," a woman's voice called as she dropped below the line of a workbench with a new cybernetic installer mechanism half-dismantled. "It's Joie."

Joie?

What the fuck?

"Joie?" he called.

Glancing over, Hanni had also dropped behind a workbench, kneeling to shoot.

At least nobody could easily sneak up on them without setting off the access alarm on the fire door at the back of the space.

"Long story, Bandi," Joie said. "Things are happening, and you needed to be brought up to speed quickly. Obviously, we don't have long before I need to run. Can we just chat like last time?"

Last time, that asshole Kehoe had brought *Mithras* himself and a Cybernaut named *Pakhet* right into the lab, after Joie and Ernesta Hernandez. Nearly had a firefight amidst precious equipment. He'd made Bandi disable *Mithras* while Joie managed to disarm the woman.

Shit.

"What's going on, Joie?" he asked, more from curiosity than anger.

"They call themselves Heecha, Bandi," she answered, one eye just enough above the counter that he could see her.

Heecha? Here? HERE?

FUCK!

"Heecha?" Sora hissed behind him, almost causing him to turn and fire.

Bandi had gotten so wound up he'd forgotten that there was somebody in the office with him.

Still, if Joie knew about the Heecha. Had spoken with them…

"Hanni, put your weapon away," he ordered.

The man turned an incredulous look this way, eyes wide and mouth fallen open.

"It's Joie Daring, Hanni," he reminded the man.

Last time, she'd only wanted answers, then had left, telling nobody about them who didn't already know.

He waited until Hanni stood up and put the pistol in a pocket before speaking. His two associates were still a little stupid about Human ways, in spite of their decades here.

Neither of them had ever been shot at by someone who meant it. Not like him.

"Joie, it's safe," Bandi said.

He stuffed the pistol into a jacket pocket as well and stepped out into the open. Joie was even more dangerous than *Mithras* had been on his best day. If she wanted him dead, there wasn't much he could do to stop it.

Joie's head came the rest of the way up. Another person peeked around the shattered door. Bandi got a good look at the second one and felt the entire freaking planet spasm under his feet.

"What in God's name did those sons of bitches do????" he screamed, mostly at the heavens.

Ernesta Hernadez's granddaughter smiled back carefully at him. Except that it wasn't. That was Ernesta herself.

He turned to Joie. Saw the same sorts of changes.

"FUCK!" he followed up.

Bandi looked to the heavens, as if they might open up and give him answers.

Or strike him dead. The Catholics around here were particular about shit that befell sinners. He'd lived among them long enough to hear stories.

Joie stood up. Bandi heard both Hanni and Sora gasp at the implications.

"I never did that," Bandi snarled, mostly at himself, while pointing at the two women. "Never once."

And snarled at the superiors that had sent him to this shithole to deal with homicidal barbarians.

"I know, Bandi," Joie said in a friendly, calming tone. "This was part of the cost I had to bear, in order to do the rest."

"Well then, you've come to the right place, my dear," he shrugged angrily. "I was just contemplating both Faust and von Frankenstein this afternoon. How can I be of assistance, and how long do you have before more people kick in my door shooting?"

The old place had been built with glass to stop anything short of a fusion rifle at short range. They hadn't been here long enough to complete all those upgrades.

He wondered how much, if any of it, would have even slowed Joie Daring down today.

Bandi turned and shooed Hanni into his office with Sora. Behind him, Joie and Ernesta followed.

"Not long," Joie said as she stepped in. "Genevieve recognized me and triggered the alarm. Carter stunned her."

"Oh, shit," Sora gasped. "*Mithras*, too?"

Bandi moved to his seat and wished that Danorak could drink alcohol like Humans did. A shot of whiskey or something right about now sounded good, from what he'd heard.

"Heecha?" he asked Joie.

"They contacted me in Hanoi," she nodded. "Extracted me, Ernesta, and Carter. Explained that a lot of other aliens are trying to decide if they should basically destroy Human civilization about now."

Bandi nodded, grimacing.

Faustian bargains. The devil always came for your soul eventually. Even aliens, apparently.

Well, it had been a good run. And longer than he'd ever imagined possible.

Time to pay the piper?

"Have you come to kill us?" Hanni asked, but he was like that. A little too wound up most of the time. Should have had a vacation before this.

Hell, they all should have taken more vacations. More relaxation time might have let them see the bigger picture.

Especially if the Heecha were here, watching.

"We are trying to save Earth," Joie said. "They've talked about starting with a Carrington Event and then getting mean."

Sora gasped. Bandi nodded. Hanni was a little too focused on his toys to have read Human history.

"And they want us out of the way," Bandi completed the thought for her.

"They want you no longer interfering with Humanity, Bandi," she said, smiling sadly. "That means off-planet and never coming back. It means that Ernesta, Carter, and I have to stop Bouchard and destroy all the things they have that might let them keep building more people like he's done, even after you're gone."

"The thermal signature," Bandi nodded.

"If you looked at me right now, I'm also running that hot," Joie said.

Bandi blanched in surprise.

"Yes, Bandi," she said. "Once we're done, I'll be in exile with the rest of you, because it isn't necessary to kill all of them. The Heecha scientist I've been dealing with says the rest will be happy for now if Humans plateau here for a while. Cyberware is okay, but not the really advanced genetic engineering."

"I don't understand," Sora stage-whispered to the room.

"It means we're done here, Sora," he said, watching Joie's face for the nod. "That we're about to be arrested and deported, like we probably should have been in the first place."

"Just like that?" Hanni asked.

"We have deliberately interfered with this planet for centuries, Hanni," Bandi reminded him tartly. "Almost certainly made it worse instead of better, with men like Kehoe and Bouchard calling the shots."

"Kehoe defected," Joie said, causing Bandi's head to snap around.

"Really?" he asked.

"Really," she nodded.

"And he's helping you undo it all?" Bandi breathed, shocked almost out of his mind.

"This is bigger than one person, Bandi," she turned serious. "Billions of Human lives are at stake. Plus however many billions or trillions of aliens more if my kind managed to escape Earth before we were ready to be friendly neighbors. That cannot be allowed. I have one chance to salvage everything before the others unleash exceptional efforts to fix this problem."

Bandi hung his head in shame. Sora was frozen. Hanni appeared to be weeping, but he'd never been the strongest personality Bandi knew.

At least his executioner was somebody he respected. Bandi could deal with that.

"Okay," Bandi said simply to Joie. "Now what?"

"Do you have any defensive systems that would prevent a matter transmission beam from working in here?" Joie asked, betraying how much she knew that should never have been a thing for Humans.

Bandi laughed.

"The old place, with the bullet-proof glass, did," he replied. "We had to move in a hurry because of you, and not everything has been moved here and set up. Another month, and it would have been, but the Heecha could have just grabbed us any time they wanted."

"You'd have fought them," Joie said, knowing him probably better than his own mother with that observation.

He would have.

But not Joie. She was right. And doing the right thing. Who was he to resist that?

"I would have," Bandi agreed. "But that time is done."

He sighed and looked around.

"Time to go home," he said.

Joie pulled out a phone and pushed a button.

"Yormevs," she said immediately. "Three Danorak and four Humans, one of whom is stunned but otherwise fine."

Four? Ah, Genevieve. Yes, a witness who had identified Joie Daring on sight. The new Joie Daring.

The one who was hunting the rest of his co-conspirators.

Bandi felt justice finally descend on him in a beam of light.

# CHAPTER 17

Valmy wanted to slam the phone's handset down. Except that, as angry as he was, it would disintegrate. The first time had been an unwelcome surprise he didn't care to repeat.

Instead, he put it carefully into the cradle and looked out over the fading sunset his window revealed.

Then Valmy drew a breath and stood. Again, care was called for, as much as he wanted to throw a chair through that window. Or shatter the wooden desk with his fists.

Even going down to the gym and sparring with some of his Project Carpenter warriors would be a bad thing, as much angry energy as it would burn off while he did.

He simply lacked the time. Somehow, somewhere, an enemy organization had suddenly stepped up their attacks against TRC. They weren't out in the open yet, but that was likely only a matter of time.

First Daring and most of her team had vanished. That Konicek and Vanlaere had been left behind meant that whoever it was wasn't ready to confront Valmy over the new Humans he was creating.

Then, six hours ago, somebody had attacked La Plata. This time, it wasn't a case of bad luck and black humor, either. Both *Pakhet* and all three of the aliens had vanished, plus the woman receptionist. Jennifer or something.

The facility had been attacked. The shattered door was all the evidence he needed. Similarly, someone had broken into *Pakhet*'s surveillance post via a window and somehow neutralized the woman.

Who?

Wasn't the Russians. They didn't know the truth, and pictures of Faulkener's head had done wonders for back-room negotiations this last week. The Chinese liked to play long games, but they were happier slowly stealing Siberia.

Valmy moved to the door and stepped outside. Most of his staff were ignorant of what was going on. They transferred through too regularly for him to trust any of them with things that might get them killed for knowing.

They might also get him killed.

Instead, he walked down the hallway to where Konicek and Vanlaere had been installed. Valmy's entire staff here in DC wasn't much. Certainly not for a Commanding General. But Technology Research Command had always been small and private.

Better that way.

He entered the office and closed the door behind him, gesturing both of them to remain seated as he took a chair.

"We have a situation developing," Valmy said carefully. "I need to brief you about things above your pay grade, because the three of us will be heading into the field immediately. Pack for southern hemisphere weather."

"Sir?" Vanlaere asked.

She'd been sent to infiltrate Daring's team, but had not been successful before the woman disappeared. Or perhaps had been on the verge, and this new enemy needed to remove Daring and Kehoe first.

"There is a research facility of ours outside of Buenos Aires, Argentina," Valmy said. "It was attacked this afternoon and the staff has vanished. All of them. The local authorities did not find bodies, either. One of two observer missions in place was also hit simultaneously, and Lieutenant Freya Malik, a cybernaut, is also missing. The other watcher was apparently not discovered, as they were able to report in, but didn't see anything useful before or after alarms were triggered at the lab."

"We're investigating it, General?" Konicek asked.

"No," he replied. "TRC will send a team of bureaucrats and analysts, once the local police finish their investigations and are paid off to leave everything alone. I need a strike team, and don't even have time to pull people in from North Carolina or Washington. Most of the people I need are, in fact, still around the Central Asia situation, packing up. Waiting for them is longer than I think we have, but I will be sending orders routing all of us to South America, regardless of their current mission. It is that important."

He stood up and looked at the ceiling. TRC had fantastic toys to detect and neutralize listening devices. Plus, he was in the middle of a building with security comparable to Cheyenne Mountain or the White House.

However, he also knew how easy it was to build better toys that outdid such defenses.

Valmy Bouchard had not gotten where he was by trusting his electronic security to someone else.

"I will brief you on the plane," he said. "The flight will be long enough to cover everything. Then we might be fighting for our lives when we get there."

"Do we know who we're fighting, General?" Vanlaere asked.

"No," he said as he exited.

# CHAPTER 18

Joie stood next to Yormevs and watched Freya through one of those invisible force field cells that Joie had been in after they grabbed her in Hanoi.

Eerie, from this side. Freya couldn't see anything, but had touched the wall to confirm that it was there, just like Joie had.

"Are you certain this is the wisest course of action?" Yormevs asked her.

Joie was still in the jeans and shirt she'd been wearing in La Plata. She had Freya's cyberarm cradled in hers, dangerous fusion disks removed.

"No," Joie said. "But she deserves this much of the truth. I wouldn't trust her in the field, but she might be an excellent agent later, after Kehoe and Mitch have a chance to talk to her."

"Are you at risk?" he pressed.

Joie smiled.

"She's good, but not that good," Joie said. "I needed her alive and unharmed before. Hard to do when you have that much skill. If she gets out of hand, you can stun her for me or something. Don't hurt her unless you absolutely have to."

"Joie, you continue to surprise me," Yormevs said, turning to face her fully. "All of your kind are regarded as violent and dangerous at all times. Lethal for little provocation. Prone to excess. And you have gone out of your way, time and again, not to resort to violence. Why is that?"

Joie paused and considered it. Certainly, all of her training since she'd been fourteen had been geared towards being the deadliest person she could achieve. And she had succeeded.

Right up until the moment that Kehoe burned her.

Broke her.

RDR-ed her.

*Revoked, Demilitarized, Retired.*

Then two years in the wilderness, just trying to make something of the remaining forty or sixty years she had in front of her.

Broken.

At least Amy had given her purpose. Place. Family.

Until Kehoe and this woman showed up at her door one night to ruin everything.

Again.

Except that Freya had been doing what she was told, like a good, little soldier. Like Joie had been once. The Army pounded that into you. Even for a civilian boss.

So she considered the question Yormevs had posed.

"Humans also believe in second chances," she said. "At least American culture does. Someone can screw up, sure, but that they can learn from it and become a better person. I've gone through many such changes over the last few years, so I understand that. Freya had the career she had planned out before the events that cost her an arm, like me. Then the surgeries and rehab to become even more like me. She's young. She could be so much more, but has to face an entire lifetime of doubt. Especially as she doesn't know who was right and who was wrong, as she was given orders to do things. I certainly had time to reflect. Some of the shit I did in the old days was flat evil. I'll never be able to undo that, but I have to try to make things better."

"And you believe Freya Malik can also make things better?" he asked.

"I have no idea, Yormevs," she countered. "This isn't about

recruiting her. It's about me doing right by her. At least as much as I can."

"As I said, you continue to surprise me, Joie," he smiled. "In good ways. I shall keep watch."

Joie nodded and stepped forward. A door appeared in front of her and Freya turned her way, moving to something like a defensive posture, but an uncertain one.

She didn't have the advantage of Sifu Wěn and the thing that woman had taken to calling Angry Elephant. It showed, but only in that Freya hadn't figured out how to fight without her dominant arm.

Joie entered and smiled. She held out the arm, shoulder first.

"Sorry I had to take it away from you earlier," Joie said. "And last time we met in La Plata. My hope is that it will never be necessary again."

Freya had relaxed a little. She stepped one meter closer and reached out for the arm, like she expected Joie to jerk it back tauntingly.

Instead, Joie handed it to her, then moved around to the woman's right.

"You'll need help socketing it again," Joie said, moving close enough to help guide as Freya watched her with eyes full of wonder and fear.

"Why?" the woman whispered.

"Because I know what it's like to have it taken away from you," Joie said, unable to contain some of the rage that came with such memories.

Together, they got it into place. Joie pulled a small handheld from her pocket and pressed the button that triggered the unit to lock in and recalibrate itself. Not that it would be off by much, but it made Freya whole again.

At least as whole as she could be for now.

Joie stepped back as Freya flexed her fingers and fist open and closed. Bent it. Rotated it.

Noted the lack of weight where all the fusion disks were sitting on a shelf in the main part of the ship.

Freya's grin was wry and twisted.

"Carter lives in terror that someone is going to blowtorch his pretty new face," Joie said.

Freya laughed.

"Not my type," she said. "Before or after."

"Agreed, but that was why I went in the door and he came through your window," Joie said.

"And you kidnapped the others?" Freya asked, turning her body more this way, but not square on. Not up on her toes.

Not poised to attack.

Her body language spoke of uncertain curiosity.

"That's as good a word as any," Joie said. "There is a war among the gods going on, though they are really only aliens, with different goals and methods. I needed to remove these aliens first. Then go after Bouchard and some of the things he's done."

"Bad?" Freya asked, obviously wondering what could top Captain Daring going rogue a second time.

Joie held out her hand to the woman. Freya automatically took it in her cyberhand.

"Warm," Freya said with surprise after a moment.

"My core temperature is about forty degrees," Joie nodded.

"And you have two arms now," Freya acknowledged.

"I needed that for the rest," Joie said. "Bouchard is building geneti-cally-engineered agents like my new form, but doing so in secrecy. My new friends think I am a physical match for what he's done. But this war must be fought in the shadows still, because there is another group of aliens out there who might decide to just crush us entirely if they learned the honest truth about everything going on."

"Can I help?" Freya asked.

"Eventually," Joie replied. "But time is tight right now and that's one thing too many on my list. Plus, you don't know enough about everything. Those that do find out what's going on will be required to leave Earth forever later, assuming we win."

"Assuming we win?" Freya pressed.

"If we fail, Human civilization is doomed, Freya," Joie said. "It might be anyway, if one of those other groups decides that we're simply too big of a threat and goes ahead and pulls the trigger. Too much can go wrong, and Bouchard has no idea what he's facing."

"He won't go down easily," she nodded. "Will he listen to reason?"

Joie shrugged.

"Even TRC doesn't know the truth, from what I've gathered," Joie said. "All the secret projects we've been part of are fairly public there. Instead, he's carved out something even more sinister, and nobody seems to know the extent of it."

"So you can't just grab him?" Freya asked. "Like you did me?"

"The lab you were watching didn't have barriers in place, like the former one did," Joie said. "But they were coming. Apparently, Bandi allowed Bouchard to have those, but only a few. Worse, they are both invisible to scans the aliens have, so they can hide things. Not even my superiors know what's going on, and they've been watching him. The rest of the galaxy, at least the key parts, are starting to panic. Not yet, but soon. That's how long we have."

"I'm not your physical match anymore, Daring," Freya noted. "But I do have a—what did *Mithras* call it?—a blowtorch I can bring if you need an anti-tank sniper when Armageddon comes."

"Thank you," Joie said. "I will keep it in mind, but we're in a tight spot and I won't make any promises right now."

"Understood," Freya nodded. "The offer is the thing to remember. You and I both took the oath because we wanted to save the world. That doesn't stop if our own people go bad. If anything, it makes it more important."

Joie started to say something, but the wall beside her thinned and Yormevs entered.

"Joie, you are needed elsewhere immediately," he said simply. "Something has happened."

# CHAPTER 19

Bandi just stared at this new Human, but the man Graydon didn't seem to be impressed. Kehoe was a little more off-put, but he'd never seen a Danorak in their native, gray coloration. Or without a wig of Human hair.

The Heecha entered, bringing Joie, but leaving the others outside somewhere.

They were aboard a Heecha ship. Bandi recognized the overall design, but he'd been away for so long that maybe this was a newer class. Something. It looked subtly wrong to his eyes.

Plus the damned smell. Sour kimchi almost cleaned out of the air, but not quite. It was amazing that nobody else noticed it.

The Heecha sat at the head of the long table. Joie and Kehoe were across. The newcomer Graydon was next to Bandi on the left.

Everyone settled.

"Tell them," the Heecha commanded.

Bandi bit back a snarl. Turned to the Heecha.

"Does Kehoe need to be here?" he demanded instead. "Or this other?"

"It will be my mission," Kehoe growled. "Mitch is my analyst. Joie is my agent. Talk, or be utterly damned. I don't care."

Bandi felt the surliness rise, but contained it. Kehoe had always been an asshole on a mission. Changing masters hadn't changed anything relevant about the man. Hardened him, if anything.

Bandi sighed instead.

"It was brought to my attention that Bouchard made a sudden and unplanned trip to South American," he said. "All well and good, except that he wasn't going to Buenos Aires, like we would have expected."

"It didn't fit context," Graydon interjected.

Bandi nodded. The man was right.

"It would not," Bandi agreed. "You don't know certain things. Nobody is supposed to know them."

"What's in Santiago, Chile?" Graydon asked sharply, leaning forward.

Analyst. Take data and refine it into information. Good ones could turn it into understanding. Graydon had that look about him. That made him doubly dangerous, if he was going to know everything about this shitshow.

"Nothing," Bandi replied, waving the others off when they got restive. "It is what comes after Santiago that matters."

"We know he's headed there?" Joie asked.

"I have all sorts of access to things I shouldn't." Graydon smiled fiercely. "Running an invisible backup and restore to servers here, so I can recompile things for reporting purposes. Makes it fast, and lets me set alerts. Bouchard triggered one, but he requested a flight plan to Chile instead of Argentina. That got escalated."

Bandi nodded sourly. Graydon might be more dangerous than Joie, in his own way. At least from what had come up over the last day or so.

Smart, while the others were generally only cunning. Lots of difference there.

"Bandi?" Joie asked.

"We happened to be on the Chilean side of the border, but working out of Argentina for political and social reasons," he sighed. "Santiago is the closest place to get any sort of aircraft capable of flying him to the volcano."

"Volcano?" Joie asked.

Bandi ignored the men in here and concentrated on her. She was the only nice one, anyway.

"You were correct, the first time we met, Joie," he said in a heavy, sad voice. "We do have a ship, carefully hidden against anybody finding it. The transmitter beams that you've used to get around made it easy to get from there to where we needed to go. I never kept a unit assembled, because that would have given your kind enough information to possibly reverse engineer one yourselves, which would have been all kinds of bad."

"How so?" she asked.

"You could have walked to the moon, instead of flying," he offered. "Mars is too far away, but putting a station about halfway to closest approach would have let you step there. Or a whole chain of such stations, so you could send robots to build new stations, then just walk over and populate them. Humans break out of their homeworld so much faster than anybody back home could have imagined. That would have pissed them off."

"Because they'd have known somebody like you was here, doing things illegally," she nodded.

He nodded back.

"Our ship is hidden in a cave in the summit crater of Espiritu Santo, which overlies the La Engorda volcano. Way the hell up in Chile," Bandi finally admitted, sealing his doom for all time.

As if there'd been any doubts left.

"And Bouchard figured out where?" she asked.

"Somebody like him," Bandi replied, pointing to Graydon next to him. "Too smart for his own damned good and playing with patterns. How, I don't know, but there is absolutely nothing of value anywhere in Chile, as far as my people and research are concerned. If somebody just kidnapped all the Danorak scientists and he doesn't immediately go to look, then that's the only other thing I know of with any value to you. So I told the Heecha here."

"I have a name," the Heecha said.

Bandi just scowled at the fucker. Kehoe and Graydon rated names. Barely.

Joie was the only one here really worth a shit, himself included.

Somewhere in hell, Faust was laughing.

"So I get to compound my crimes, Joie," Bandi said, turning to focus on her again. "I get to make certain that a Human discovers the ship that brought me here fifty years ago. They'll start a crucifixion when they learn that, then move up to something cruel and painful."

"So you're Jesus of Nazareth, now?" Kehoe asked.

"I'm the guy that was trying to get you silly monkeys out of the stone ages," Bandi retorted sourly. "But that's all done and gone. Joie I trust. If Bouchard gets it, you all are absolutely screwed, because I'm certain that a lot more people are watching Earth these days. That's why we had to hide it so well. Tell me, Heecha, how well are you hidden from the Watchers?"

At least the son of a bitch had the decency to look chagrined. Bandi'd snuck down here with Sora and Hanni in 2057, after a major Party operation to provide the right opening. When the guards were still half-asleep.

If the Heecha were here, so were a bunch of others.

"Well enough, Danorak," the creature replied tartly. "And not everyone out there objects to our actions. You're the one who's pushed too many too close to retaliation, however."

"I'm just a research scientist," Bandi said, hearing echoes of Nuremberg in his words.

The Soviets had made damned certain that he watched those films. All of them. That he understood what fate might be his, if he decided to not work for them.

Only their implosion in 1991 had allowed him to vanish without being hung as an old Nazi, regardless of the truth.

"You are an admitted criminal, caught red-handed," the Heecha announced. "The list of your crimes boggles the mind and will run many pages when we finally bring you to a court of justice."

"Leave a bunch of blank pages for me to fill in when we get there," Bandi snapped. "You folks don't know the half of it, pal. Not yet, anyway."

"Bandi," Joie interrupted before he got up a head of steam. "How do we stop Bouchard from stealing your ship?"

"By stealing it yourself, Joie," he sighed. "By flying the damned thing right out of the mountain and probably inserting it into a safe orbit somewhere. If you land on the ground, the Heecha's friends will probably just destroy everything rather than risk further technological contamination."

"Further?" the Heecha snarled and started to rise.

Bandi rose to match him.

Joie surprised everybody by slamming an open palm down on the table top. Worked, too. Bandi nearly pissed himself in surprise. The Heecha sat right back down.

"Are you two done?" she demanded.

Bandi sat, sheepish. Took a breath.

"Everything I've done to date was just a week ahead of what Humans were already doing," Bandi said. "Yes, crimes. Fine. Incarcerate me forever. All I did was compress what they'd already been doing. Two whole generations just during World War Two. Another couple before the Americans got to the Moon, using, I might add, technology they stole from my lab in Irkutsk in the first place. They'd have gotten there without us. Maybe not by now, but you people have no idea how smart this species is. I didn't understand until I'd lived with them for several generations."

"Bandi, assuming I do steal the ship, why orbit?" Joie asked.

"Because folks will notice," he sighed again. "They'll have to come down here and deal with everything, including Humans, immediately. My people won't be able to secretly recruit an army of your kind. Nor will Bouchard."

"Why are you telling me all this?" she asked.

It was just the two of them now. The other three were silent, as they should be. Irrelevant, in the grand scheme of things. Kehoe would do the thing where he was in charge. Graydon would tear apart all the little details and make pretty pictures of it. The Heecha was merely Bandi's warden.

Joie would have to save them all.

After this long, he had developed an attachment to Humanity, even with all their warts and wrinkles.

"Because I finally understand Faust, Joie," he admitted. "I have lived long enough to see what evil is and how seductive it can be. I screwed up. You are the only person I know who can salvage anything from this mess."

# CHAPTER 20

Valmy studied the night sky out the jet's window, that endless darkness of the Gulf of Mexico before they were over land again and racing down to Chile.

If someone had finally discovered his pet aliens, it was only a matter of time before they found the ship. It should still be there. Only a deep analysis of old data from satellites watching for nuclear missile launches had noted anything, and then only in the sort of perfect vision hindsight could get you.

"Sir, everything is confirmed," Konicek called, stepping out of a small office and entering the main cabin.

Vanlaere had been meditating a few rows aft. She came forward.

Valmy turned away from the night and studied the two agents he had with him.

More of his people were coming, but nobody else was close enough unless he delayed.

The three of them would have to risk it.

He gestured them to sit.

"In oral records, it is called the Santiago Incident," Valmy began.

"Oral, General?" Vanlaere asked.

"We're dealing with aliens, soldier," he nodded. "I always assume that most of our systems are going to be compromised by them. Thus, some systems are air-gapped and never connect to the outer world. Other things are never written down, or were typed on a mechanical machine and only stored as paper. This is one of those."

They nodded. Probably understood that they have moved into territory where even the President and Joint Chiefs didn't need to know. A few Senators in DC were informed, but only knew enough that they could be counted on to force the Defense Department to keep funding TRC without many strings attached.

And their fervent hope that Valmy Bouchard perfected his treatments that would eventually make them young and immortal.

It was an even easier way to bribe politicians than money, once you got hold of their dreams.

Konicek and Vanlaere were suitably awed. And frightened. This was one of those secrets you took with you to the grave.

"Orbital sensors had recorded something, but nobody noticed anything until I ordered a review of the data, wrapped around a certain year," Valmy said. "The aliens arrived to talk with us in 2057, so I went looking for evidence of how they'd arrived."

He leaned back and rubbed the bridge of his nose. Once upon a time, he'd needed glasses. Then laser surgery. Eventually, cybereyes would have been on the menu, except that he'd found a better way.

Still, some habits die hard.

"Something happened in the mountains east of Santiago," he continued. "An ancient volcano on the border with Argentina. An unexplainable surge of energy, followed by changes to the terrain itself."

"Building a base?" Vanlaere asked/guessed.

"Overnight," he replied. "Or at least in only a few weeks, as we had older images that showed a difference when they were done."

"Has anyone ever investigated?" Konicek asked.

"No," Valmy said flatly. "Too much risk that they might notice aircraft flying close. The best we've been able to do was make sure that certain espionage satellites kept that location in their footprint, scanning passively and photographing the scene regularly."

"So we don't know what's there?" Vanlaere asked.

"We do not," Valmy confirmed. "However, I have had unknown enemy agents take out two of my primary teams in the last month, without leaving any trace. Without anything else to go on, I have to gamble right now. This is why we can't even wait for the rest of the team to get here from their various deployments. Nor could I route them to South America without giving away too much."

"What do we expect to find there?" Vanlaere pressed.

"Possibly an alien base," Valmy replied, watching both recoil in surprise. "With any luck, an alien starship that we can understand and steal."

"Steal, General?" she asked.

"It belongs to the aliens near Buenos Aires, Vanlaere," he nodded. "They've been here for fifty years and never told us anything at all about it, so I have nothing but supposition and circumstantial evidence. But if they were not willing to tell us about it before this, they are not in a position to argue now, if someone else has captured them. We must move first."

"That's why you needed a high-altitude rescue helicopter and cold weather gear waiting for us on arrival?" Konicek asked.

"Yes," Valmy replied. "We will transition directly to the coordinates in question and force our way in. Not even the Chilean military will be allowed to assist, because they would confiscate it themselves. I will not allow that."

They fell silent at that. He did as well, with nothing useful to say at this point until they got there and started the next phase.

Twelve hours from now, in possession of a starship he could tear apart and understand, maybe replicate, he might be the most powerful person on Earth.

Or he might be starting a war with aliens.

# CHAPTER 21

Ernesta stared at the closed door and asked herself again if this was a smart idea. What she thought to gain from it.

She didn't know.

It was the middle of the night, Guadalajara time. Joie had emerged from her meeting with Yormevs and the others then sent everybody to bed, saying that they would eat a heavy breakfast before their first mission to truly attempt to thwart Kehoe's old boss.

Maybe that was what had brought her to this door, unable to sleep with the kind of nerves she hadn't faced in years.

Decades, at this point.

She just knew that she didn't want to be alone tonight. And didn't want to miss her opportunity, were something to happen tomorrow.

There were always regrets. Sometimes, she wondered if that was the single most powerful Human emotion in existence. Certainly, it had moved more people farther than love or hatred ever had, even if they had been much more quiet about it.

She didn't want regret.

Ernesta knocked instead, waiting on the balls of her feet for the door to open.

It was late.

Too late?

Except that it opened, sliding sideways into the wall. Mitch stood there, still dressed from earlier, though looking tired.

"Am I intruding?" Ernesta asked nervously, unable to believe the sound of her own voice.

Her, the most dangerous woman in Guadalajara. Nervous.

But Mitch smiled.

"Not yet," he said, stepping back and to one side. "Come in and try harder?"

It took her a moment to process that.

He wanted her to intrude?

She could do that.

Ernesta crossed that threshold in the deck and the door closed behind her.

The room was dimmer than hers usually was. Lights dialed down halfway, with a clamshell laptop computer on the desk in one corner.

"Been doing more research," he said sheepishly, grinning in a way that made him even cuter. "Trying to find out what's going on in Chile."

"Any luck?" she asked.

Ernesta drifted to the end of the bed, the spot closest to his desk, and sat. Mitch moved to the desk chair, but turned it around to face her.

"Hints of something in 2056," he said. "Some weird research project initiated by Bouchard six years ago, but I can't find any record of results. Given the systems I have access to, they were never put on the right servers. But knowing where let me find a when."

"Would he leave it where someone else might find it?" she asked. "I rarely trust important things to computers. In fact, I have a woman mechanic on staff whose primary job is repairing old typewriters, just because the US government loves to insert their AI systems everywhere, permission or not."

He blushed a little and shrugged. Guilty, himself.

Then he reached a hand over and closed the machine entirely. Not shutting her out of that conversation, but turning himself entirely to focus on her. It was like a spotlight had come on, his eyes boring in on hers.

"Obviously, you didn't come here for a late night briefing," he said. "Or did you?"

"That depends on your definitions, Mister," Ernesta laughed. "I might have had ulterior motives. We have not had a chance to really discuss certain things. I didn't feel like they should wait until we got back from Chile."

He nodded, lips pressed together. Listening.

She could see why Joie had been so attracted to the man. And why it wouldn't have worked, having heard what kind of person she used to be.

Before being transformed into someone else. The second time. And now a third.

Ernesta had merely grown up and grown old, having two ex-husbands she wasn't on particularly good terms with, now that she had grandchildren.

Her first transformation had turned her back into a young woman. With everything she'd known as an old one.

Including an appreciation of how little time anybody had.

Mitch waited. Watched her, but didn't say anything. Patience, in a way most men didn't understand until they were much older. Old soul in a young body. Where had she heard that before?

"I could be coy," she said finally. "Offer subtle misdirections and innuendo, but that's just wasting time I don't have. None of us have. And I've talked to Joie about it previously."

She watched his eyes. He nodded, still smiling. Patient.

"What I really want is to come here tonight and ask you to make love to me, Mitch," Ernesta said simply. "Joie has extremely nice things to say about you, but she's not jealous of you or me. As both of you have said, you've moved past being lovers and become friends instead. That sounds lovely, but I have needs. And I would like you to take care of them. Now."

He stood. Reached out a hand. Drew her to her feet. His hand was cold, but that was her body temperature being so much warmer than it used to be.

Most clothing left her overheated, but walking around in a bikini top and islander wrap might do terrible things to everyone's concentration, so she was in jeans and a silk blouse.

Mitch pulled her closer, but she stepped into the man. Wrapped her arms around his back and pressed herself against his chest.

She was young again, but still much shorter than Mitch. He leaned down as she tilted her head back, enjoying her first real kiss in…

Wow, that was a long time ago.

She'd been doing something so very wrong. Or had she merely grown old and given up hope of being personally happy? Most men her age were busy chasing after much younger women.

Like she was now.

Except that it was just the flesh. The soul was an ancient crone.

But the crone had needs. Reawakened desires perhaps. Or merely no longer thwarted?

She'd seen much of herself in Joie Daring, during that first meeting in Guadalajara. How Ernesta had been at that age. That vitality.

She broke the kiss with Mitch and leaned back to study his face. His eyes.

Calm. Careful. Patient.

Ernesta let go of her deathgrip about the man's middle and unbuttoned a cuff. Then the other, leaning back into his arms as he held her up.

Her blouse buttons went next, one at a time surrendering, but it wasn't a burlesque. It was simply removing it so that they could move on with more interesting business.

Not wasting time that none of them had.

Her blouse slid off her shoulders, leaving her bare. His smile warmed her.

Mitch leaned down and kissed her on the shoulder. Then the neck. Cheek. Lips.

She nodded.

He would take his time, but get the job done, just as she expected from things Joie had mentioned.

She pulled his shirt over his head and kissed him again.

# CHAPTER 22

Joie considered the approach from the safety of the ship. Gray walls. Warm temps, but not that warm. Her, Ernesta, and Carter, plus Yormevs standing at his console.

Six thousand meters elevation. Glaciers. Wind. Possible whiteout conditions on short notice, though right now the weather satellites promised a gloriously pure sky.

She missed having a blowtorch in her right hand today. Not enough to bring Freya along, but enough to have asked Yormevs to steal her three specific sets of alpine gear.

They were dressed against the cold. White against the snow. Ernesta had a long-barreled semi-automatic pistol that wouldn't notice the freezing temperatures. Joie had a carbine and a pistol matching Ernesta's.

Carter had just finished doing a once-over on a previously new-in-box M37A1 *Firelance* Squad Anti-tank Rifle, identical to the one he'd used in Hanoi, just over a month ago.

*Just a month ago? Wow.*

Carter was still getting used to being smaller than he'd been. Only Human, as he'd laughed more than once. At the same time, she wasn't sure she knew many people as at home with such a weapon as that goofball.

Yormevs had turned the temperature in here way down, so that nobody was sweating as they took their spots on the platform. The man himself was bundled against the cold, but he had a steaming mug of something on a counter nearby.

"Are you ready, Joie?" he asked.

"Everybody put your goggles and scarves on," she called, doing the same herself and pulling her hood up.

It was going to be bone-chilling where they landed. Yormevs could only get them so close because of the shielding devices that Bandi and his folks had left in place to hide their ship.

"Comm check," she said aloud.

"Good here," Carter replied, his voice in her earpiece.

"I hear you," Ernesta said.

"Base traffic is good," Kehoe noted.

He'd be in touch, wherever this ship was hiding. Not much the man could do, except that he also had Mitch next to him in their operations room, accessing all the systems that TRC had, with a permission level at least as good as General Bouchard did.

Joie looked right and left. Carter and Ernesta were ready. Joie turned back to Yormevs.

"Do it," she ordered.

Light.

The universe changed, but that was coming back to the world. They were atop a mountain in Chile. Way beyond roads, where only trained mountaineers might visit. Or desperate people.

She wasn't a mountaineer by any stretch of the imagination, extensive arctic training notwithstanding.

The breeze was solid, but not hard. Seattle on a nice day, rather than Chicago in a storm or the Santa Ana winds down at Pendleton. Early morning visibility was measured in kilometers, with a hazy sky.

Nobody flying above them currently, but that was just a matter of time. According to Mitch, Bouchard had landed Santiago, transferred to a helicopter, and was headed this way as fast as it could go.

They had minutes, but she couldn't have done this any earlier.

Not safely. Top of a glacier in the dark was barely possible for her and maybe Carter, but not Ernesta. Risky even now.

"We've arrived," she announced, mostly for Kehoe. "Spotting my surroundings. Nobody else present."

Bandi had marked the place on the map. If they'd thought that Bouchard couldn't find it, she might have let him wander about, but the Danorak had used their own matter transmitters to hollow out a chunk of mountain big enough for a ship to enter.

The need to possibly flee later meant that they couldn't just bury the garage door again, so they'd made something that looked like natural rock. At least well enough from orbit.

Nobody came up here without a lot of warning, most of the time. Nothing to see, and there were easier ways to summit the peak behind her if you were that kind of person.

That left the bowl they had landed in.

"Moving now," Joie said.

She had a small backpack, along with the carbine. The pistol was on her hip. Her gloves weren't thick enough to prevent her from getting to it and using the weapon, but she really needed to find an outcome that didn't involve a firefight on the top of this mountain.

If nothing else, Bouchard would have told someone where he was going. Others would come later. Possibly more like Bouchard and Vanlaere. The Chilean Army, if nothing else.

It was now or never.

Joie moved.

Carter had appointed himself overwatch. She'd read his reports of shooting down that police helicopter in Hanoi. At the time, she'd thought he'd gotten unlucky with a shot to kill the tail rotor.

Since then, listening to him, she'd come to understand that he'd done that on purpose. Specifically not killing anyone he didn't have to.

Or wasn't being paid for.

A helicopter out here today would draw fire. Hopefully, Bouchard hadn't brought a gunship.

Better, maybe they could get inside before all hell broke loose. If she was in control of Bandi's ship, that would make it better for everyone.

Everyone.

Scree under her feet. Loose shale broken off the face of the mountain by glaciers and time as well as stuff liberated by alien energies.

At least she knew exactly where to head.

A glance back and both Ernesta and Carter were trailing closely.

No predatory animals at this altitude.

No others, anyway.

The sun was exactly high enough in the eastern sky that they could see what they were doing. Cold as fuck, but she was dressed for it and had everything covered for now, plus small backpacks with extra gear against emergencies.

"Moving upslope," she announced, just so Kehoe could keep track.

The bleedingist-edge satellites these days could pick out movement as small as a human, but none of those were pointed this direction. Hardly any had the range to look south of the equator without a lot of prep time.

Bouchard hadn't given them any, though that might change.

She moved as quickly through the scree as she dared, paying attention to the softness underfoot that might cause it to slide away under her. The only saving grace was that they were in the bowl here, so she didn't have to worry about any cliffs that would tumble her unlucky ass down the mountain.

Just make her look silly and amateur.

And let Bouchard catch her.

She hiked.

"Mitch, any luck hacking a satellite or radar system?" she asked idly.

Again.

"Negative," he said. "I mean, I could, if we wanted everyone in DC asking why and looking over our shoulders. Didn't think it was worth it at the present time."

"Agreed," Joie said. "Wishes and fishes."

That got laughs from the others. Nobody had set out on a life's course that involved hiking in the bowl of an extinct Chilean volcano looking for an alien starship.

At least nobody sane.

Not that she wanted to contemplate those thoughts either.

Still, they made rapid progress. Most of the scree was in larger lumps that had held avalanches in place, or had already tumbled, so she quickly got to solid rock and could move. No trail, but that wasn't a surprise.

According to Bandi, nobody had come up here in more than a decade, and then only to check the maintenance systems.

She made it to the spot he'd marked on maps. A cleft in the stone that looked natural and was not. Hollowed out by Danorak systems that might be weapons and might be something else.

Joie stepped to it. Into it.

From here, the door was obvious. Only from here. You had to be standing in the notch looking.

Metal door, except that it was painted to look like the striated stone around it. Rectangular in the opening. Not to Human dimensions. Not to Heecha, either. Too short for what she expected. And too wide. Like big dwarves from some fantasy epic.

Apparently, every species did it their own way, if they weren't expecting to accommodate strangers.

Like, say, an illegal base on a proscribed planet?

It would have been nice to have Bandi on the line, but Yormevs didn't trust him. Not with things that could be activated by a word. Or sounds that had once been capable of disabling a man like Carter.

"We're here," Joie told Kehoe. "Looking for the keypad. Got it."

She found it quickly enough, covered over with a painted plate.

American systems used a standard pad with four rows of three buttons across. Went back to the first push-buttons phones. Heecha used something similar.

Danorak put them in a circle with a larger button in the middle.

And she didn't know their numbers to be able to read it. It was like the first time she'd had to read Chinese, slow and deliberate.

Joie ended up counting.

"Activating the door now," Joie said, wishing she was more certain.

Bandi had told her the combination. A combination. Maybe it opened the hatch. Maybe it initiated a self-destruct sequence like all the bad science fiction movies did when the bad guys were about to capture a vessel.

Something.

So she counted. Pressed. Counted again.

"Here goes."

Captain Daring, that badass *chika* warrior, held her breath and pushed the big button in the middle.

Nothing.

Then the door retracted about a centimeter with a ripping sound before it silently slid sideways the rest of the way into the wall.

Joie remembered to breathe and was extra thankful that she'd taken a potty break just before the jump, else she might have peed her pants at that sound.

"It's open," she said, awestruck.

Up until now, she hadn't really *believed*.

"Carter, what's in the sky?" Ernesta asked, at least paying attention to the perimeter.

Joie was a little too locked in presently.

"We're currently clear," he replied. "No idea how long."

"Let's get inside," Joie ordered, stepping across the threshold.

Bandi had described it, but only in vague terms.

Garage. That was the term. Low and wide like the door. Not all that well-lit. Maybe a hundred meters long, a third of that wide. Twenty tall. Flat floor with a polished surface and a slight tilt down to her left.

Bandi had said that it was to keep the space drained. Worked, as the floor was dry.

It was the ship in the middle that caused her to gasp. Ernesta, too, a moment later, when she entered.

Long tube on short landing pylons rather than wheels. Thick wings emerged from the bottom of the cylinder, about midway, flaring out into a delta configuration, with the passenger compartment also widening some. Vertical stabilizer like a shark fin at the rear.

They had entered near the needle-tipped prow. Joie moved to her left to get a better view.

Cockpit forward with space for two pilots, lit just enough to see seats inside. Ovalish windows down the side for passengers to see, but the aft compartment was dim enough to be all shadows.

Joie glanced back.

"Carter, close the main hatch," she said. "Maybe they won't find it and this was all a false alarm."

"You really believe that, Daring?" he asked.

Joie shrugged. Wishes and fishes.

Bandi had told her that every death was a subtraction of possibility from the universe, in one of those quiet, private moments when he'd been trying to make amends for centuries of evil. Killing Bouchard and the others wouldn't really do any good.

There were others who knew. Without stopping all of them, they would be back here again soon enough, facing this same problem.

Joie needed to solve it today.

Somehow.

Still, she pulled her goggles down and untied her scarf enough for Carter to see her scowl. He nodded and pushed the button next to the door.

Everything slammed shut with a solid thump.

Joie turned her attention back to the alien starship.

And all that it represented.

# CHAPTER 23

Valmy was aft in the helicopter with his two agents, plus a representative of the Chilean Army who had made it clear with his body language that he thought all of Valmy's stories were a load of horse shit.

And they were, but the fewer people who even suspected the truth, the better.

Everyone wore helmets with comm gear, but Valmy hadn't said anything since takeoff and the others had matched him.

The pilot had been quietly bitching about flying directly into the morning sun, but that couldn't be helped. They'd already delayed long enough that the sun was up for him to see.

Even Valmy wasn't crazy enough to try something like this in the dark.

Or maybe desperate was a better term.

In a month, he could drop an entire battalion of specialist troops up here to hold the bowl of that old volcano, but he didn't have a month.

Maybe not even the week it would take to get more of his Project Carpenter troops into place.

Not with somebody out there hitting so effectively that people simply vanished.

First Pham. Then nothing. Had they been lulling him back to sleep?

Daring and most of her team in Hanoi, but only most. All four of the people inside the laboratory in La Plata, plus one of his surveillance people, but not the other one.

Were they toying with him? Leaving people behind to up the horror quotient of the disappearances?

One survivor who didn't know anything often just muddied the waters.

"General, we're about to arrive," the pilot said over the intercom, bringing everyone to a higher state of alert. "Swinging around for the left side to see."

Valmy's side. He turned to look out. Vanlaere was across from him, with Konicek across from the Chilean major who still didn't know anything.

Bowl. Titled, but the caldera of an extinct stratovolcano. Cone broken off and collapsed inward. Glaciers around them, but not everywhere.

A century ago, it might have all been glacier. Or not. Didn't matter today.

He looked at the spot where before and after photographs had suggested an excavation. Instant and impossible, but somehow done, with tons of stone rubble suddenly apparent where it hadn't been before, and none of the ridges above changed.

Like a giant mole had burrowed out a den, then closed it behind them, leaving only the dirt.

"Your orders, sir?" the pilot asked.

"Find a spot where you can set down," Valmy replied. "If you can, shut down for a bit while my team looks around. Otherwise, you'll need to return to Santiago, refuel, and standby to extract us later."

"What's here, General?" the major asked.

"I don't know," Valmy replied. It was even honest. "I suspect many things, but we need to know now."

The man was in semi-warm gear, but not sufficient to spend a day on the mountain. Nor a night, like his team was geared for.

At least the forecast predicted a week of clear skies and calm winds. Being trapped up here would be a pain in the ass. Having to find a way to hike down to one of the tourist lodges well below would be foolhardy.

At least he was willing to play the fool.

"And you three are just going to hop out and look around?" the major asked, somehow keeping the sneer out of his voice. Certainly wasn't idle curiosity.

"That's right," Valmy said. "Pilot, can you find us a stable spot, or are we dropping a skid long enough to bail out?"

"Stand by, General," the pilot replied.

Everybody waited. It wasn't out of his hands, but that was because Valmy had spent the flight down and the ride over coming up with every possible contingency response he could think of. They had arctic gear and food. Backpacks with tents and blankets more advanced than anything a civilian could buy on the open market. Comm gear capable of reaching any of a dozen satellites, to the point that he could brief a Senator if he needed to, from here.

*Dear God, please don't let it come to that.*

The pilot had been chosen from experts at high-altitude rescue. The helicopter was configured for it as well. Any edge Valmy had been able to think of, against an unknown enemy.

"General, I can put you down and pick you up later," the man said. "However, there is no place I can see that looks stable enough to hold my weight with the rotors off. Orders?"

"Put us down and prepare to come back for us later," Valmy decided. "What's your safe margin?"

"I can orbit for an hour without risk, sir," the man said. "After that, returning to base to refuel and recharge will be necessary."

"Understood," Valmy said. "Three departing as soon as you are ready."

He nodded to the major. That one wasn't coming along. Period.

The man acknowledged that, though Valmy had no doubts that he would call ahead to Santiago to have gear assembled for himself. Probably also a full alpine rescue team as well.

Witnesses that Valmy didn't need.

Ergo, make sure that he didn't need to be rescued later.

The pilot brought the craft in delicately. Right on the edge of a field of scree that looked almost like oatmeal with cinnamon sprinkled on it.

The left skid touched stone and flexed just enough to be stable.

Valmy nodded and Vanlaere jerked open the door. Konicek handed her the first pack and she tossed it out. Two more rapidly followed, then she went. Valmy followed. Konicek trailed, slamming the hatch shut and waving the pilot off.

Rotors surged and the beast leapt into the air.

Valmy grabbed his pack and pulled out a belt holster he strapped on, with a pistol rated for these conditions.

Konicek did the same.

Vanlaere was kneeling down, studying something.

"Lieutenant?" Valmy asked.

"Animal tracks headed that way, sir," she said, never looking up as she pointed to a nearby rock face. "See where the snow was knocked when those rocks were flipped? Except that there would be no animals up here, so I assume people."

"How fresh?" he asked, reaching for his pistol automatically.

"Minutes, General."

# CHAPTER 24

To Ernesta, it looked exactly like the sort of thing you'd get if you told a budding three-D modeler to make you a starship that had to land on the surface of a planet regularly. Or an artist that you needed a cool piece of art to use on a book cover like something from her library back home.

She followed Joie into the larger space, studying the sleek, aerodynamic lines of the thing. It was painted a white darker than old parchment, when she had unconsciously been expecting metallic gray of some sort. Marker lights on various corners and spots like her personal jet had.

All told, bigger than a business jet. The central cylinder was roughly the size of a commercial passenger liner, even though the wings were stubby and blunt. Comfortable long-term for three, assuming Bandi had been the pilot for Sora and Hanni on the most recent trip.

Ernesta moved around Joie when that woman kind of staggered to a halt, but Joie, for all her brains and experience, was a soldier and a secret agent. She certainly didn't read lurid science fiction and space horror in her spare time. Unlike Ernesta.

So Ernesta took point. Carter was walking sideways, unwilling to ignore the front hatch they had come through, but drawn to a real, honest spaceship.

"This way," Ernesta waved the other two into her wake as she passed the point and moved down to the left side.

American designs put the access hatch on the left, looking forward. Bandi's was on the right. Midway. Just ahead of the wing.

The wing itself was interesting. More than half a meter thick, like a solid plate of metal that the top of the ship had been rested on and welded to. Again, she'd been expecting an aircraft wing, sloped to generate lift.

Bandi had engines capable of carrying the thing into orbit. Into deep space.

Into the galaxy.

And some wag had painted racing stripes on it. Faint, but three distinct lines in blue, green, and red. No wider than her smallest finger, so invisible at any distance. And faint.

Aspirational, rather than decorative, as it were.

Ernesta moved to the wing and found the control box under a small plate that would lock shut when the engines came on.

Everything used codes instead of keys. Bandi had told them that he'd always been in a panic that he would lose a key, or be arrested and have to break out, without whatever had been in his pockets at that moment.

So all the information was in his head.

Ernesta typed in the code and pushed that same style of middle button that Joie had used to access the flight deck.

The ship beeped and a door opened in the side, hinging down from the bottom to reveal steps as it came to rest in front of her.

"It is safe?" Carter asked.

"Who are you and what have you done with *Mithras*?" Joie asked sarcastically.

"Somebody chopped off his head," Carter joked back. "He's dead now and this new guy isn't bullet-proof."

"I don't seen Bandi trying to kill us," Joie replied.

Ernesta had to run with that. She didn't have the personal bond with the alien that Joie had somehow developed, even though she'd been there for almost everything with him.

Joie had that touch.

New Joie. Old Joie had been much more violent and linear. Ernesta had heard those stories as well.

Ernesta led anyway. She was the one who had dreamed of starships.

The steps were wrong, but that was alien architecture. Too deep and not as tall as she was expecting. Still, she got up to the top. Looked in.

Smelled alien smells that had been cooped up inside a sealed environment for a long time.

Danorak had a scent that put her in mind of freshly roasted hazelnuts. Dark and brown. They all wore Human scents to mask that, but this ship still held them.

Ernesta entered a room she took to be a dining area and kitchen, with space forward where folks could sit and read or watch stars go by. A hatch up to the bridge deck.

Lights had come on automatically when she'd opened the hatch, so Ernesta could see the carpeting underfoot. Clean and shallow, but better than raw metal.

Looking to her left, she saw another hatch that led to four cabins aft, according to Bandi, with a machine shop, storage, and a room to monitor and fix engines at the very back.

Starship.

She entered and the others followed, the first Humans to ever do such a thing. At least as far as Bandi had known.

Carter was quietly cursing under his breath, but he was like that. Joie was still a little in shock.

How do you get up in the morning and handle jumping from the cybernetic age to the interstellar?

She turned to Joie. All of this was her mission.

Joie's eyes were a little wide, but she took a breath and smiled.

"Kehoe, we're inside Bandi's ship," Joie said simply.

Ernesta was just sorry that history wouldn't record those words, like Armstrong first walking on the moon. Maybe she'd ask Yormevs for a copy of the recording later.

History was being made today.

"Shit," Kehoe replied. "You really did it, didn't you?"

Again, rather appropriate, but Ernesta didn't take these sorts of things nearly as serious as the soldiers around her.

"We don't have long," Joie announced. "Bouchard is somewhere close. Maybe already arrived."

"I can fix that fucker," Carter countered.

"No, Carter," Joie said.

"But…"

"I said no." And Joie meant it. Ernesta could see that in the woman's eyes. "Killing people doesn't solve a God-damned thing, Carter. Not now. We're too deep in the hole for that."

"Then what do you think we should be doing?" the no-longer-big man demanded.

"We need to get to the cockpit," Joie said.

"Fly this beast out where God and everyone can see it?"

"Yes," Joie said. "I have a plan."

What said plan might be, Ernesta had no idea. At that moment, an earthquake struck, knocking them all to the ground. Or the deck.

"What was that?" she asked from her knees.

"Breaching charge," Carter replied with deadly certainty in his eyes. "Bouchard's here."

# CHAPTER 25

Valmy followed Vanlaere as she ascended. Everyone was armed. Safeties might be on, and they might not be. He trusted the trigger discipline of these two, and the helicopter wasn't armed so he didn't have to worry about that.

The morning sun lit things like an art gallery. Good, and bad.

In the movies, there was always rain and darkness—maybe fog—to add to the ambiance.

Here, he was stalking someone, though he had no idea how they'd gotten here ahead of him. Visibility had been fantastic from above, so he would have seen someone else flying around. And the chances of someone ascending this peak on foot today were laughable.

At least he had a chance to confront his enemy, whoever they were.

Valmy had wondered when this day would come, but he was too close to back out. Plus, he had upgraded himself to be even a little better than the youngsters with him. The Commanding General, as it were, even after everything else shook itself out.

Vanlaere stalked wild game. He watched over her, ready to shoot while her eyes were down. Konicek would be watching their flanks.

She knelt again and touched something. He had been in an office for too long. He saw what she'd pointed at, but wasn't sure he'd have noticed it on his own. His skills at forestry had atrophied.

Human footprint, left in some snow when someone had walked by.

Someone was here, and already out of sight.

Ambush? Possibly.

Except that nobody had been killed yet, as far as he knew.

Just vanished without a trace.

Still, he flipped the safety on his pistol off and scanned the ridge-lines around them.

Nobody.

Nobody visible, he corrected himself.

Snipers were invisible, usually after they struck as well. Like Faulkener in Hanoi.

Vanlaere led him to a cut in the rock, not far from the piles of stone that had appeared one day on a satellite image.

"Tracks seem to lead here, General," she said quietly. "Then vanish."

"There's a door, then," he replied, looking.

Konicek took overwatch, back turned to them as he looked for trouble. They had radios to talk to the helicopter, but the less the pilot and the major ended up knowing, the better.

"Here," Vanlaere said after a moment.

She flipped open a panel that had been cunningly hidden to appear as part of the native stone, revealing…

A ring of twelve buttons around a thirteenth?

Weird. And wrong, as he didn't recognize any of the symbols.

At the same time, he'd been working with aliens for many years. And this spot potentially contained a hidden spaceship.

But the placement gave him a clue.

Valmy turned and saw a spot in the rock, squared off for a door. Something. Rough, but raw where it looked to have been opened recently. Like, in the last five minutes?

"Thoughts?" Vanlaere asked.

"No idea what the code might be," he said, pointing at the panel. "Blow the door."

"Sir?" She was shocked.

"Someone is ahead of us, Vanlaere," Valmy reminded her. "And they went in. We cannot wait for them to emerge."

She blinked twice, then shifted gears.

"Konicek, you're better with explosives," she said. "Trade me."

Valmy stepped back and watched Konicek get to work, pulling bits and pieces from various packs and assembling them on the face of the rock quickly.

Detonator in place, the man waved them all back and out of sight around the edge of the stone.

"Ready to detonate, General," Konicek said calmly, device in hand.

"Blow it," Valmy replied. "Then be ready to get inside and find out who we've been chasing. Remember, however, that I need prisoners. Dead people won't tell me enough to understand what's going on."

"Clear!" Konicek called after nodding.

Valmy opened his mouth and closed his eyes.

The sound was over so quickly he almost missed it, a crack like a bullet, then a rumble through his boots.

He moved first, even faster than Vanlaere around the corner.

The charge had mostly done its work, but the door was still intact. Harder than Konicek had anticipated, and the man had been a little heavy on the explosives.

Valmy holstered his pistol and slammed his entire left side into the door. At least it bounced as much as he did.

"A hinge held," Vanlaere called. "Or something."

Valmy stepped back as Konicek dug out a small charge and stuffed it into the gap that had been revealed.

"Step back?" the man asked.

Valmy just turned his back to it.

"Go," he ordered.

This time, the sound was much louder, unmuffled. Something bounced off his back, but didn't feel like it had penetrated the jacket or the armor under it.

He turned back and looked.

Mostly gone.

"Stand clear," he said.

Valmy took a few steps back, got a flying start, and launched a hard front kick.

The metal surrendered.

# CHAPTER 26

Joie knew she'd run out of time. If Bouchard was using explosives, then he must have seen them. Seen something.

Knew he wasn't alone on this mountaintop.

And confronting him right now didn't solve her greater problem.

Everyone kept forgetting that one.

What the hell had happened to Romana?

Joie knew that a matter transmitter like Yormevs was the best explanation, but he claimed not to have done it. That just left everyone else in the galaxy.

She moved to the cockpit.

If Bouchard was using explosives, he meant business.

Through the hatch, she saw two seats, just as Bandi had described them.

Preflight was relatively easy, because Bandi hadn't been a pilot. The ship did most of the work for you, rather than forcing someone to deal with ten thousand different knobs and gauges. They were there, but only for nerds and adrenaline junkies who wanted to tweak things.

She threw herself into the chair as a second, smaller explosion went off. Light suddenly filled the space as the door to the garage collapsed inward, followed a moment later by two bodies rushing into the space.

Joie hit the friendly, purple button designed to activate the autopilot system. A screen came up in a language she couldn't even begin to understand. Again, Bandi rescued her.

A smaller screen showed a white spot where the hatch was open aft. She touched it and heard the door start to cycle shut.

Movement on her left was Ernesta taking the co-pilot seat. Hopefully, Carter hadn't been stupid enough to charge into an unnecessary battle when she'd turned her back on him.

New Carter wasn't the self-destructive lunatic he'd been when his skin would stop bullets.

Lights came up with a hum of power that communicated itself through her seat.

A flight yoke not too different from others she'd used rose out of the console and Joie grabbed it with both hands. A throttle on her right, just as Bandi had described it.

In front of her, the garage door that the ship had been backed into opened by scrolling up, just like a Human would have done it.

If Humans had built secret bases for starships in the Chilean mountains.

Two figures in front of her. Not even that far away. Chelsea Vanlaere she recognized immediately.

The other one was General Bouchard.

They locked eyes.

Joie pressed the throttle forward a notch.

Bouchard raised his pistol and pointed it right at her.

In the movies, the hero would utter some rude profanity as he made his escape, but she didn't have it in her. She hadn't escaped anything. Even getting away right now would just move the battlefield.

And expand it tremendously.

She had no choice.

Instead, Joie smiled and shrugged. Around her, the ship lifted a meter and began to move forward at a slow walk.

Bouchard shot at her.

Son of a bitch!

Except that it wasn't glass between them. Transparent enough to leave a scar of copper where the bullet hit and bounced straight up, but didn't do anything.

Then she was past him, accelerating outwards into the clear morning sky.

Joie looked for the helicopter that had to be here somewhere. Found it. Turned the yoke instinctively, like she was playing a video game, to avoid him.

She notched the throttle forward two more clicks and pulled back, suddenly riding a rocket pointed at the sky.

Now came the hard part. She had no idea where she could take a ship like this. Or who would suddenly be able to see it, on radar or whatever the other aliens might use.

"Joie?" A voice startled her.

Kehoe.

Shit. She'd been focused on everything and forgetting to keep up a running commentary.

"We're away in Bandi's ship," she said aloud.

"Gathered that," Kehoe replied sarcastically. "You just showed up on Yormevs's scanners, so apparently whatever cloak Bandi was using is located in the space, rather than wrapped around the ship. Everyone can see you."

Joie looked out over the wing at the ground receding rapidly. Hardly any g-forces pressing her back, so she had no idea how hot she was running.

Really freaking fast.

"And nobody can catch me," she replied. "Yormevs, are you somewhere in orbit where I can rendezvous? Or can you be when I get there?"

A long pause.

"Are you certain that such an action is wise, Joie?" the alien finally responded.

"No, but everyone is about to discover the truth," she said. "Some of it, anyway."

"Can you understand any of the screens in front of you?" he asked.

"Negative," Joie laughed. "Non-Terran language unlike anything I've ever seen before. I can fly it. Control speed. Presumably land it somewhere because it's smart enough, according to Bandi, since it was designed for a civilian to operate. That's about it."

"Very well, Joie," Yormevs said with a sigh. "We shall meet you when you get to orbit. I shall walk you through the process of a proper orbital insertion that is stable enough for someone to come aboard who can handle the vessel professionally."

"Thank you," Joie said.

She glanced back and saw Carter strapped into a jumpseat, smiling weakly at her.

Three of them against a hostile universe?

Bring it.

# CHAPTER 27

Valmy closed his mouth before he caught any flies, like his grandmother had always warned him.

That had been Joie Daring piloting. Plus someone else he didn't know.

What the hell was she doing here? Last known coordinates for the woman had been Hanoi, just before she had disappeared from a hotel surrounded by a full team, most of whom had vanished with her, save for the pair he had with him right now.

He'd fired automatically, but Valmy hadn't been surprised when his bullet didn't even scrape the ship. The Danorak had told him how advanced their tech was compared to Humans. That would include metallurgy.

And it had been a spaceship. Some kind. Physics was physics. He trailed it out into the open and watched a star receding into the western sky.

For a thing going to orbit, there had been remarkably little sound. And no wind blowing him backwards like he'd have gotten had he walked behind a jet.

Joie Daring had just stolen an alien starship, right out from under his fingers.

He looked at Vanlaere. She had the same shock in her eyes that he felt.

"Was that...?" she began.

"Daring," he nodded back to her.

"But..."

Valmy shrugged. None of it made a damned bit of sense. Konicek walked close, so pale that he could hide in the nearby snow.

"Sir?" the man asked.

Valmy turned back to the cave behind him. Base. Something.

He entered and noted how smooth the walls and floor were, like someone with a giant knife had cut out a slice of cake then closed the box again.

There was light in here, but that seemed to be something quartz-like in the roof letting it in, rather than some advanced technological gadget his scientists could unravel.

The space was empty. That ship had been the entirety of value and Joie Daring had just stolen it.

How?

Better, why?

Who was she working for?

Valmy holstered his pistol and turned back to the outside. The sound of the helicopter was getting louder, so he presumed the major was landing.

He walked out and confirmed that, Vanlaere and Konicek trailing in his wake, all of them crestfallen.

The pilot was still excellent, touching a skid just right for the major to open the door and hop out, then lifting away so there was quiet to talk without screaming in each other's ears.

"General Bouchard, what the hell was that?" the man asked in a voice working really hard to be calm instead of frightened or angry.

Valmy smiled ruefully at the man.

"I could tell you," he replied. "At that point, however, the US Army would have to take you into protective custody for an extended period of time. I'm certain it wouldn't be too many years, but you would have to be isolated until we determined that your knowledge wouldn't compromise certain operations and endanger my agents."

Pure bullshit, but almost automated boilerplate when dealing with Congresscritters who didn't have the necessary security clearances to be asking certain questions.

For a Hispanic man, the major was about the same color as Garrison Konicek right now.

Valmy waited for the man to irrevocably damn himself. The major seemed content with ignorance.

His loss.

Valmy would have asked, but that was the kind of man he was. He turned to the helicopter and waved for the pilot to return. There was nothing to be gained at this point by staying. He could send troops later to remove the door and whatever electronics could be salvaged, but it wouldn't be anywhere as useful as an apparently working starship.

The pilot saw his signal and came back in to land. Everyone boarded and helmeted up.

"Where to, General?" the pilot asked, skipping entirely the part about sharing the skies with something that had looked vaguely like the old delta-wing jets that the European air forces had dabbled with in the early jet age.

"Back to Santiago," Valmy said. "I need to make some calls."

# CHAPTER 28

Ernesta would have liked to have been frightened by the whole affair, but that would be a lie. She'd never been one to dream of being a princess in a tower. No, she'd had a ray gun in one hand saving the galaxy from monsters and evildoers.

Fifty years later, she had gotten her chance.

Pity she couldn't understand a damned thing on the various screens and controls in front of them. Joie, however, was flying it like a natural. Or a video game.

"So, please pardon my abject ignorance," Carter suddenly said from behind them. "Is now a good time to ask what your actual plan is?"

"That was Bouchard," Joie said.

"Pity I didn't get a chance to blowtorch the son of a bitch, then," Carter demurred.

"What would that have solved, Carter?" Ernesta asked.

She'd spent enough time with Joie now, a sister of the soul if not the flesh, to have a better grasp on the woman's thought processes.

Violence solved every problem, true, but rarely was it the *best* solution.

"The man in charge would have been dead," Carter replied smugly.

"It's an organization, doofus," Joie piped up. "Thousands of people have to be involved in one way or another. Ernesta's organization didn't suddenly shrivel up and die because she's not in Guadalajara. TRC would have to appoint a new Commanding General, but there are already deputies of various departments who handle things when the top man is out of the office. And whatever research he did suggests entire laboratories and teams of people. They probably think they are curing cancer and solving immortality, because he certainly didn't tell them the truth."

"Granted," Carter replied. "Still not following your logic."

"That's because you want to blow things up," Joie teased, glancing back over a shoulder at the man.

"Fine," Carter huffed. "And?"

"And there is at least a third player involved," Joie said.

"Whoever took Romana," Ernesta suddenly understood.

Joie was playing a game in at least three dimensions, where everyone else was simply playing chess. Complicated, but flat.

"Correct," Joie nodded. "Yormevs denies that the Heecha did it. The Danorak didn't, at least Bandi and his ilk. That leaves somebody else."

"Do we presume someone who can't appear as Human?" Ernesta asked, cycling back through the piles of SF books she'd read in a lifetime as a secret nerd.

"Maybe," Joie shrugged. "But I can't find them until they want to be found."

"So you had to go steal Bandi's ship?" Carter asked.

"We just appeared on everybody's radar systems," Joie replied casually. "I could probably turn on whatever they used as a cloak to hide when they arrived, but I didn't bother asking."

"Because you need someone to find you," Ernesta nodded. "Will they be friendly?"

"One can only hope," Joie said. "We're flying into orbit in a way that nobody else can do. Not riding a rocket with massive fuel consumption. According to Bandi, it will fly rather like an aircraft until we get high enough, then we'll have to use something like vectored thrust to maneuver. But we're centuries ahead of anything on the ground."

"This thing got guns?" Carter asked.

Because of course Carter would ask that.

"Negative," Joie laughed. "We are a passenger jet with an extended range."

"What about FTL?" Ernesta asked.

Joie turned a confused face towards her.

"Faster Than Light," Ernesta explained. "Warp drive. Hyperspace. Folding space/time. However they get somewhere when a light-speed journey is measured in years. Like in the vids or on television."

Joie nodded at that.

"No clue," she said. "Bandi said they have it, but that I couldn't activate it unless I got stupid. Looking at all these controls, he's right, because I'd have to be randomly pushing buttons and I have no intention of trying something that foolish. We've got lights, power, air, and some sort of pseudo-gravity. I can get us up high enough, then Yormevs will flatten us out into an orbital insertion and do something to dock. That's enough for now."

They rode in silence for a bit, everyone consumed in their own thoughts.

Ernesta reveled in doing something from some of her favorite books.

"Anybody else hungry?" Carter asked the room.

"You don't need to munch constantly," Joie replied.

"Habit going back before you were born, young lady," he scoffed humorously. "I just eat tiny snacks these days."

"Stay out of the kitchen," Ernesta said. "Chances are that something in there will poison you."

"Oh, I got snacks," Carter laughed. "Been doing this a long time. Just figured I should ask. We might be a while getting wherever we're going."

Ernesta waved him off. She'd lost all those kilograms that age had put on and had no interest whatsoever in gaining them back.

She happened to be looking out the windshield as darkness

engulfed them, watching the curve of Earth itself, with that thin line of atmosphere as a haze around it.

Something shimmered into existence, just off their right side bow. Something huge and off-white, like a giant space shark about to chomp on them.

Then light swallowed her whole.

# CHAPTER 29

"WHAT?" Valmy screamed into the microphone.

He'd been communicating in coded phrases with his team in DC. Everything spoken in obscure evasions, because he was certain that the entire planet was listening in on the conversation, but they were still a few minutes out from landing at Santiago and he'd needed things in motion.

"Confirmed, General," the operative on the other end of the line said. "Target designated Alpha simply vanished off our radar three minutes ago. There was a bigger blip for about eight seconds, then nothing at all. Subsequent scans have turned up nothing. Not even debris as we might expect had the craft exploded."

Valmy kept all the insults and abuse inside. This was merely the commander of a radar installation that happened to have the best view of the skies over the South Pacific, where Daring had been flying.

Woman didn't even know that you rode into space west-to-east to make it easier to insert. Less fuel needed.

Did she even need fuel? How did an alien starship work?

What were Daring's limits?

Valmy was certain of one thing right now. He was too exposed. The aliens had given TRC certain devices that they used to hide from other aliens. Such had somehow been used on the mountain behind him, as well as the facilities in La Plata.

He had a few of them in the States, protecting labs as well.

It suddenly felt like a war had been declared. Or escalated. Hadn't they all been playing quiet games for years? The one alien supposedly had first come to Earth in the 1920s, left in the 90s, then returned in 2057. Almost fifty years ago, and he'd been keeping an exceptionally low profile for that whole time.

Valmy was exposed. Out on the tip of the spear with only Vanlaere and Konicek. They were good, but there was an unknown enemy out there who had decided to up the stakes.

He needed to get to safety.

If such a thing existed.

"General?" the man on the radio asked.

"I will be aboard my jet in under an hour," Valmy announced. "Assemble all your data so that it can be transmitted. We'll take it from there."

"Understood, General. Working now."

Valmy signaled to the major to cut the line and leave them on intercom. The man nodded a moment later, eyes still wary but as yet unwilling to step over that line and fall fully into the sorts of security that would come with actually knowing the truth.

Valmy considered him.

"I appreciate that this is Chilean sovereign territory up there," Valmy said slowly. Carefully. "As you now know, there is much more going on. I would request that you do not put troops up there to interfere with my investigation until we can do it as a combined effort. I will be briefing the Joint Chiefs shortly. They will no doubt be in touch with your superiors. This situation must be handled with care, or everything we might have gained will be lost. Do we have an understanding?"

Valmy knew that he was putting the man into an impossible situation. Things unknown and vague threats. At the same time, it should protect the major from getting in over his head.

The man nodded. Held out a hand. Valmy shook it.

He only needed a few days to put a team up there, including a few scientists who might be able to understand whatever tech had been left behind.

What Valmy didn't know was if he had that much time left.

# CHAPTER 30

"WHAT?" Taylor screamed at the alien.

Daring had gotten in successfully ahead of Bouchard. Rescued Bandi's ship from being confiscated.

"She just vanished off all of our sensors, Kehoe," Yormevs repeated.

Sounded sincere. Sad. Like the ship had gotten all the way to orbit and inexplicably exploded.

Would that stupid, Danorak fuck have set her up like that?

"Where's Bandi?" Taylor demanded, already angry enough to get answers.

However he needed to.

"We will go speak with him now," Yormevs nodded. "Mitch, could you join us please?"

Taylor stood up and felt the stiffness in his back. They were in an operations room with computers he could have had Stone requisition from stores, watching various feeds from Mitch as the man poked into TRC systems and whatever else he could access.

Mostly, audio feed from Daring, because they didn't dare tap some of the systems they needed. He agreed with Mitch on that. Too much risk of people looking the wrong way at the wrong moment.

Mitch rose as well. Taylor looked around the conference room.

Bland, with moss-colored walls and carpet, possibly designed to put you in the mood of a friendly swamp someplace.

"Where's Stone?" Taylor asked in a much less belligerent voice.

"I believe he is currently training with Sifu Wěn," Yormevs replied.

Taylor grunted. Without much else to do, the man had leaned back into a martial arts background the last few days. Those two were still Human, as folks understood it.

They might have also just turned into his only remaining agents.

"Could you ask them both to join us?" Taylor asked in a finally-friendly voice.

"Certainly," Yormevs nodded, then led them out into the hallway.

They paused at a door long enough for Stone and the Cantonese woman to join them, both a little rank from sweat.

Showers could wait. Answers could not.

They got to the suite where Bandi Algom was being held. Better than a jail cell. Less than freedom to explore the ship. The man had been reading a book when they entered. Taylor didn't even recognize the language the cover was written in as they moved to a large dining table and sat.

"Trouble?" Bandi asked, looked this way.

Taylor turned to Yormevs.

"Could you explain it in terms all of us would understand?" he asked politely.

Mentally, he was shuffling everything, wondering if there were any other agents he could somehow kidnap and press into duty, with whatever lies he had to tell. *Pakhet* came to mind.

With the two he had, definitely second-string compared to Joie. Still better than nothing.

"Joie was able to access your ship, Algom," Yormevs noted. "She was there ahead of the one called Bouchard, but he accessed the facility with explosives, so she immediately flew it out of the bay and launched for orbit."

Taylor didn't know the word the Danorak muttered, but he got the general gist of it. Something any of their mothers would have washed their mouths out with soap for using.

"Without shields," Bandi grumbled.

"That is correct," Yormevs said. "She could not read the panels to know what to do, and asked us to meet her in orbit, where we could put a crew member aboard to handle those things."

"And then she vanished, didn't she?" Bandi asked.

Taylor perked right up.

Bandi grimaced like he'd just sucked a lemon dry.

"Well, I wanted to go out with a bang, I guess," Bandi said, looking at the heavens overhead before returning his gaze to Taylor. "Do we know who got her?"

"The vessel was uncloaked for only a few seconds," Yormevs said.

"Long enough to grab Joie and the others, put a pilot aboard, then everybody cloaked again?" Bandi asked, nodding as he went.

"That is a valid presumption," Yormevs agreed.

"English, please?" Stone grouched at everyone, a little before Taylor did the same.

"We use an electromagnetic shielding system that renders us invisible to most scanners, except at short range," Bandi spoke. "It also prevents the matter transmission beams from working. I had one around my old lab in La Plata, but hadn't gotten it installed in the new place yet. There was another one protecting the ship on the ground. Joie wouldn't have been able to activate it without a lot of training."

"Not helpful yet," Stone growled.

"Someone else has a ship in orbit," Bandi snapped. "Hidden. They dropped their cloak long enough to capture Joie and the others, then vanished again."

He turned to Yormevs.

"They did capture her, right?" Bandi asked.

"We found no evidence of an explosion," Yormevs nodded. "However, we remain at a significant distance so our data is fragmentary at best."

"Can I see it?" Mitch asked.

Every eye in the place turned to the man. Taylor grinned.

"Analyst," Taylor reminded the others. "Really freaking amazing at taking odd tidbits and assembling them into useful intelligence. You've seen what he's been able to do for me. Maybe he can do it for you as well. We've got nothing to do right now, unless you plan to dump the rest of us back on the surface to be arrested by Bouchard."

"That would gain us nothing, and potentially cost us everything, Kehoe," Yormevs replied. Then he turned to Mitch. "What would you need?"

"Who are you folks all hiding from?" Mitch asked. "I've heard no mention of any sort of law enforcement or space navy organization running around, like Humans might do it. Instead, I hear about the Danorak and the Heecha as species. Tribes, almost. Who's the most dangerous, most powerful tribe in this region of space? The one you're hiding from?"

Taylor grinned at the two aliens, their own mouths fallen open in shock. But they were both scientists. Not agents. Most certainly not analysts.

Yormevs kind of sputtered. Bandi's grimace was back.

"Myself, we're always hiding from the Brakhua," Bandi said stubbornly. "They do see themselves in a law enforcement way, keeping things honest. Nobody is allowed to claim Earth, so nobody has resources here. The Brakhua have been known to stick their noses in anyway."

"Good," Mitch said. "So you had several seconds. Were there any passive cameras recording images, even at this distance, that we could magnify and clean up? Or access Human spy satellites that might have seen something? They tend to be extremely high altitude, so they can stay geosynchronous over a specific ground location. Who can we tap? What data can we steal?"

Taylor wanted to laugh. These folks really were amateurs at the espionage business. At the same time, he understood that he was exceptionally good, and had been blessed with amazing teams, both in operations as well as folks like Mitch.

Yormevs was blinking too fast for normal. Taylor put that down to surprise. Emotional overload.

Humans did something similar.

"We will get you what we can," he managed.

"Include ship silhouettes of Brakhua vessels," Taylor inserted. "Three dimensional models that can be rotated to compare."

More blinking. Top-notch scientists. Keystone cops agents.

And while the three operatives he might have to send out into the field weren't as good as Joie Daring and the other two, nobody else probably was either.

Still, Taylor felt the entire weight of Humanity descend on his shoulders.

What idiot had decided that he had to save the universe?

# CHAPTER 31

Joie watched the light fade, expecting to be in another prison cell like she'd been that first time when Yormevs had first grabbed her from Hanoi.

A quick glance to either side didn't reveal Ernesta or Carter, but they could easily be in their own cells.

She didn't expect the person standing across from her, pointing some sort of weapon.

"Romana?" Joie gasped.

Romana was dressed in black. Pants over ankle boots. Belted tunic over that, with a hint of a gray collar underneath at the neck. Black beret on her head with a logo Joie didn't know.

And the gun. Whatever it was, Joie had no doubt that it was a gun. Lethal or not, she couldn't tell. Didn't really want to find out.

"Joie, do you have any idea what kinds of trouble you've caused?" Romana demanded angrily.

Joie studied the woman. Party-partner. Dancing fool. Occasional sidekick. More-than-occasional troublemaker.

She also straightened from the defensive stance she'd fallen into. This was Romana.

She hoped.

"Actually, I do have a pretty good idea," Joie grinned.

"Your scans show you are no longer entirely Human, Joie," Romana said darkly.

Joie nodded.

"That was necessary," Joie said simply. "Bouchard has slowly been turning out a number of Advanced Model Humans. AMHs. My assumption is that he's eventually going to form a global army and then attack the aliens that had up until now been thinking they were in control."

"How much do you know?" Romana demanded, shocked.

"I was the one who captured the three Danorak who have been behind it the longest," Joie said. "With the help of a group of Heecha. Who are you working for?"

Romana studied her long and hard, scowling like she did.

Romana's family had come to the United States in the late 1970s, escaping the communist takeover of Vietnam and fitting right into being another facet of American life quickly. Ethnically, mostly still Vietnamese, but wholly American. Wholly TRC, though she'd never been upgraded with cyberware.

Joie looked closer, using some of those new senses that Yormevs had baked into this form. Genetics, rather than cybernetics.

Romana had changed, as well.

"How did you come to be flying that ship, Joie?" Romana asked, ignoring Joie's question.

She could do that, holding the only gun in here.

Joie glanced down and realized that she was back down to the jeans and T-shirt she'd been wearing under all the thermal gear. And they'd taken the time to strip the silks she'd been wearing under that to stay warm.

How long had she been in the beam?

Still, it was Romana. The woman who'd held her hair so she didn't drown, face down over a toilet. Who'd gone dancing with her to obscure places, meeting strange and interesting men. Like Mitch.

"Bouchard knew there was something there on that mountain," Joie explained. Might as well get it all out so everyone could figure out how to salvage the situation.

The bad guys could have gone ahead and destroyed Human civilization anytime they wanted, give the state of their tech. They had to have been holding off for a reason.

Joie just had to find it.

"How did he know?" Romana demanded.

"Mitch found references to something, but they weren't written down in a database he could access," Joie replied. "Air-gapped."

"Mitch?" Romana demanded. "MITCH?!? What the hell's he doing here?"

Joie sighed.

"Kehoe recruited him when they started chasing me all over hell and gone," Joie said. "If you want the whole story, that's going to take a while, so we might as well get some comfortable seats and coffee. Mitch and Kehoe were back at base with the aliens, monitoring the operation. You've got Carter and Ernesta somewhere, since they were with me."

"The records tell me that you had *Mithras* with you, Joie," Romana accused.

"He's a new guy, Romana," Joie explained. "They took out all the stuff inside him and reset him to Human, like they did with me. Then upgraded both of us, because we had to stop Bouchard and TRC from whatever terrible shit they were doing, before folks like you finally got angry enough to do something irrevocable."

"Anybody but you, Joie, and I'd say all that was a load of fresh pig shit," Romana replied.

"Oh, it is," Joie agreed. "It's also God's honest truth."

"Who's the woman agent with you?" Romana demanded. "You called her Ernesta?"

"Ernesta Hernandez, of Guadalajara," Joie nodded.

"The **crime lord**?" Romana snarled. "More bullshit. This woman is twenty-five."

"It's her," Joie said. "They reset all three of us to that age when they did everything else. Carter was in his mid-fifties before this. Ernesta helped me when I was on the run from TRC. She'd kept helping me after I returned to the fold. Then she went rogue with me when I asked her."

"There are a lot of angry people extremely nervous right now, Joie," Romana accused.

"You think I don't know that?" Joie snapped back at one of her best friends in the world. "I'm out on a ledge here, trying to keep everything from catching fire, because Bouchard is absolutely playing with matches. As were the others. Who do I need to meet to explain it all? You're in somebody's uniform, so I assume that they recruited you into going rogue, same as me. I did what I had to because that was the only way I could convince you folks to come out of the shadows long enough. Otherwise, boom. The world ends one day and most of Humanity goes with it."

Romana started to say something, but a pleasant gong interrupted.

Joie rolled back off her toes and took a moment to actually see the space where she had…*materialized*. Say it for what it was.

Yet another alien starship. Yet another player. Hopefully, the only other one right now, and not just a new third side against whoever would pull the trigger to dump Earth into the stone ages overnight before a fourth showed up.

Metal walls more like a US Navy aircraft carrier. A little cramped, but she'd been on two ships before this, and assumed that Romana's bosses might be a physically smaller species, so this was normal to them.

Metal deck underfoot, painted a marbled gray. Door behind Romana, but the room itself was sized more like a bedroom than a prison cell. Entirely empty save for the two of them.

Then the door behind Romana opened and another alien walked in.

This one wouldn't ever be able to walk the streets of La Plata, even in disguise. Upstate Maine, maybe, but they considered anyone born more than sixty kilometers away to be an alien to be looked down upon with disdain and ignored.

Even a short, skinny humanoid with lavender-hued skin. Maybe one hundred and fifty centimeters tall. Lanky-feeling, in spite of the height. Almost lizardlike build.

The newcomer was also dressed in black, but it felt softer. Like maybe Romana was a warrior and this guy was a REMF in a nice suit, though such an insult was probably uncalled for.

Rear Echelon Motherfucker. The ones that stayed behind in air-conditioned bases while sending agents out into mud and squalor. Kehoe, on a bad day.

Still, the alien did feel like a REMF in the way he studied her.

Joie had a head and shoulders on the man. And a lot of kilograms.

Still, she'd done all this so she could meet this person.

"Good morning," Joie said.

She and Romana had been…arguing in English, so Joie had started there.

Most of the time recently, she had spoken in Spanish, because of Ernesta and Bandi. Everyone had been fully fluent.

"Good morning, Captain Daring," the creature replied in a melodious voice that seemed to be more used to a tonal language like Chinese or Vietnamese. Not that English was much better.

Joie nodded deeply. Maybe this was the person—guy?—that had the answers she'd been lacking.

Or the trigger finger poised to wipe out Humanity.

"I have been following your conversation with Agent Pham," the person continued. "We lack a great deal of the context that the two of you take for granted, but one word stuck out as I listened. You mentioned going rogue."

"That's right, sir," she said, automatically. "I had been forcibly retired from service two years ago. Then my former bosses attempted to reactivate me as something of a last resort when nobody could explain what had happened to Romana. She simply vanished one night out of a secured base. I presume in a flash of light."

The man(?) seemed to smile at that. The face muscles made a motion similar to how she'd have done it.

"Go on," he said.

"Then Carter did turn rogue, having been lying to me earlier," Joie said. "Again, long explanation with a lot of details and a dead, Russian Ambassador. As I was hunting him down, a group that call themselves Heecha used a matter transmission beam to kidnap me from Hanoi. We came to an understanding and I've been working for them recently, trying to find a way to stop my old bosses at Technology Research

Command before they frightened someone, presumably you, into causing an apocalypse."

"Indeed, Captain Daring," the man confirmed. "As you noted, the basis for a long and complicated conversation."

"Is Bandi's ship safe?" Joie asked. "I had only intended to keep it out of the hands of everyone on the ground, but if you have us, then it needs a pilot to get it someplace where it won't fall later."

"Such was taken care of when you were taken into custody," he nodded in a Human way. "The stealth circuits were also activated, so it has vanished as well. You mentioned Heecha and Danorak."

Joie nearly got whiplash from the way he turned the conversation, but nodded.

"Danorak scientists have been working with parts of Humanity secretly for almost two hundred years, according to their story," Joie said. "The Heecha came for me and my two friends a month ago."

"The Danorak have told you truths?" he asked.

Romana stirred, but Joie suspected that her friend been a prisoner of these folks for a stretch before being recruited to change sides. Maybe about the time Joie had been unretired by Kehoe.

"The one in charge is named Bandi Algom," Joie replied. "I think he has had an ethical crisis recently where he came to understand the evil that he had perpetrated previously. He helped me, even before I had to go rogue against TRC. He has helped since."

"Agent Pham speaks highly of you," he said. "But only in the past tense."

Joie nodded and shrugged.

She'd been broken by Kehoe. Driven Mitch and Romana off because she'd preferred to wallow in depression and self-pity.

It had taken Amy to start her healing. Then all her new female friends like Celeste Graydon, Sarah, and Ernesta, plus a whole cast of nameless women who had seen a sister in need and responded immediately. Anonymously.

Because helping a complete stranger was a Human thing Joie had never understood. At least until the Army had no longer been her family.

"I would have stayed retired," Joie admitted. "Until Kehoe knocked on my door one day several months ago. Romana had vanished and nobody knew how. At the time. Several of us have been in a beam at this point."

"You spoke truth about the threat to your world, Captain Daring," he shifted gears again. Directions. Something. "Many have proposed triggering the apocalypse you suspected. Especially when we detected a Human flying a Danorak ship. That would have been unspeakable."

"Indeed," Joie replied with a grimace. "I had to keep it out of Bouchard's hands. My allies would have been fine, since they could have known how to hide it. You'll do."

"The Heecha you mentioned," he said. "They are close?"

"I asked them to meet me in orbit to take care of the ship," Joie replied. "Not knowing that you were there to do it. I suspect that they will remain hidden for now. Possibly panicking themselves, as you've captured many of Kehoe's agents."

"Is this Kehoe friend or foe?"

"He was my boss in the old days," she said, gesturing to Romana. Gods, it was so good to see her. "Our boss. He was something of an enemy when this started, because I didn't want to come back. He was the hound and they made me a hare. Later, we came to an understanding, so that I would help them try to find Romana. Then *Mithras* went rogue and we had to hunt him down. The Heecha appeared at that point and things got weird."

"Lady, you have no idea," Romana said with a laugh that was good to hear.

"How do we save the world?" Joie asked.

"I think we will need to hear your entire tale, Captain Daring," the man said. "Then we will make decisions."

Joie nodded. She'd done everything to bring it to this moment.

Hopefully, she could pull it off.

# CHAPTER 32

Valmy boarded the craft and immediately turned left, sticking his head into the cockpit and surprising the woman flying. The other pilot, the male, must be aft sleeping.

"File a flight plan for immediate departure," he ordered, waiting for her to nod. "Destination Andrews. Take off as soon as you can get clearance from the tower. We will change course over Mexico for a location in the Rockies that we will approach below radar, flying nape of the earth, but do not mention that to anyone. We are under top secret orders. Questions?"

"Negative, General," she said, already flicking switches. "Andrews, with a deviation probably midway between Guadalajara and Mexico City. I'll need to study the maps for best timing on that."

He nodded and pulled the hatch shut, isolating her from what was about to be said aft. He had a pair of stewards who generally kept a low profile, but they had as good a clearance as anybody in TRC that handled Project Carpenter agents. They would keep quiet.

Konicek was closing things up. Vanlaere stowing bags. Valmy gestured the stewards to remain aft in the galley for now as he sat.

The three of them got settled and buckled in, even as the jet began to roll.

Things were in motion.

"Some of our allies are not Human," he said simply by way of introduction.

Konicek gasped. Vanlaere nodded. She must have seen or known things from Daring.

"At this point, I presume Daring has gone turncoat, though I'm not sure why," he continued. "That she stole the alien ship and did not talk to me tells me all that I need to know. I presume she is behind the disappearances of our alien friends and one of their watchers in Argentina."

"And the ship vanished off radar in orbit?" Vanlaere asked.

"Stealth technology better than anything we have," Valmy nodded. "I was able to locate their base on the timing of their recent arrival in 2057 and attacking any possible anomalies with some of my AIs. It still took years and a lot of Human work, weeding out all the false positives. I'd been holding that location in my back pocket against need. The only person who could have told Daring were the aliens who had been working with us."

"Since 2057, General?" Vanlaere asked.

"He claimed to have first come in 1928, Lieutenant," Valmy said with a grin. "Might be immortal, or at least extremely long-lived. We don't know. But even that little told our scientists that is was possible, so they started working on how to do it."

"*Mithras*," Vanlaere stated. "He was supposed to live for several hundred years, if I recall correctly?"

"You do, Vanlaere," Valmy said. "All of the Herakles agents had that upgrade, as do Carpenter agents."

"We were told a doubling, sir?" she asked hesitantly.

He smiled.

"Herakles agents were selected with a different set of criteria. Three of them are dead now. Three will continue to be watched closely for a long time," he said. "The three of us should be around at least as long."

Valmy rather liked the recoil of shock that embraced both of his agents.

He'd selected people for personal loyalty, rather than patriotism. It had taken a much wider net to find the sorts of people that he could slowly twist around over time, when it would become clear that the US Government didn't have their best interests in mind.

Hell, Valmy had commissioned a few studies that gave the United States less than thirty more years before it finally disintegrated, though a Civil War like the Nineteenth Century was unlikely. Just a collapse as all systems cascaded into failure like dominos.

He would need his army commanders already constructed and ready to go at that point, assuming that the labs producing them might be destroyed. Or the factories supplying chemicals.

Something that made it impossible to make more, until he could rebuild.

Valmy had a definite end-point that he'd been racing against for two decades now.

"Sir?" Vanlaere managed.

"You were not told, Vanlaere," he acknowledged. "Specifically, because Carter Faulkener took that knowledge and started looking at a much longer horizon than his handlers would. Eventually, he decided that he didn't want to work for TRC anymore, and became a terrorist. Note the Russian Ambassador. Fortunately, he's dead now and no longer a threat to my plans. Our plans."

"What are our plans, General?" Konicek asked.

Yes, the loyal soldier, fitting himself into a proper hierarchy with Valmy Bouchard at the pinnacle. Yet another reason Faulkener had had to die.

And now Daring would have to join him in hell.

"The aliens originally wanted an army of Humans to go conquer the universe," Valmy said. "At least, that was the story I was given and what I've been able to research from old German and Russian archives. The ones that came here intended to force Human development rapidly ahead. As planned, they had expected the entire arc of our twentieth century developement to take more like three hundred years, maybe longer, so they needed us ready for interstellar technology on a specific date."

"What date was that, sir?" Vanlaere asked.

"The larger alien civilization was planning to come down and invite us to join them at that point," Valmy smiled. "Because we would have moved past our warlike, primitive selves and been more social."

"Like Europe before the EU more or less fell apart?" she asked.

"Very much like that," he acknowledged. "We would have presumably either destroyed ourselves or settled down."

"And now?"

"Now, some folks have been meddling for nearly two centuries," he said. "We are technologically far in advance of what those other outsiders were expecting. Had Daring not stolen that ship, we'd have been able to take it apart and perhaps build our own."

"Sir, were we going to go conquer the aliens?" Konicek asked carefully.

"We were going to be in a position to negotiate a far better deal that passively accepting whatever they offered," he replied, sidestepping the salient points.

*Going to* and *able to* were matters of intent. Valmy didn't even know how many were out there, other than only a few looked enough like Humans to walk the streets of La Plata.

Was that why they'd needed Daring? An agent? Was that what had happened to Pham?

Were the bad aliens already here, and getting ready to do something?

The President would love nothing more than to host a press conference in the White House Rose Garden, introducing bonafide alien ambassadors. The EU and UN would want in on the act.

Valmy had no doubts that everyone would want a piece of that action.

He needed to move quickly if he was going to seize control.

Perhaps it was time, thirty years early.

"Sir?" Vanlaere asked. Must have seen something in his eyes.

"We are approaching endgame, Vanlaere," he told her. "It might get ugly before it settles down."

# CHAPTER 33

Ernesta noted that she'd been stripped back down to comfortable clothing for indoors. Blue jeans. Plain, red T-shirt. Socks, because those boots were too warm.

Joie was there in a small chamber with a big table dominating the center. Carter as well.

"Romana Pham," the other Human woman introduced herself.

"A lot of people have been looking for you," Ernesta nodded. "Are you doing okay?"

The woman gaped at her. Probably everyone had forgotten to ask that, but none of them were parents, let alone grandparents. Ernesta brought an extra something to the conversation.

"I am," Romana answered.

They all got settled.

"This is Tanerhald," Joie introduced the other person. "He's of the Brakhua."

Lavender. Ernesta had a blouse almost exactly that color that she wore usually in the fall. He was small, too, but the man looked fast and sleek. Eight fingers instead of ten.

Ernesta also noted four other Humans around the outside of the chamber, standing like guards in uniforms identical to Romana's.

Armed like guards, while she didn't even have her phone or wallet with her.

A bit over the top. It almost looked like a bad sci-fi vid, where the costumer went a touch heavy-handed with the visual metaphors.

Ernesta might have to have a chat with someone about better fashion choices later. After Joie worked her charm and magic on them first.

At least someone had provided mugs of coffee from the smell, as well as a carafe in the center of the smooth, black-finished table.

Ernesta glanced over at Carter, next to her, and gave him that special Mom look to remind him to behave. He occasionally forgot.

She could tell now by the blush that appeared. He wasn't a bad guy. Just a goofball who didn't always think things to their logical conclusions before jumping in.

"So, Captain Daring, we have assembled," Tanerhald said.

"Call me Joie," she said automatically. "Everyone else does."

"Joie."

"I to have to go all the way back to the beginning," Joie said. "Well, not the beginning, but from the point when I was sent to La Plata to chase down Carter here, the first time. Before everything happened when I was forcibly retired by the TRC and Taylor Kehoe."

Ernesta listened as Joie told the story again. She really did have a way with words, and had made enough peace with things that the anger was mostly subdued. Plus, Kehoe wasn't here, though he had changed remarkably since she'd first grabbed him by the hair and put a pistol in his ear.

Some men learn.

"And then I appeared in a room with Romana across from me," Joie finally finished up, having drunk an entire mug of coffee and part of a second one. Ernesta had largely been silent, save to interject a few points. Carter had wisely refrained from dirty jokes or social observations. "Then Tanerhald walked in and filled in a few points. We're all here. How do we stop Bouchard from all the things he has been doing? How do we stop the Brakhua and others from what they have planned?"

"You would speak for the Heecha, Joie?" Tanerhald asked.

He did have a lovely voice. Deep tenor without the resonance of a baritone. Powerful, though, rather than thin like it might have sounded on a small Human male.

"Since they haven't chosen to appear, I will presume so for now," Joie said. "You have the comm gear that allowed us to talk to them when we were on the ground, so at some point I can ask them to join us."

"You think they would?" Tanerhald asked bluntly.

"They wanted to keep folks from destroying my homeworld," Joie said. "That you have Romana on your side says the same thing. At the very least, we have a commonality of purpose that should allow us to be allies. I appreciate that it might only last until we solve our common foe in Bouchard, but that must be enough for now."

"Have the Heecha warned you?" Tanerhald asked.

"That I know too much to be allowed to remain on Earth afterwards?" Joie asked sharply. "Yes. And both of my friends here chose to undergo the same genetic modifications, knowing that if we were successful, we would all have to accept permanent exile from Earth. That was the price required. We understood that ahead of time. If I thought we could somehow find and deport everyone with the wrong knowledge, I'd help you start beaming them out now, and we could create a Human colony somewhere safely distant while we let everyone else settle in and recover."

Ernesta liked the way Tanerhald's eyes got a little bigger. They looked Human enough. It was the skin that was alien. And the sleekness of the bones in his head. Predatory, like a hawk.

Tanerhald's mouth opened to speak, then closed again as he reconsidered his words. Interestingly, he turned to Romana. Ernesta watched that woman grin.

She'd heard many stories about Romana Pham. From Joie. From Carter. From Kehoe. Even Mitch had been willing to share a little, though he was not one to kiss and tell.

"You were correct," Tanerhald told Romana.

"*This* is the woman I knew before, Tanerhald," Romana said with a hint of triumph in her voice. "This is *Captain Daring* as she was in the good old days."

"Bad old days," Joie corrected her friend. "The days when violence was a first response, rather than a last one. We've got to change. To grow up."

Romana gave her friend a look of surprise, but Ernesta supposed that she only remembered the *badass chika*, as Joie called herself. Or the depressed ex-soldier working in a coffee shop and some mornings unable to even get out of bed.

Ernesta had seen Joie growing up, if she could be rude enough to say that. Celeste and Sarah, plus the others. Strangers helping. Powerful mojo that had caused Joie to rethink everything.

And convinced Ernesta to help someone who might have been one of her worst enemies in another life.

"To grow up, Joie?" Tanerhald asked.

"Bouchard's automatic response when I flew away with the ship was to shoot," Joie told him. "My first response was to escape, so that the situation was contained, when it could have spiraled badly out of control. Imagine if Bouchard had been aboard, instead of me."

Ernesta noted the shudders in Tanerhald, as well as Romana and the nameless Human guards around the walls.

"Still, it might have helped, had you taken him into custody," Joie acknowledged. "He's the driver behind all this, and removing him might have given us time to identify everyone else involved before they could do anything desperate."

"You believe that we should remove him from the playing field?" Tanerhald asked.

"Eventually, it will become necessary," Joie said.

Ernesta leaned forward now, drawing all eyes to her.

"Most of Humanity has no idea what is going on," Ernesta reminded everyone present. "They go about their daily lives in ignorance of the things out there. Of people like you, watching in the darkness. Bouchard's actions provoke a communal retribution that is unwarranted on any sort of ethical basis."

She paused, eyeing Tanerhald and Romana, grateful for those silly books on first contacts that she had devoured.

*Wasn't all of science fiction busy asking one of three questions?* **What if? If only? And if this goes on?**

"Bandi, Sora, and Hanni are neutralized," Ernesta reminded them. "Yormevs has them in custody, along with poor Genevieve who is just an innocent here. That lab grinds to a halt, though I am certain from my other contacts that the state of cybernetic research has spread to the point that it will continue moving forward elsewhere. After all, Bandi was always trying to push the envelope, but to do so slowly enough to not be noticed by folks like you."

"You have been modified greatly," Tanerhald pointed out. "Genetically."

"And the price was exile," she countered. "Before you came along, we expected Yormevs and the Heecha to take us away, so that the rest of the world could continue to live on in ignorance. Now, the only change is that the Brakhua would be our jailers instead. Bouchard must still be stopped. Costs have already been borne and will continue. The Heecha needed Human agents. The Brakhua even more so. How can we help?"

"You assume we desire your help?" Tanerhald asked.

"You did not destroy the ship," Ernesta pointed out. "You recruited Romana to your side. As Joie noted, at the very least we have a commonality of purpose. How do we save all the billions on Earth before they have to suffer the collective punishment for the crimes of a few?"

She leaned back and watched. The guards around the walls—the Human ones—stirred at her words. Romana did as well.

Tanerhald would still make the decision. He turned to Joie and leaned forward, tenting his hands in a most Human manner and resting his chin on them.

"What would you do, Joie?" he asked.

Ernesta let go a breath silently. If they were going to listen to Joie Daring, there was yet hope.

At least for some of them.

Bouchard still had it coming.

# CHAPTER 34

Joie looked around the room she had been assigned. Her and Ernesta. Carter had a room with a pair of beds all to himself.

She was utterly exhausted from talking all afternoon.

"I can't believe he got away," Joie said, sitting on the one bed. "They held us in that damned beam for almost two days before they let us out? And didn't say anything?"

"They also had a tiger by the tail, Joie," Ernesta told her soothingly. "They didn't realize that you might be a pussycat if they asked nicely."

Joie had to laugh. In many ways, Ernesta had pretty much replaced the mother Joie had grown emotionally distant from over the last decade. Same age. Nothing at all alike in personality.

But a friend when she'd really needed one.

"Bouchard knows too much," Joie said. "And he knows we're involved, because I saw him recognize me. You were just some *chika* I picked up on a street corner to help, and I doubt he got a good look at Carter. Right now, we've got to do something."

"We need Mitch," Ernesta said. "And not just for someone to scrub my back in the shower. Or yours. We need his brains."

"Agreed," Joie said.

She stopped when a chime sounded at the door. Doorbell?

She hadn't even checked to see if they were locked in after Romana had escorted them to these rooms to settle.

Joie rose. Ernesta moved onto a flank like a wingchick in a bar.

Romana stood there.

"Hi," she said awkwardly.

"Should I depart so you two can talk?" Ernesta asked.

"No," Romana said, turning to her. "You should be here. We don't have a lot of time to catch up, and I've just come from a meeting with Tanerhald."

"Come in," Joie stepped back and gestured. "Make yourself at home."

She wasn't prepared for Romana to get a running start and take a flying leap onto the nearer bed.

Just like that one time in…

"Bogota?" she asked.

Romana grinned and pulled all the pillows out so she could pile them up and rest against them. Boots came off and got tossed into a corner.

Joie felt a weight slide off her shoulders that she hadn't even appreciated was there.

"Bogota!" she laughed.

"I feel like I'm missing something," Ernesta said.

"We'd just finished a mission into Venezuela, and had some down time," Joie said, stepping to the other bed and flopping onto it, only without the flying bit. "That was how she entered the hotel room we were going to share, before heading out and hunting for a dance hall."

"I see," Ernesta offered blandly.

Joie watched her friend pull out the chair from a table in the corner and sit. In many ways, the space was configured like any hotel room she'd ever stayed in, save that the colors were a dark, forest green and there was no balcony.

"So talk, pipsqueak," Joie instructed her previously unindicted co-conspirator.

Romana grinned. It was like three years vanished, until Joie saw a young woman forming the third part of a triangle on the other side.

Shit, three weird years.

And a chance to start all over again? Twenty-five was her age when she'd been blown up in Egypt. When Ernesta had moved into upper middle management for her grandfather.

"Tanerhald had a lengthy talk with his people after our long afternoon," Romana said. "I wasn't there, but he's willing to use you as an agent, within limits. Certainly, it helps me."

"You got upgraded, didn't you?" Joie asked.

"Yeah, but not to the level you did," Romana turned serious. "Better than Human. Are you better than Bouchard?"

"Dunno," Joie replied. "Yormevs seemed to think that I needed to be good enough to take on someone like Carter unarmed, so he pushed. Plus, we weren't ever going home, so he didn't have to worry. And we're both sterile."

She caught the grimace that flashed on Romana's face.

"You, too?" Joie asked delicately.

"As you said, necessary if I wanted to save the world," Romana said. "They don't want advanced Humans loose in the galaxy, so I won't be able to have kids."

"I'm sorry," Joie offered.

That had been one thing she knew Romana had been looking forward to in a few years. Retire from the Army, find some dude, and settle down. Part of the reason Romana had never gotten cyberware.

That, and not having been blown up. Still, she was a normal woman who could walk into places even Joie couldn't, if they were paying attention with the right scanners.

"Cost of doing business," Romana repeated with an offhand shrug that didn't fool Joie one bit. "Anyway, Tanerhald sent me to talk to you. He wants to meet with Yormevs, to see if the Heecha are willing to come in from the cold and help. And he sends his apologies that he let Bouchard escape. Standard paranoia on his part, augmented by me, when I saw who it was and what they'd done to the three of you. The Brakhua nearly shit themselves before I convinced them that I could talk to you."

Joie nodded. Water under the bridge at this point. Bouchard had filed a flight plan for DC, then vanished off radar and Tanerhald's people hadn't had any reason at the time to be tracking him from orbit. Just one of thousands of aircraft in the skies at any given moment.

"Ernesta and I were just talking about that before you got here," Joie said. "She thinks we need Mitch."

It was telling, the way Romana's eyes slid around to Ernesta. Questioning.

After all, they'd all shared him, in the biblical sense of the word. Romana hadn't been able to make it work any better than Joie had, but that was the nature of the business. He had been on the outside, so they couldn't tell him certain things.

He was an inside man now. Ernesta had taken advantage of that. Hot babe with an old soul, and all that.

"Why?" Romana asked oh so delicately.

"He's a superb analyst," Ernesta said with a grin. "Kehoe needed him to track everything and make sense of it, especially when he didn't have access to hundreds of other analysts working the data because we've all gone rogue. And the man's smart."

"Duh," Romana said. "Are you two an item?"

"Maybe?" Ernesta replied. "There have been conversations, but nothing solid."

Romana surprised Joie by nodding and grinning.

"Good," she offered. "He needed someone like Joie. That was obvious. And Joie has to like you to smile right now. So I like you."

Joie felt a stab of emotion knife her in the gut. She was back in Seattle, outside the train station, when one woman looked at the situation and got another woman involved.

That sisterhood Joie had never realized even existed.

"So now what?" Joie asked.

"You willing to call that Heecha and browbeat him into surrendering?" Romana asked. At least she was smiling. "Tanerhald won't do it any other way. That man's been committing crimes only a level or so below the Danorak, even if he had good intentions. That just means less jail time at the end."

"I can ask," Joie said. "Won't make any promises, because you've given Kehoe several days to fall back on contingency plans and grow a little desperate."

"What's he got?" Romana asked.

"Sergeant Stone," Joie said. "You remember him?"

"Gruff old coot who used to be Airborne," Romana nodded.

"Him," Joie nodded. "*Pakhet*, aka Freya Malik. Another cybernaut like me, with almost the same hardware."

"She's out of her league here," Romana said.

"She is, but she offered to come anyway," Joie said. "And Kehoe doesn't have much more."

"That it?" Romana asked.

"One other," Joie grinned. "My Sifu from DC. Wěn Cōng Mǎ."

"Oh, shit," Romana whispered. "Her?"

"Yup," Joie nodded back. "So Kehoe might be desperate, but he's not alone."

# CHAPTER 35

Taylor sat at the head of the table and considered his options. Three of them.

It was rude to think of them as the second string, but that was only a comparison to the team he'd sent to South America, who were varsity stars in any operation.

Mitch was here as well, but he was the bloodhound, bleary-eyed from two days of diving into Defense Department systems and trying to find a lead on Bouchard. Man had simply vanished somewhere over southern Mexico.

Gone.

"Any luck?" Taylor asked anyway.

"We know a great deal more about things than we used to," Mitch replied grumpily. "However, at present, I don't know which of about a half-dozen places he might have landed. All low-key airstrips without proper tower control. From there, he could have gone to any of fifty places I have mapped, or however many I can't."

Taylor nodded, commiserating with the man. Solo, he was still worth more than all of the folks Taylor had left behind in DC.

He turned back to his second string.

Stone. *Pakhet*. Sifu Wĕn.

"Should we go through the same upgrades as Daring?" Stone asked in a gruff voice. "Or will that take too long?"

Taylor considered it. According to Yormevs, the reset to youth and upgrade was getting almost standardized, having been done three times now. And extracting cyberware and replacing it with grown parts for Freya had been sped up as well.

Still, he was looking at a week of downtime if they committed to it. Or sending one agent instead of a team.

What did he do with a white guy, a Cantonese woman, and a black woman? Pretty much anything he wanted, considering the range of languages spoken.

However, he had no clue where to send them.

Plus, he was almost dead certain that Bouchard had gone to ground in the States.

"Let's hold off on that," Taylor said. "Mitch, how narrow was your search?"

"Range of that jet, assuming he didn't pause to refuel and recharge somewhere," Mitch replied.

"If we eliminate Mexico and Canada, how much does that help?"

"Almost none," Mitch shook his head. "Maybe ten percent of options move off the table. I need something that wasn't written down in a computer. Air-gapped system, or verbal orders without electronics."

"And that's normally when I send someone in to steal them," Taylor agreed. He turned to Stone. "Where would you hit, if you wanted radar logs that were above top secret?"

"Bases like Edwards out west," Stone replied immediately. "Cheyenne Mountain for NORAD, because I guarantee you they have it somewhere. Doubt any civilian spot would have it, unless an airport like San Antonio happened to have them pass through the control zone while heading northwest."

"Not northeast?" Freya asked.

"Too many people around," Stone nodded. "Lots of open space in the west that got transformed into things. Even a bunch of old, secret missile bases from the twentieth century that never got decommissioned, just disarmed when the missiles were retired. Big hole in the ground with secure enough facilities to survive a nuclear strike. Some of them are huge."

Taylor studied the man. Stone had done a little of everything in the service before finally retiring to a desk job because his back wasn't up to jumping out of transports or helicopters anymore. If he knew about such places, that was because he'd been in a few. And those were the sorts of secrets that you were supposed to take to your grave.

Assuming you were still loyal to the DOD.

He looked over at Mitch, but Graydon just shook his head.

"Asked Stone about that," he said. "Added a few places. Again, all of them are active, so if we hit one, alerts go out everywhere and we have task forces of Special Forces troops dropping in a box all around us quickly. Have to be right the first time."

"How did everyone miss the ship Joie stole?" Sifu Wěn asked.

She'd been so quiet up until now that Taylor almost thought she was asleep.

Playing possum instead.

He studied her.

Fifty-something. Built kind of like the Buddha, except possibly as fast as Joie had been upgraded to. Stone spoke in awe of her skills, and he taught various martial arts on the side back home.

She'd been sandbagging everybody.

"Beg pardon?" he asked, just to buy a few seconds to think.

"The ship that Bandi hid," Wěn smiled. "It wasn't there, then it appeared when she took off. What were they using to hide it?"

"There is a field generator," Mitch spoke up. "I asked Yormevs about it. Whatever happened to Joie in orbit was somebody turning one off just long enough to presumably grab her and insert a pilot who then turned the one on…Shit."

Wěn smiled. Taylor was still a little lost.

"Talk to me, Mitch," he said.

"She's suggesting, probably correctly, that Bouchard must have something similar," Mitch nodded to the woman. Taylor watched her grin. "Bandi had something before we made him move, and hadn't installed them again because he was feeling a little lazy. There's one in the mountain in Chile. Probably a few that Bouchard conned him out of over the years to protect some of the more critical facilities from someone beaming in to steal shit."

"Or plant a bomb and blow the place up," Freya noted.

Taylor understood and concurred. How easy would it be to just put the right-sized bomb in someone's living room, instead of having to drop it on them? Or tasking Joie or Carter with breaking in and doing it?

Taylor rose from his seat and walked to the comm thing next to the door. They weren't locked in, but he was feeling too lazy to walk to the office where Yormevs would probably be right now.

He keyed the button.

"How may I assist you, Kehoe?" the alien asked immediately.

"Is there a way you can do some sort of hard scan that notices spots where someone has a shield up to cloak themselves?" Taylor asked.

The sudden, drawn-out silence on the line was at least better than a flat denial.

"I will bring one of my technical experts to your space where you can ask," Yormevs said. "I am not sure I even understand the question."

"That's fine," Taylor replied. "Thank you."

He returned to the table and sat. The others watched him, Wěn grinning ever-so-slightly.

Yormevs and a shorter Heecha arrived a few moments later. Introductions went quick, but Kehoe didn't figure he'd ever see the person again. Instead, they piled a heap of technical questions on them instead.

Which turned into a long conversation in a tonal language, presumably Yormevs translating everything into Heecha. The other person thought about it and replied with a single word.

Taylor knew the answer before Yormevs even opened his mouth.

"Maybe."

"What would it take to be certain, one way or the other?" Taylor asked.

More translation. The shrugging of the shoulders was apparently a universal thing with bipeds. At least Heecha and Danorak. Good to know, since one of these days he expected to be living with them.

Out there.

"We will do some investigating," Yormevs promised.

Better than nothing.

Then a third Heecha, this one maybe female, but Taylor wasn't sure, entered, walking right to Yormevs and whispering in his ear. Several back and forth, none of which he understood.

Then Yormevs paled. Eyes huge. He turned to the room.

"Joie Daring is on a comm," he said in a small voice. "She would like to negotiate."

Taylor nodded. Smiled, even.

Trust Joie to pull it off, whatever it was.

"So let's talk," Taylor said.

# CHAPTER 36

Valmy studied the walls around him. Concrete. Rough-poured and painted several times, but no effort had ever been made to make them pretty.

The whole facility was like that. Sturdy, when measured on the scale of nuclear weapons, back in the era where accuracy had meant good enough to explode at low altitude and maybe take out the base.

Maybe not.

People had been wound a little too tight in those days, Americans and Russians—back when they'd been communists instead of gangsters—facing off with lots of missiles, primitive radar systems, and an assurance that if one side tried to launch a surprise attack, the other would cut loose with enough firepower to annihilate the world.

At least the Russians had pretty much fallen back to where the Brits and French were these days. The Chinese and Indians were still bitter enemies, but Pakistan and Saudi Arabia also having nuclear missiles meant that any fuckup there only ended life from the Mediterranean to the East China Sea.

A lot of old missiles had been decommissioned a century and more ago, irrelevant as technological advances moved them to submarines and aircraft. Plus a few in space that nobody talked about, even today.

Most of those weapons weren't nuclear. Hypersonic cruise missiles could take out command and control facilities rapidly with minimal collateral damage.

Still, nobody wanted a general exchange. In the modern era, that had turned into the Shadow War, where enhanced agents like *Mithras* or Captain Daring had done things at a personal level, allowing everyone plausible deniability later.

Crime was, after all, in the eye of the beholder.

So TRC had been able to take over a bunch of old, decommissioned missile silo facilities, a few even built in the middle of the twenty-first century when some of the South Asian Cold Wars had threatened to get out of hand again.

But the place was ugly. Someone had obviously gotten a fantastic deal on a particular shade of green that was too dark to be called mint and too bright to be goose shit.

Everywhere. Probably still better than raw concrete, but he wasn't entirely sure.

When this was all done, he had already made a note to increase the budget for interior decorations at places like this. More colors of paint, if nothing else.

The green reminded him of insane asylums from old movies. And not in a good way.

He'd been sitting on his bunk, mostly meditating.

Trying to figure out what the hell had happened to Daring.

He'd ordered her burned two years ago because Valmy was still confident that she'd worked a deal with *Mithras* to bring him in alive, when she was supposed to take the man out, and then be so badly injured that she had to be retired.

Hell, if she hadn't been so broken in the first place, she would have been a perfect candidate for Project Carpenter.

As it was, she was too good to be left running around.

And she'd proven that, retracing her steps to South America in spite of one of the biggest manhunts in the last couple of decades chasing after her. Found the aliens. Broken into their lab. Compromised everything.

Valmy still didn't think that Kehoe had made a wise choice,

bringing the woman in instead of eliminating her, but Valmy hadn't been prepared to deal with the blowback of issuing orders to take Captain Daring down.

Too many Senators still had fond feelings for the woman.

Back in the field, she'd even managed to kill Faulkener this time, eliminating one of Valmy's biggest headaches and public relations issues with Congress.

Then vanished.

Only to appear in Chile, stealing his spaceship.

And then it had vanished.

Who had her? How many other players were out there, maneuvering?

What person had been able to convince Captain Daring to walk away from her country? Her oaths?

Valmy didn't have any answers, and that stupid green paint was starting to get to him.

He rose from the bed and checked his watch.

Close enough to dinner for governmental purposes.

He needed to stay hidden in the tall grass for a bit, while other elements of TRC and the larger Intelligence apparatus started digging in for some questions.

Something had gone desperately wrong, and for once, Valmy had no idea how to deal with it.

# CHAPTER 37

Joie sat in a control room like they used when launching rockets. Screens, knobs, switches, the works. Heecha had ears more or less like Humans, so she even had a headset with microphone, like those folks in the old moonshot videos or SF movies.

It had taken a little time to get through, mostly because Kehoe and Mitch had apparently been in a meeting somewhere, with Yormevs, when she'd called on the channel they'd been using.

That, and a lot of confusion she'd created at that end.

Tanerhald and Romana were present. Ernesta sat next to her.

Carter had even gotten off his ass to join them, wonder of wonders.

Checking the clock, it was evening on the East Coast. About dinner out west. Joie wondered what Celeste was making tonight. Or Sarah.

It was weird, not being either in combat planning mode, or just so depressed that getting to the coffee shop on time for her shift was a chore.

But then, she'd only been a civilian in her own mind for maybe a year now. After nearly twenty thinking about the green.

And she'd only had hope since she and Ernesta had returned to Guadalajara.

The line came live from the other end. They were putting it out on speakers in the room for everyone to hear, but she had the only mic.

"This is Kehoe," he said.

"Does this qualify as me suddenly banging on your door late at night and uninvited?" Joie asked simply.

Pause. Recalibration. Maybe returning to that first moment when he'd stomped back into her life, after burning her and leaving her to die, emotionally if not physically.

"Maybe," Kehoe said after a few moments. "Freya is here as well, if that helps."

Joie smiled. *Pakhet*. Freya Malik. Another Cybernaut like Joie had been. She'd been Kehoe's bodyguard that night, because nobody had been certain of the reception Joie would give them.

If they'd have talked to Amy, she might have set proper expectations, but Kehoe had been too full of himself in those days. And Freya was just a soldier.

At least until their world had turned upside down.

Joie had only a small bit of responsibility for that.

"So I met some interesting people after I last talked to you," Joie continued. "Yormevs won't be thrilled, but these are some of the folks he was probably hiding from. And an old friend nobody has seen in nearly a year showed up."

Another long pause. They weren't speaking a code designed to hide from outside listeners. At least not Human ones. Yormevs and Tanerhald had both assured her that Human systems weren't capable of understanding these signals as anything but random hash.

Joie didn't trust that, but hadn't wanted to insult their naivety on the subject. If it was out there, someone had built a machine to figure out what the hell was going on.

"How's she doing?" Kehoe asked carefully, tacitly acknowledging who was here.

After all, this had started as a means to find out what had happened to an agent codenamed *Tyche*. Romana Pham, who had vanished from a training base in the Virginia mountains in the dead of night.

At least everybody involved knew how it had been done now.

"Really well," Joie said. "She suggested we pool resources. The folks up here have the same sort of interest as Yormevs, and are willing set hostilities aside while we sort everything out. Bouchard has vanished, and nobody has a good idea how to find him. We need Mitch."

"I was just having that conversation down here," Kehoe laughed. "We have some ideas, but no clue if they would work. Hang on."

Joie waited. The tone of the audio had changed, suggesting that someone had muted him from that end. She looked around and caught the smiles from everyone, aliens included.

It was still weird, talking to people to solve problems instead of beating them up or using lethal violence to eliminate the issue.

Everything the Army had trained her in seemed to be almost exactly wrong on the topic.

But then, war had more than once been described as *diplomacy gone wrong*.

"So folks at this end are a little nervous, Joie." Kehoe was back. "They'd like the locals only to meet at this point, if we can come up with some neutral ground. Something about dropping shields for about two seconds, then hiding again and running somewhere else."

Joie turned to Tanerhald. Watched Romana lean over and whisper in his ear, which turned into a quick conversation.

She, Romana, and Kehoe could have entire conversations with a few, key words. Carter, to a lesser extent, because he'd been in and out of trouble for so long, but insiders had a language.

Romana must have used the right words with him. His face cleared and he leaned forward to push a button at this end, no doubt muting her.

Joie waited.

"Your honor on this thing?" he asked.

Stilted, so it probably sounded different in Brakhua. Or whatever their language was called.

Intent was obvious. He would let her go down there, if she promised to behave. And meant it.

Joie was beyond that at this point, wondering if she could get the others to come back here. Tanerhald had more resources, if he was the regional law enforcement, which was the impression she got, cultural translations notwithstanding.

"Indeed," Joie replied simply.

Tanerhald nodded then.

"Go with my blessing," he said, flipping the switch again and bringing her live.

"Kehoe, we've got agreement at this end," she said. "Let me make a few calls and hopefully I'll be able to give you time and space coordinates. Most likely in the morning, depending, because I've been running hard here and would prefer to be rested before we go after the next stage of things."

"We'll be waiting for your call, Joie," he said, and cut the line.

Joie nodded to Tanerhald and he cut their end.

Joie sighed. Much of it on her shoulders, but not all of it. She'd gone from alone to a whole pack of folks. A family, of sorts.

Found family, which seemed far better than the one she'd ignored. At the same time, Joie was finally willing to admit that the fuckup had been entirely hers. Lots of cousins wanting to engage her, but she'd been too focused on army things to talk. Being a good student instead of a *barrio chika*, as it were. Getting her grades up and keeping them there so she could go to West Point. Staying out of any trouble that might prevent her from making it. Studying all the time instead of doing family things with her blood relatives.

Then the Army had been her family, until it hadn't.

But she'd had folks willing, once she'd gotten over herself.

"So I understand that you can insert a signal into the cellular network as though it was a regular call?" she asked Tanerhald.

He nodded warily.

"Can you put my name on the caller ID?" she pressed.

"Which one?" Romana asked.

"Real name," Joie grinned. "Birth certificate and everything."

Again, a quick conversation between Romana and Tanerhald. Obviously, she had thrown herself wholeheartedly into working with the Brakhua, and Tanerhald had come to rely on her. That would help.

"Yes, we can do that," the man finally said.

Joie gave him the number and leaned back to wait.

A few moments later, she heard a ring in her headset. It almost went to voicemail, but finally someone picked up.

"If you think this is funny, so help me…" the woman on the other end said.

"Hi, Celeste. It's Joie. I need another favor."

# CHAPTER 38

Joie had eaten breakfast here that first morning in Seattle, on the run and still nervous about just showing up on the doorstep of the people who might have turned into her in-laws, had things worked out differently. Wasn't likely at this point, but she did have yet another mother out there.

They were down on 15th Avenue eating. Her, Ernesta, Romana, and Carter. Everyone dressed casually for a gray, drizzly Seattle day.

The place was done brasserie style, with the cooks on the far side of a low wall where anybody could watch. Better than a lot of joints around here, because the kitchen was open all day. Too many bars that only served dinner, though old timers had assured her that it used to be much worse.

Still, the food was heavy in a good way. Eggs any way you wanted them. Bacon or sausage. Drop biscuits or English muffins or toast. Potatoes or some seasonal side veggie.

COFFEE!!!

Yormevs had coffee, but he'd stolen it from a grocery warehouse for her. Romana had gotten Tanerhald to select a slightly better brand, but that was a low bar to clear.

Seattle still took their coffee seriously, dating back to the 1970s when Italian Coffee Shops as a business concept got started down by the Public Market. Before taking over the world.

She'd come back here because they had a full barista on staff, and not just drips in pots. While she'd been eating, a number of folks had come in solely to get coffee in a paper mug and leave again.

Serious business.

They'd eaten. Burped happily, because she hadn't had a nice, heavy, American breakfast in a while. Even Ernesta's people had been a little iffy on the concept of gravy.

And COFFEE!!!

Joie leaned back and smiled at the universe. If that was a last meal for the condemned, she could have done much, *much* worse.

"So who is this woman again?" Carter asked.

But then, he'd been kind of doodling during the briefing.

"Mitch's mom," Joie said.

Ernesta was a little nervous, but that might be a meeting future in-laws kind of thing. Romana remembered Celeste, and had probably eaten dinner there in similar circumstances, as another potential daughter-in-law.

At least Mitch had good taste in women.

"And she's going to host us in her kitchen?" Carter asked, a bit dumbfounded. "Just like that?"

"Remember when you and Kehoe couldn't find me in Seattle, Carter?" Joie asked. "And Kehoe went up to the mountains with a team to talk to Mitch that first time?"

"Yeah, you bloody vanished," Carter nodded.

"Celeste insisted that she and I drive to the southern border in her Subaru," Joie grinned. "Camping along the way, before she dropped me off to visit some other friends while she went all the way to El Paso, just to mess with Kehoe's systems."

"She must like you," Carter shrugged defensively.

Then it hit her. Carter Faulkener had been that lone wolf warrior like they'd trained her to be, except that it had led him entirely astray about the time she'd been in middle school. He'd spent decades in the shadows, unable to trust anyone, because of the bounty the DOD had put on his head.

He didn't have friends. Or hadn't, before now. He had her and Ernesta. Kehoe and Mitch to a lesser extent.

And that was about it.

"She does," Joie promised. "This will be a safe place for everyone to meet and sort out what we need, in order to go after Bouchard."

"What's she like?" Ernesta asked nervously.

Joie and Romana shared a knowing glance. They had a few minutes before they needed to leave, so the two of them took turns talking about Celeste Graydon, power behind several thrones and school boards around here. Upper class busybody and wife of a retired architect who lived on Capital Hill adjacent to the really nice, old money in Seattle, all of whom owed her favors and probably feared her a little.

Finally, the alarm in Joie's head went off. She got them out of the booth and into the tiniest drizzle misting things. Walked the few blocks over and up.

The door opened as soon as she knocked and Joie found herself almost tackled by the tiny woman.

"JOIE!!!!"

Romana got the same treatment, which was good. Ernesta got a hug, but didn't have any expectations except a friend of theirs.

Celeste glared up at Carter and Joie watched the man blush without a word being said.

"Just so we're clear," Celeste said.

"Yes, ma'am," Carter replied diffidently.

All of them got shuffled into the big kitchen and dining room at the back of the house.

Donovan Graydon had been given permission to be gone all day. Orders, really. Celeste expected him and his friends to have a marathon D&D game over pizza and cheap beer while his house was hosting a summit.

And Celeste understood good coffee. Everyone got a mug and settled.

Then there was a knock at the front door.

# CHAPTER 39

Mitch hadn't slept much last night. Too wound up. It was the home he'd grown up in, but right now Joie was there. Romy. Ernesta.

What man wanted to face three recent girlfriends who have had a chance for a long chat with his mother?

Except that Mom liked Joie. Had liked Romy the few times they'd gone out to dinner. Maybe wasn't sure how Ernesta fit into everything.

He knocked. Mom answered.

He got a hug and a kiss on the cheek. Everyone else got dutifully greeted and led inside: Kehoe, Stone, Malik, and Sifu Wěn.

He saw Joie first, but all three women were up and engulfing him in a big, group hug before he got a chance to react. Probably just as well. Ernesta ended up with an arm around his waist when the other two settled back and hugged the others.

Mom was watching.

"At least you have good taste in women," she said quietly. Approvingly.

He felt Ernesta blush. Shit, he blushed.

Then someone handed him a mug of coffee and he made it to the dining room table, stretched with every extension leaf like Christmas day. Interestingly, Kehoe was across from him and Joie was on the end. Mom was at the bottom, closest to the kitchen and the coffee pot.

Mitch studied the evolving social dynamics of the room as people took chairs.

He couldn't not do that. Then he turned to Joie.

But for her, he'd still probably be up on that mountaintop, studying the horizon for a sign and occasionally painting. Had he made the world a better place by coming down and signing up with Kehoe?

Mitch hoped so. But this was Joie's game. He watched.

"Talk to me," Kehoe said simply, looking back and forth between Romy and Joie.

Joie nodded to Romy.

"There are nervous people out there," Romy began, looking carefully at everyone. "They've woken up to the fact that Humans have been accelerating in their development from the previous several centuries. Nobody in the galaxy is supposed to do that. Nor have they, from what I've learned."

"We had help," Kehoe nodded.

"The wrong kind of help," Romy growled at the man. "The Danorak may have already done too much for everyone else to be comfortable. Only Joie's suggestion has caused my new bosses to withhold the blade."

"Who are you working for now?" Kehoe asked.

Not indignant. Mostly curious. They'd all defected, more or less, so he had no high horse to be sitting upon.

"The Brakhua have largely taken it upon themselves to keep places like Earth isolated," Romy replied. "But they can be a little heavy-handed. My understanding was that Joie's Heecha friends were trying to get in and eliminate the Danorak infiltrators so that the Brakhua didn't come down and crack heads together."

"Joie?" Kehoe turned to her.

"We have to remove everyone who knows, Kehoe," she said. "Not just Bouchard and his warriors, but the scientists doing the research. All their notes need to be corrupted beyond salvage, anywhere somebody might have backed them up."

"That's thousands, potentially tens of thousands of people, Joie," he said.

"Not cybernetics research," Joie said. "They're okay from what I've been told, because they have the same sorts of tools to shut that shit down as you did. It's the genetics that frightened them. Those folks threaten the whole galaxy. But if they are removed from the Earth permanently, everybody else maybe has a chance to live a normal life without an alien apocalypse. Plus, I suspect that the Date of Contact has been moved up drastically to deal with all the aftermath once the current generation gets to understand how close we got."

"Point of order," Mitch said, unable to help himself. "We haven't saved the world yet. Bouchard vanished, and that has to mean he's getting nervous. That, in turn, will make all our friends nervous, because the whole US military might get called in to do stupid shit at some point. We have to find him and remove him before he starts making a bunch of new killers because we've backed him into a corner. How do we do that?"

Everyone had gone deathly silent, so he had their attention. And an understanding of how freaked out he was about the whole thing, in spite of the good they had done. He'd been hired by Kehoe as an analyst. That one dude who takes fragmentary evidence and intuition, and produces solid intelligence from it.

"Before you called, we'd been talking about asking Yormevs if the negative of those defensive screen things could be detected," Kehoe said, back to switching his attention between Joie and Romy. "Can the others detect something like that?"

"No," Romy said. "That was why the Danorak had been able to hide. Eventually, we might have found them, since apparently they weren't using them recently, but maybe not. Their ship would have been invisible. Same as wherever Bouchard has run off to."

"With the data I have right now, I can't nail him down," Mitch confessed. "We have theories, but once we hit someplace, the whole Defense Department is likely to react, so we'll only get one chance."

"What happens if we fail?" Stone asked, gravelly voice as usual. "If we go in someplace and he's not there? Or he gets away from us?"

More silence. Bad silence.

"Tanerhald probably pulls the trigger at that point and shuts every-thing down, just because it will have gotten out of hand," Romana said in a dark, heavy voice. "The other species tend to draw back at that sort of thing, but that's part of the Brakhua thinking. Better to kill most of the Humans now than to let them loose in space. The needs of the many vastly outweigh the needs of the few, especially as warlike and crazy as Humans can be. At least until we grow up."

"So we've got one chance to do this?" Kehoe said, looking around.

All eyes settled on Joie, but that was right. They were all here because of that woman. At times he was sorry it hadn't worked out, but it had given him a chance to know Romy better. And maybe really get to know Ernesta well.

Because if all three of those women had to leave Earth forever, Mitch couldn't see himself remaining behind.

What were the odds he'd be struck by lightning a fourth time?

Joie took a deep breath. Gulped audibly at the enormity of what she was about to say.

Carter spoke instead.

"I might know someone," he said simply.

# CHAPTER 40

A day later, Joie wasn't surprised that Carter had dragged her to a dive diner up in Everett. Those seemed to be his sort of place. Ernesta and Mitch had gone in earlier as a cover, looking like a couple doing a late breakfast. The others had returned to the two alien ships, with Kehoe monitoring things while Yormevs apparently fidgeted next to the man.

Joie had been given a small earring that could put sound directly into her eardrums via some magic, as well as pick up everything said within about two meters of her.

Carter swore by the food in this place, telling her before that they deserved a Michelin star, if they could only convince someone to buy better coffee. It was Seattle, you couldn't swing a dead cat without finding better coffee, so the owners must have liked it black and tarry.

She'd had one sip after they sat down and agreed with Carter that it needed a lot of stuff added.

"Remember, you only need about a quarter of what you used to," she said to him.

He was on the inside of the booth next to her, giving her access to move quickly. Neither of them was armed at the moment, but Yormevs or Tanerhald could grab them in a flash of light if necessary.

Hopefully, Earth wasn't being put out of its misery today.

"I'm working on that," Carter muttered back. "Helps that they shrank my stomach. I get full so fast it's like I didn't eat anything."

"You're eating like a normal person, dork," she laughed. "Granted, that's been how long ago for you?"

"Too long," Carter muttered darkly. "I'm almost as old as Ernesta, at the end of the day. However, I did give up living for a stupendously long time to do this."

"And you have a lot of bad habits to unlearn," Joie turned to look at him.

He was growing in a beard that was a darker shade of blond than the hair on his head. Chestnut, maybe. Made him look almost distinguished, for all they looked like kids. And he hadn't cut his hair in a while.

"Going for the hippy look?" she asked with a grin.

"Ernesta suggested a lumberjack look to try to blend in better," he rumbled. "Still a lot of folks out there that might recognize the face, in spite of being fifteen centimeters shorter. I'd hate to be nabbed for something the old guy did. Even if I got away, they might run my prints and then you'd have one hell of a time explaining things."

Joie nodded at that. He did look better. Not remotely her type, but he was consciously trying to act less like a juvenile delinquent than he had been. To listen to the folks around him. Her job was to help with that.

Help him understand what it meant to have friends.

Her own wakeup call had been a little brutal.

The waitress returned and got their orders. Joie did a meat and cheese omelet, with some broccoli and spinach thrown in, simply because they'd made the mistake of offering her a 'build your own' option.

Carter did the SOS. Shit on a Shingle like you got in the army when the cooks were running behind or had had a shitty morning. Biscuits, split and buttered. Meat tossed randomly on. Hash browns on one side. Gravy over everything. Cheese over that.

Joie knew she'd be burping all day if she ate that many carbs and that much grease.

Carter seemed to thrive on it, even shrunk down.

They waited. Small talk just to make small talk. Anything she said was going to be recorded by both alien sides, so she skipped several topics when he asked, including how she'd managed to get to Guadalajara.

No reason to drop the feds or the aliens on the *Pedros* if they hadn't figured it out already, after all.

She would miss Sarah as much as she missed Celeste, but the Army had been exceedingly good at teaching her to value duty over self.

Pounded that into both of them, though it hadn't stuck as well with Carter.

Or maybe it had gotten buried under all the other things, until Yormevs had dug the original Carter Faulkener out and shown him to the light.

Yeah, that was more likely it. They'd all three been born again, metaphorically, if not literally. There was no roadmap for how to handle being young and exuberant after you'd hit middle age and settled. Shit you'd learned and knees that didn't hurt.

Carter and Ernesta were both winging it. Joie was just recovering from the depression of the last two-plus years.

Joie picked her up as soon as the woman entered. Carter called his old contact *Irene*, because that had apparently been the name the woman had been using when he'd met her more than a decade ago.

Thai bones in her face and that golden coloring to her skin. Short and broad in the shoulders and hips. Busty. Wide, flat face that was attractive, but not beautiful. Sharp eyes.

They made eye contact and Joie felt the woman's appraisal. Then Irene scanned the rest of the room, but didn't seem to notice the others.

Mitch had his back to her and Ernesta was a better undercover agent than just about anybody Joie had ever met.

Irene approached, waving down the waitress as she did.

"Coffee, please," Irene told her. "No food for me. And I'll need extra cream and probably extra sugar, because he'll have used it all up."

"Saved you two," Carter grumbled under his breath.

Joie grinned.

They were almost like an old, married couple in that way. He'd said that when setting up this meeting, but Joie hadn't grasped just how closely the two of them had to have worked for those sorts of casual assumptions to come up in public.

Irene sat. Studied Carter and blinked so hard she almost fell out of her seat. Moved to Joie's face again and stared, mouth open.

"It's complicated," Joie said. "Yes, that really is Carter. No, you don't want to know because the price of that knowledge will haunt you for the rest of your life."

"You paid for it," Irene noted.

"Rest of my life, as well, Irene," Joie nodded. "The costs are that high because the price of failure is even worse."

"Failure?" Irene asked. "Your friend here asked me to meet with you two because you needed information. Previously, he'd been on the run from specifically you and everyone else for things he'd done for some folks elsewhere."

"Hanoi," Joie said simply, watching the impact of her words on Irene. "That was where I caught him. Brought him in. Things have gotten…*squirrelly* since then."

"Oh?"

"We made a deal with some people you don't ever want to meet, Irene," Joie said. "They did this to us. When we're done, they'll remove us entirely from the playing field and you will never see any of us again."

Irene blinked. Euphemistically, they would all have to die for what they knew. At least that was the little, white lie Joie was implying.

Because technically true was the best kind of true.

"He said you were looking for someone," Irene nodded to Carter now, not saying his name out loud.

Possibly folks around here knew the name. Or maybe she was that superstitious. Either way worked.

"US Army General Valmy Bouchard," Joie said in a quieter voice. Limited to this table. "He is playing with fire, Irene. Playing with Armageddon. We have to stop him, and do it right now, before things happen and you get to watch Human civilization melt down."

Irene mouthed the words, eyes huge as the implications sank in. Joie nodded.

This woman was a smuggler, primarily. A fixer. You had a need, usually for something illegal or at least hard to find. She found it for you. For a price.

Like getting Carter to Vietnam, looking for Romana. She hadn't been there, but he'd been asked for a price, a favor for one of the major crime lords in Hanoi, and had paid it.

Granted, it had been the Russians. Carter probably would have done it for free, maybe paid them, but he had a deep and ancient hatred of those folks going back a generation.

Joie had never had the security clearance or mission need to be told what had happened back then. Still, everyone who knew Carter knew his opinion on the Russians.

"Melt down," Joie repeated. "Possibly end. As in Armageddon itself. We'd like to stop that. To save the world. I need help finding Bouchard."

She leaned back and watched.

Irene turned to Carter and Joie felt him nod, bristling that he was the one Irene would trust.

*Seriously? The world has to trust Carter Faulkener to do the right thing?*

*That was when you knew shit was bad.*

But that was Old Carter. Mercenary. Warlord. Terrorist. Punk.

New Carter had friends, even if he was still too tough to admit the need.

They hadn't given him any choice in the matter.

And he had Irene, who might have been his best friend in the world, in the before time. An old, married couple sort of thing.

"What am I allowed to know?" Irene asked finally, not much more than a whisper.

"My people think he has gone to ground in the Western US," Joie said. "Flight from Santiago, Chile that went off the radar in Mexico, but there have been no indications that it crashed. And there would be, with the systems we can access. He's air-gapped himself."

Irene nodded at that. An air-gapped computer was one where you only touched a network that didn't have any connection to the outside world. If it wasn't physically on the internet somewhere, nobody could touch it.

Bouchard had gone somewhere that didn't register his presence. Ergo, air-gapped.

To Joie, a mark of panic. Which just meant that he understood what had happened in orbit, even if he didn't know who had done it.

The walls had started closing in on him.

"I get the feeling that suddenly I'm on the side of the good guys," Irene said bleakly. She turned to Carter. "How the fuck did you let that happen?"

Carter shrugged. Then he grinned.

"She can be mighty persuasive," he said, nodding at Joie. "And the shit I've seen…"

He smartly let that trail off.

Irene could live the rest of a normal life if Earth survived.

Joie and Carter would be boarding somebody's spaceship, probably Tanerhald's, and leaving forever, hopefully with nobody the wiser at what had almost happened.

Cost of doing business.

"Damn it, why do I have to be a hero?" she asked in a quiet, angry voice.

"Because the folks I'm working for intend to destroy the world if we don't find Bouchard, Irene," Joie said bluntly. "Right, fucking, now."

That got through.

Like Carter, Irene was mostly bluster. He'd said that, too, but Joie hadn't believed. Hadn't understood the psychology of their pairing.

The unspoken trust that bound them. Not quite wedding vows, but maybe as close to friends as either of them had been allowed to retain in this business.

Joie held out her hand to the woman. Nodded for Irene to take it.

"Hot," Irene said, confused.

Joie elbowed Carter, he did the same, until they were all holding hands.

"We're not Human anymore, Irene," Joie said. "I can't say more, or you'd have to come with us forever when this is all done. There are angry people out there, who see us as a threat that must be neutralized. They've given me one opportunity to do it, before they step in with a big, fucking hammer."

Irene went white. She blinked. Let go of their hands.

Food arrived, and they ate in silence, Irene watching and processing while Joie and Carter pretended that it was all perfectly normal.

In the background, Ernesta nodded as she and Mitch rose, paid, and departed.

The waitress cleared the empty plates and refilled their coffee with crappy sludge, bringing more cream and sugar without having to be asked, as they'd already emptied everything.

Irene drew a heavy breath. Settled. Studied Carter for a long moment.

"So this is goodbye?" she asked.

"Most likely," he said, holding out a hand that she took. "It's been fun."

Irene nodded and turned to Joie.

"Contact you on his emergency number?" she asked.

"Yes," Joie replied simply, trusting that the computers routing such a call would forget about it before the CIA or any other agency managed to figure themselves out.

"I'll do what I can," Irene promised.

"Thank you," Joie said. "Carter has told me that you were one of the only people on this planet he could trust. I'm glad I got to meet you."

"And I, you, Joie Daring," Irene breathed. "Wouldn't have missed it for anything."

Joie slid out of the booth and left a couple of counterfeit bills on the table that the Department of the Treasury itself couldn't have detected. But a nice week's bonus for the waitress.

A way to put a smile on the woman's face.

If only for one last week.

# CHAPTER 41

Valmy was in a space that had been mission control for the silo, back when it had been armed with world-ending missiles. Old-fashioned consoles originally designed for monitors with tubes, then updated later. Still the thick, angled metal. Still had that 1970s feel so endemic to many US bases.

Set the design once and then just keep building it forever?

He looked at Chelsea and Garrison and wondered if that sort of thinking had caused a lot of the problems he was facing today.

They were alone in here. Without weapons, the space had no purpose, so folks used the other levels for training and social space. He'd made it clear that anybody even acknowledging their existence would be facing a stint in Leavenworth measured in lifetimes, so other than nods in the chow line, he was left alone.

So far, nobody else had found them.

Partly, that was the device Bandi Algom had given him to install atop the old launch silo. It supposedly blocked other folks from scanning him, or getting to him. Valmy didn't understand how the tech worked, but it had kept them safe so far.

"I have a problem," he said to the two.

"Can we call in more help?" Konicek asked.

Most of his people were headed home from Central Asia now that the Russians, Chinese, and everyone else had finally backed off and started moving troops home. Standing down, as it were, from the sorts of heightened efforts that would need them to take a few weeks off to recover from. Sleeping two to three hours at a time with a pistol under your pillow, while staying ready to be sent on a mission on ninety-seconds warning, that wore on a person.

And it had been necessary.

"No," Valmy decided after a few moments of thought. "Issuing those orders would tell our enemies where to look for us. How to find us. I've got teams headed to DC and Seattle, plus instructions to send a force of regular troops to Chile as fast as we can negotiate a joint mission with the locals. Daring is coming for us."

"Do we assume all the ones who disappeared are with her?" Vanlaere asked. "Kehoe, Graydon, and Stone?"

"Would they have defected?" he asked her. "You were the closest to them?"

"She can be charismatic, sir," Vanlaere replied. "With *Mithras* and Hernandez dead, I could see her easily tipping Graydon. Kehoe would be harder. Stone will follow orders."

"So let us assume that we're facing those four, plus whatever resources whoever has them can supply," Valmy said.

"Who has them?" Konicek asked.

"Aliens," Valmy said simply. "I'm not sure which ones, but my group in Argentina have all vanished, as has the ship we were trying to recover. Assume infiltrators, but I also assume that they will look Human. Human-enough."

The two of them had heard enough to nod instead of recoil in abject horror. It was like dogs. Some folks had an utter terror, while many were blasé.

"We're defensive," Vanlaere noted. "Holed up and safe presently, but that limits us. How do we break out?"

"I've needed the resources of TRC around me while I considered my options," Valmy said. "We've managed to steal or reverse engineer a few things from our pet aliens over the decades. Nothing sufficient to turn the tide right now, but I feel like we've come down to endgame, and need to draw some things out of the cupboard."

"Such as?" she asked.

"I've been holding off on offering treatments such as you two underwent to outsiders," Valmy said soberly. "In a way, dangling the possibility in front of people in order to keep our funding levels high while we did research. Project Herakles was a reasonable success, but it created monsters like Faulkener. Big and burly. Project Carpenter has refined that to the point that we all look normal."

"Who are you thinking of bringing in from the cold, sir?" Konicek asked.

In from the cold. An old espionage term, for an agent that was on the outside, guessing, and needed to be rescued. Informed.

Made dangerous.

Valmy nodded to himself.

"This is a secret you need to carry deep," he informed the two, waiting for them to nod. "Your upgrades supposedly double your lifespans, meaning that you will not really feel the advance of age until you are twelve or thirteen decades old."

They nodded as he spoke. Old briefings, often repeated.

"That is a lie," Valmy said. "Only a handful of folks are aware of the truth at present. I expect to live at least four hundred more years, and there are suggestions in the latest research that aging is a disease that can be defeated entirely, instead of held at bay for a time."

"Defeated, sir?" Vanlaere asked.

"Defeated," he nodded. "None of us are fertile. I'm not sure that can be fixed, but if we could make people live forever, we need to control population ruthlessly, anyway."

They both stirred uneasily, but Valmy had spent more than a decade considering the shape of Human culture that he intended to create.

Republican government as currently constructed worldwide would eventually have to give way, if only because it had been founded and secured on the notion that politicians would eventually age and die, opening space for younger generations to step into their space.

Perhaps political terms in office needed to be extended to ten and fifty years at that point? At least as an interim step.

"Eventually, there will be an entire caste of people who were functionally immortal, troopers," Valmy said simply. "Not the entire species, if we need to keep birthing new generations, but things will fold into two, distinct layers."

"Won't that knowledge drive more political instability, sir?" Vanlaere asked. "Revolutions initiated by folks on the outside?"

"Exactly why it has been kept quiet, Vanlaere," he said. "But it will also be necessary to neuter such organizing pressures by offering those rebels the treatment. Making them one of us."

"Trojan horse," she offered.

Valmy understood. Let some radical tell you he has seen the light and will work to uphold the new system he is part of, while quietly working from the inside to destroy it.

"Power is one of two choices," he replied.

That death was the other one was a given. He would be playing with fire at that point.

"So who do we need to contact and initiate, General?" Konicek asked now.

"A couple of Senators and House Chairmen," he said. "I've been waiting a few days to see if our security is compromised, because the aliens have unknown capabilities."

"Should we alert the rest of the base to prepare for an assault?" Vanlaere asked. "Daring is an expert at penetrating supposedly-secure facilities."

"They are already alerted, merely by me being present," Valmy smiled. "Once I make a few calls, it will be time for a couple of training exercises around here."

# CHAPTER 42

Looking around the starship's empty mess hall with half a mug of coffee in one hand, Mitch would have liked more than one night and one breakfast with her up in Everett, but the deal with the aliens had seen him remaining with Yormevs while Ernesta returned to Tanerhald. Along with Joie and Romana.

Romy.

Something.

He wasn't sure at this point, having moved on from the first two women emotionally. And all three would be leaving, one way or the other, when it was done.

"You look pensive," a voice interrupted.

Stone. Sneaking up on people like he did.

"Thinking about tomorrows," Mitch replied. "Wondering if Tanerhald will decide that we all know too much and have to leave, instead of Joie and the others."

"Hard call," Stone nodded.

Instead of continuing, the man moved to the coffee robots Yormevs had *acquired* from *somewhere* and pushed buttons. Careful, deliberate motions. Push the exact button correctly the first time, then move on.

That described the man that most people just sort of took for granted. Even Kehoe fell into that mistake from time to time. Over-looked because he didn't draw attention to himself.

Stone joined him when the robots were done gurgling.

"If it were me, I'd make a clean sweep of things," Stone said simply. "Too many people know too much, so I'd just grab 'em all and haul them off to a friendly planet somewhere, then keep them under constant observation for the rest of their lives, importing videos and consumer goods from Earth to keep them connected to their heritage."

"You don't think someone is going to go ahead and land a ship on the White House lawn and say *We come in peace*?" Mitch asked the older man.

Not that much older. Harder years. Stone was only a few years older than Mitch, but they had been vastly different. Enlisted at eighteen. Coming up on twenty years' service, though currently Unlawfully Absent. Technically kidnapped, if anyone asked, and being held against his will.

Or something.

Mitch had lived a much softer life. And never shot anybody, unlike Stone.

"They'd have done that already," Stone growled as he sipped his coffee. "Could do that tomorrow. No, they're giving us one chance to take care of their problems, before they drop the hammer on us."

"Think we can?" Mitch asked.

He and Stone had been two guys at opposite ends of a party, most of the time, with Kehoe between them. And the others. This was one of the first times the pair of them had *chatted*.

"I think that if Captain Daring can't do it, nobody else would have gotten close," Stone replied. "That's about as good as I can estimate right now. We've got Kehoe planning and you looking. I'm at loose ends a lot, since he doesn't need an office manager, so I've spent time training with the Clever Horse."

"Who?"

"Cōng Mǎ," Stone chuckled. "Her name means clever horse, translated roughly out of Cantonese."

"I did not know that," Mitch observed, a bit surprised.

But he supposed that a guy like Stone didn't have anything to do except wait while the big hitters did their things. Planning. Training. Preparing. At least Mitch could dive headlong into various databases, looking for things that weren't there.

Or were too well hidden.

Which kind of described the whole situation.

Mitch was about to say something when the hatch opened and Kehoe entered the space, Yormevs hot on his heels.

"There you are," Kehoe said. "Carter's contact came through."

Mitch rose automatically.

Finally, something he could do.

# CHAPTER 43

Joie was on her bunk, legs crossed and meditating. Ernesta was reading something on a tablet Tanerhald had gotten for her. Something cheap, trashy, and with a lurid cover featuring two spaceships fighting in an asteroid field. At least last time Joie had asked.

The door chimed. Then opened a moment later. Romana stepped in, followed by Carter and Tanerhald.

At least they'd both gone to bed dressed enough for barracks, since her room had suddenly turned into a meeting.

Joie watched the three standing there at the foot of her bed. Ernesta put her book reader down.

"You tell her," Romana said to Carter.

Carter actually looked embarrassed, which wasn't an emotion Joie would have thought he was capable of understanding, let alone feeling.

Did this mean he was growing up?

"Irene called," Carter said simply. "Gave us the name of a place, but Romana's friends can't figure it out."

Joie turned to her former sidekick and best friend with a questioning look.

"Feels like a base name, but a quick look at the records didn't turn anything up," Romana replied.

"We probably need Mitch, then," Joie noted dryly.

Trust between the two alien sides was not particularly well developed at this point. Angry cops and neighborhood vigilantes both trying to achieve the same goal, but in different ways.

"That's what I told him," Romana nodded to the small alien leader.

Joie turned her attention to Tanerhald. Lavender skin. Bones that reminded her vaguely of a lizard, like a character from one of Ernesta's books made into a vid.

"I need my whole team," she said simply. "Without a lot of complicated nervousness. If I convince them to uncloak or whatever it is, can I ask you to only grab the Humans and leave the Heecha alone for now?"

The man stewed. Alien. Whatever. Dude In Charge.

Angry cop, asked to let the neighborhood vigilante group off with a warning.

By the burglar who had discovered that one of the neighbors is really a serial killer or something.

Shit had gotten weird.

"There must be a resolution to this, Joie Daring," Tanerhald replied in a stiff voice.

"I understand," Joie said. "But without them, I can't do this, and you'll end up doing whatever it is you originally planned. You have to tell me how badly do you want Humanity to survive as an industrial, technological species, Tanerhald."

She watched the man rock back onto his heels, physically as well as metaphorically. He'd been playing the heavy through this whole tragedy, and it looked to Joie as though nobody had ever asked him what he wanted out of everything.

Or rather, what outcome would be *enough*.

"Humans are too dangerous, Daring," he began, then waved her off when she opened her mouth. "And I understand that removing the troublemakers will reduce the threat. You are violent, unstable, and prone to destructive urges."

"We're not asking you to welcome us into galactic society," Joie offered. "I wouldn't want us out there myself. And you won't just sail home afterwards, if we succeed, so you'll be able to see if it works or if too much damage has been done to our joint culture by what Bandi's bosses initiated two centuries ago. Do you want me to succeed, Tanerhald?"

Again, rocked to his core.

He'd come in here like a bank robber with a gun, waving it around like a magic wand. That never worked, except to control people who wanted to survive. A lot of folks never stopped to think what they really wanted, once everything they had been planning went sideways.

"Can you, Joie?" he finally asked. "Succeed?"

"We're down to the part where Humans say *or die trying*," she replied. "I intend to die trying. The others all signed up for that much even before we knew you existed, so not much has changed on that axis. But you control the cards. I can convince Yormevs, I think. You have to promise me now the opportunity to try. It comes down to you."

Not the conversation he'd been expecting when he walked in here. That much was obvious in his eyes.

But the aliens were growing nervous. Desperate.

Did they want Humanity to survive?

She waited, having made her case.

Tanerhald surprised her by turning to Romana.

"I understand now," he told her. "You said it, but I had to see it."

"What?" Joie asked.

Not demanded. Asked.

Softly, instead of roughly.

"Romana told me that you could make me *believe*, Joie," Tanerhald replied. "I doubted her. I was wrong. What do you need to succeed?"

"I need my friends," Joie said. "Let me talk to Yormevs and I will convince him to meet you halfway, then we can go after Bouchard together."

Joie unfolded and slid to the edge of the bed, meeting Ernesta doing the same. They both rose with matching grins. One Romana shared. Even Carter seemed to get it.

They could win.

Together.

# CHAPTER 44

Joie had prepared herself for a number of different answers from Yormevs. A flat no wasn't one of them.

"Why not?" she demanded, feeling the harsh glare of accusation from Tanerhald behind her.

It was a communications room, or something, where she'd been taken. Space to sit, plus a Brakhua female(?) she hadn't been introduced to handling comm. Control panels with a lot of options. Headsets and microphones, plus overhead speakers.

Like before, she needed to use the gear Yormevs had supplied for Chile. Signals that came from anywhere, because the shield scattered their source. Radio, without triangulation, just so everyone was hidden from each other.

"Because those dipshit Brakhua don't understand Human technology, Joie," Yormevs replied in an angry voice. All the worse because he had to know his frenemy was listening in. "If you are serious, then you need to come here. Mitch has the connections into the various computer systems that he needs, but that took us months of time to set up. The Brakhua would probably require at least a year. No, you must come over to my ship. He can even come with you, if he has the courage."

Joie took a deep breath as the bodies around her all gasped at the same moment. Now was exactly the moment when Yormevs could fuck it all up, if he wasn't careful.

So could she.

"Stand by while I mute the line at this end," she said, turning to the commtech and nodding.

That woman pushed a button on the console, hidden among dozens of others, and nodded back.

Joie focused her attention on Tanerhald.

Brakhua got darker when they got angry. And this was anger, not fear or embarrassment. This was a general somewhere, wishing to verbally rip somebody a new asshole in public.

Joie took a breath. She was surrounded by Ernesta, Romana, and Carter, but Tanerhald was the one who mattered right now.

"I'm sorry," Joie said delicately. "Is he right?"

Never push. Another lesson she'd been picking up from Ernesta. And Bandi, weird as that has been. You can lead the conversation, but forcing it was like pushing wet spaghetti.

Tanerhald's jaw muscles stood out like he was grinding his teeth in rage. His eyes spoke volumes.

But then, nobody likes to be shown up by a lesser enemy. Especially when you've underestimated them. And it looked like Tanerhald had with Yormevs.

Tanerhald nodded. Slowly. Almost painfully.

"If time is of the essence, as you say, then maybe he's right and we need to do this from his ship," Joie said. "I promise you that I will return afterwards."

"And me," Carter barked. "Though I'd stay here as a hostage or something if I thought it would help."

Joie felt her jaw drop open. Looking at her two friends, at least she wasn't alone.

Carter Faulkener? The notorious terrorist warlord, offering himself up instead of sending someone else?

He grinned ruefully as everybody was staring at him.

"Somebody's gotta, Joie," he murmured. "They won't trust it otherwise."

She nodded gratefully. If nothing else, she'd lived long enough to see that goofball grow up.

What the fuck was the world coming to?

"Tanerhald?" Joie asked.

Long, painful moment. Previously in supreme control, suddenly the man wasn't. And didn't know how to handle it.

Joie could offer all sorts of advice on the topic. And Tanerhald had never had to listen to his ear cook or smell his eyeball shorting out.

Tanerhald sucked a deep breath in, then released it through his nose.

"Yes," he said in a pained voice.

"Thank you."

Joie smiled and turned back to the commtech. That woman did something and the line was live again.

"Yormevs, he has agreed," Joie said. "We'll need your coordinates, and in about fifteen minutes, I'll need you to drop your shields so we can send a team over. Then Mitch and Kehoe can get to digging with what Irene found for us."

"I'm relying on you, Joie," Yormevs replied in a questioning voice.

"So is the rest of the galaxy, Yormevs," she said. "Let's not fuck things up at this late a date, please?"

"Understood," the man sounded chagrined now. "Fifteen minutes."

Joie felt her emotions kind of flow out of herself and leak all over the table. Ernesta put a hand on her shoulder and strength seemed to radiate from it. Joie drew on that. Romana and Carter added their hands a moment later, giving her enough to stand up.

Joie towered over Tanerhald, but the Brakhua were all a tiny species, compared to Heecha or Danorak. At least physically.

The other two were cowards, at the end of the day, unwilling to stand up in the light of day for what they believed, while the Brakhua in Tanerhald had taken it upon themselves to protect the galaxy from threats like Humans.

"I'm coming with you," Tanerhald announced.

Joie wondered if her jaw would break, as many times as it had fallen open in shock recently.

"I was only planning on taking my team over," she said shakily.

Tanerhald smiled and it was suddenly filled with warmth.

"No," he replied. "You told that shitbird Yormevs Coeurle that you needed all your friends if you were going to succeed. I would like to be included in that category, Joie Daring."

She wondered if she was going to cry, then just let it, tears rolling down her face. Ernesta leaned in and wrapped an arm around her waist, not quite holding her up, but close.

Joie opened her mouth, but couldn't make anything come out.

Tanerhald's smile, however, got bigger.

She drew warmth and strength from it as well.

She could do this thing.

All the galaxy was at risk, but she had friends she'd never imagined possible.

# CHAPTER 45

Bandi refused to remain in his room, regardless of what that Heecha had advised. At least that fool hadn't tried to order him or anything. Then they might have had words. And punches.

Instead, he was down in the big messhall that the Heecha fool had ordered cleared of all tables and people, leaving only a empty auditorium. The Heecha was probably behind several sets of sealed frame doors with weapons, but Bandi had also refused to cower before the Brakhua.

What were they going to do? Execute him for uplifting a primitive species?

Not a lot of change there. And he honestly did have it coming. Hadn't been his idea, lo those many centuries ago, but he could have refused. Could have stood up and said "Wait one damned minute" when it came up.

Except that he hadn't. The Party had commanded a thing, then ordered him to manage it.

And he had. Oh, how he had.

And look at where it had gotten them.

At least he could look at the Creator of the Universe soon and know it had taken a Human to beat him. Deep in his soul, where he never even whispered it to himself, Bandi knew that the others were frightened of that more than anything else.

That Humans could be that smart, as well as that dangerous.

So he had a mug of coffee in one hand, ankles crossed as he sat in the only chair, wearing a cheap suit that needed to be pressed as he leaned back and waited. Fool Heecha were afraid to be here. Afraid to stand up and admit that they'd been sneaking around the law.

Bandi didn't have too many shits left to give.

And Joie needed him.

The lights filled the room for a moment like glowing water, filling every nook and cranny.

At first, he'd wondered if the Brakhua in charge would take a moment to grab everybody they could off this ship in that moment of vulnerability.

But it was Joie in charge, not that idiot Kehoe. Well, idiot was a strong term.

Asshole. Like *Mithras*. Before.

Both were getting better.

That meant Bandi had to, as well.

Joie was in the center when the tide of light receded.

As she should be.

Surrounded by Ernesta and Romana, of whom he had only heard about and now finally got to meet in person. Carter, so small that he was almost a stranger.

And a stranger.

Shit. Really?

Bandi rose to his feet, though being taller than the Brakhua wouldn't matter much. Any being who had accompanied Joie wasn't about to be intimidated by height.

Hell, he might not even be impressed.

But Bandi's maternal predecessor had told him to walk to his execution with pride.

Of course, she had been deep into the Party and their beliefs that assholes like the Brakhua needed to be taken down, so she'd been expecting him to eventually be caught.

What was the Human term? Oh, right.

Frog-marched up the stairs to the scaffolding, to be hung from the neck, may somebody's god have mercy on his dumbass soul.

Bandi didn't have high expectations.

But Joie needed him.

So he walked over the little man and bowed.

"Bandi Algom, currently a prisoner of the Heecha," he said with a sardonic grin on his face.

"Tanerhald," the Brakhua replied. "Currently?"

"It's not like I'm going to be set free later," Bandi shrugged. "You'll likely take everyone else into custody when she's successful."

He ignored the little man now and turned to hug Joie. Just because.

Danorak were not a particularly tactile species, but he'd spent so much time on Earth or thinking about it that he was culturally Human these days.

Whatever that meant.

Joie had been surprised, but hugged him back. Ernesta was expecting it.

Even Carter smiled.

"Romana Pham, it is a pleasure to meet you in the flesh," Bandi said to the last member of Joie's other team.

She hugged him instead. It was good.

"Where is Yormevs?" Joie asked.

"Probably hiding in the linen closet under an old quilt," Bandi replied with as much disdain as English allowed. And it was a pretty flexible language that way. "Come, I shall escort you to where the old woman might be."

"It's good to see you, Bandi," Joie said as she caught up and walked beside him.

He smiled.

Whatever else he had fucked up in his long life, at least he had a friend like Joie.

# CHAPTER 46

Joie had been surprised to arrive in an empty room. Well, Bandi had been there. She wasn't entirely sure what it meant that Yormevs and the others were not, but Bandi was headed toward where they had been meeting on this ship.

And walking slowly enough that Yormevs might have time to emerge from whatever den he'd been hiding in and meet them there.

"How are you doing?" she asked Bandi.

He looked relaxed. More calm and centered than any of the times they'd met before.

All the stress and guilt gone?

"Trying to undo all the stupid shit I have spent several Human lifetimes accumulating," Bandi shrugged. "Won't matter much at the end, but even a wee bit now might tip a lot of scales."

"I see," she noted.

Had they all gone to hell, at least in their minds, and were looking for their redemption?

Perhaps Joie had only gotten there first, because she seemed to be leading a large number of folks this time.

They got to the big conference room and Bandi opened the hatch with a theatrical flourish.

Yormevs was there, looking a little flustered. Mitch and Kehoe as well. Stone and Sifu. Even Freya Malik.

Mitch had the Heecha equivalent of a laptop computer in front of him, no doubt deep in TRC's computer systems like a tapeworm.

Joie walked over to Mitch and kissed him on the top of his head, where it was getting a little thin. Then Kehoe, before he could escape. Sifu grinned so Joie kissed her forehead as well, then Freya.

Stone harrumphed, so he got his on the lips, which surprised the shit out of him.

Joie grinned and sat. Mitch got kisses from Romana and Ernesta, once Joie had set an example.

She smiled at Yormevs, possibly in an even greater panic that she might kiss him as well.

It felt like the day for it.

She might ambush him later.

Eventually, everyone got settled. Tanerhald ended up directly across from Yormevs. Bandi was sitting next to her like a guy all set to do color commentary for a football match.

Joie let them scowl at each other for a few moments.

"Yormevs Coeurle, this is Tanerhald," she introduced him.

"I'm aware of who he is," Yormevs grumbled. "Rather famous back home."

"Oh?" Joie asked, turning to the Brakhua.

He shrugged in an *aw, shucks* kind of way, but remained silent.

"This is my team," she announced, making sure everyone understood that.

The Humans were already there. And one Danorak. Eventually, the two newcomers would come around.

"Carter, tell Mitch," she said.

Carter pulled a paper from a back pocket of his jeans and slid it across.

"Name of a base, but nothing shows in the records we can access," Carter offered. "No clue what that means."

"It means that the Defense Department officially sold the land and struck it from their records," Kehoe broke in. "TRC has a couple of side corporations that deal in real estate outside of official government channels, for exactly that reason. Lots of old places shut down like that. Not all of them are in civilian hands these days."

Mitch nodded and started typing. Joie would have been utterly lost. Romana assured her that more analysts would have to take several days to find the piece they needed.

Mitch required four minutes. Which was why Kehoe had hired him in the first place.

And why Joie had found him so hot before. Well, he was still hot, but she was in a different place these days. Romana seemed to be as well, which left Ernesta a clear field to try her luck with one of the most amazing people Joie'd ever met.

Amazing men. She had a couple of amazing women handy.

Friends.

"Got it," Mitch said. He turned a scowl to Kehoe. "TRC owns it, but doesn't list it in their own systems?"

"Told you, kid," Kehoe laughed. "We do a lot of crap like that under the table. The Russians and Chinese got AI systems almost as good as ours, so sometimes we have to obfuscate the living shit out of things, just to be sure."

"What is it?" Joie asked.

"An old missile silo facility in northeastern Colorado," Mitch replied. "Looks like it held Skyhawk ballistic defense missiles at one time, part of the innermost ring of such bases built in the mid-twenty-first century for Cheyenne Mountain. Demobilized sixteen years ago, but that appears to be a change of front door keys and an adjustment of personnel, once the missiles were cleared out."

"Lots of those places," Stone laughed. "How did we miss it before?"

"Because I'm looking at a scan overlay from Yormevs's systems and it's not there," Mitch replied.

"Not there?" Kehoe asked. He paled. "Shit. La Plata."

"Explain?" Joie asked.

"Bandi had systems in place to keep folks from beaming in or even scanning that he was present," Kehoe said, turned to the man. "Did you give Bouchard any?"

"A few," Bandi nodded. "Securing the bioengineering labs against detection. I don't remember any in Colorado, though."

"Assume he figured out how to copy them," Joie said. "Or thinned down defenses elsewhere to build himself a bolthole. Unless someone wanted to drop a nuclear missile inside with him, those places are probably hardened against anything we can do from the outside."

"Then you'll have to get inside," Stone spoke up sharply. "Quiet like. Mitch, is the place in regular contact with DC?"

"Stand by," Mitch said.

"What are you up to, you old pirate?" Sifu Wěn asked with a knowing grin.

"Bases like this tend to be entirely self-contained," Stone turned to her, face serious. "That means a lot of DOD and others pass them by entirely. At the same time, that means that they don't just call Tacoma or North Carolina to confirm something. Especially if it's somebody they know."

"Who would they know and not immediately sound every alarm they have?" Kehoe demanded.

"Me," Stone replied. "Always in the background, but I bet you that I know half those men and women on sight. If I roll up with a truck, with orders Mitch inserts into a system that they can access, then the main team can be deployed inside his defensive zones."

Joie studied the man. He had demanded to accompany them at Hanoi. Everybody was the hero of their own story, after all.

"Kehoe, you come up with orders that have Sergeant Stone pulling a truck up to their loading dock for secret delivery," Joie said.

She considered the others. Her, Ernesta, Carter, and Romana could get in. But that didn't feel right.

"Freya, I'd like you in the truck with Stone because you should also be known to folks, so that will help them relax," Joie said to her. "Plus, you two can provide backup if things go wrong."

"Backup?" Freya asked.

"You got a blowtorch," Joie grinned. "Stone, do you know what those emitters generally look like, in case she needs to blow them up?"

"Do," Stone nodded. "Usually centered at ground level. In La Plata, we had to put it on the third floor, just in case. Here, I'm guessing they'll be disguised as radio antennae."

"You two sort out how to cover our rear flank," Joie ordered.

Ordered?

Kehoe was the guy in charge, but it was her team. Weren't Bandi and Tanerhald here because of her?

That left one person.

"Sifu, my feelings have not changed," Joie said. "Four of us have been upgraded sufficient that Yormevs and Bandi both think we are a match for Bouchard and his troopers. You have not, because there wasn't time and I wanted to give you the chance to remain on Earth later if possible. I still need you."

The woman smiled, and it was like all the rest of the weight slid off Joie's shoulders.

"I am here for you," she said.

Joie sighed and smiled.

Then she turned to Stone.

"What are you rated to drive, assuming we can't find an automated truck for this?" she asked.

"Anything with wheels or tracks," he grinned. "Never got into piloting whirlybirds, but that was because only Warrant Officers and higher get to be pilots."

"And you didn't wanna," Joie nodded.

"Still don't," Stone confirmed.

"That works, though," Joie approved. "Mitch, you, Kehoe, and whoever else you need, go figure out how to get a load or big container inside the base. Yormevs, I need you to drop me someplace without telling everyone else. Stone, you're coming with me, but you will keep your mouth shut afterwards."

He turned serious.

"Where are we going?"

"To get you a truck."

# CHAPTER 47

Joie had made Stone dress like a tourist, which included leaving behind all the knives he was notorious for carrying in pockets, bags, and wherever else. Jeans, T-shirt, even running shoes instead of boots. It also made him a little grumpier than usual, but she wasn't about to bend.

"Where are we?" he asked, staring in disbelief at the bright sun and warm day.

"Calexico, California," Joie replied with a grin. "When you were chasing Celeste and me south, this is where she dropped me while she kept going east."

The American side of the border fence still struck her for the overall grunginess of things. Mexicali, not all that far away across the fence, had a lot of tourist money poured into making things pretty and bright.

She tugged on his elbow and Stone fell in beside her, looking like her dad with his gray hair and overall grizzledness.

She walked a few blocks from the alley where they had been dropped off, and turned into another alley behind several shops.

It looked like a junkyard back here, but it always did. At least five cars and pickup trucks in various stages of repair. Or stripping. Hard to tell around here. Part of that was camouflage.

A head popped up when Joie whistled. Pedro *Dos*.

"Oh, shit," he muttered a little too loud. "She's back for more."

Juan-Pedro popped out a moment later and grinned.

Joie walked close and got a hug from both men. Stone held back a little.

"Stone, these are the *Pedros*," she said. "They'll help."

"*The Pedros*?" he asked. "That's their name?"

"Uh huh," she laughed. "Pedro *Dos* and Juan-Pedro."

"Up to no good, Joie?" Juan-Pedro asked.

"We are," she said. "And it will top anything you've seen yet."

"No shit?"

"No shit," she confirmed.

"Let's get you inside, then," *Dos* said. "*Uno* needs to know."

She followed him into *Uno*'s office. Listened to the man carry on a perfectly normal conversation in German while his face got white and his eyes got big watching her.

Pedro *Uno* snapped his fingers and pointed at *Dos*. *Dos* grabbed a bottle of Coke, opened it, and handed it across, getting one for Stone as well, though Joie demurred.

"We about to be arrested?" *Uno* asked after he hung up.

"I need a tractor that can haul a standard fifty-three-foot trailer someplace in Colorado without arousing suspicion," Joie said simply. "Stone here will be driving it into a secret US Army base while I sneak in from the back with a full team of folks."

Juan-Pedro whistled quietly.

"You US Army, Stone?" *Uno* asked.

"I bleed green," the man replied succinctly.

"What's in the base?" Uno asked. "How bullet-proof does the paperwork need to be?"

"Civilian rig hauling a cargo for a national distributor is good enough," Stone said, ignoring the first question. "We'll have perfect orders and records when the soldiers at the gate look us up."

*Uno* whistled. So did *Dos*.

"As for the rest, I need him to get a container inside, with my team secretly aboard," Joie said. "This goes back to what was going on the first time I came through. Stone was chasing me then. I recruited him and Kehoe since."

"Wow," *Uno* offered blankly. "Shit's serious."

"As serious as it gets," Joie agreed. "I needed to move quickly, so you were the first folks I thought of. Not sure you'll get the truck back if something goes wrong, so make sure it can't be traced to you."

"It was wrecked in a flashflood in '96," *Dos* chimed in. "Insurance never got the claim since we bought it cash from the owner. Stripped the VIN and put it on one of ours that was a match. That should get you in."

"The truck you took me to Mexico in?" Joie turned back to the man.

"Best I got," *Dos* nodded. "Anything for you."

"Let's go look at it," Joie said.

"You do that," *Uno* said. "I need to make a call. Sarah would never forgive me if she missed you, and I get the feeling you two aren't going to be around for long."

Joie smiled. *Uno* was right. On both counts.

Time was tight, but this might be her last chance to see her friend.

# CHAPTER 48

Joie heard Sarah come around the corner, recognizing the clack of her heels on the pavement.

Stone was up in the cab with *Dos*, doing manly stuff that must have involved an ongoing string of dirty jokes from the laughter coming out of the window.

She turned and grinned.

"What the hell did you do?" Sarah demanded, stopping a meter away, gesturing, mouth open as she took all of Joie in. "I mean, I know you didn't like the implants, but…"

Joie blushed. Sarah was another mom to her, or mother-in-law if she'd had any kids even remotely the right age to marry off.

"A lot has happened," Joie said, taking her by the arm and leading her off into a corner from the profanity and laughter out of the truck.

"Is Ernesta okay?" Sarah asked.

"She's fine," Joie reassured her. "I'd have brought her, but then I might have had to bring everybody. Romana is fine, too. We found her."

"Romana?" Sarah gasped. "Good. And you?"

"Obviously, some changes," Joie said. "The boys didn't comment, or maybe didn't notice."

"They noticed," Sarah smiled. "But they know better than to say anything."

Joie nodded. Yeah, they probably had noticed, but she hadn't volunteered anything, so they hadn't asked.

"You can quietly tell *Uno* and maybe *Dos*, after I'm gone," Joie said.

"Gone?" Sarah asked.

Joie nodded, then gave Sarah a greatly expurgated and condensed version of the last several months, leaving out names but conveying that a lot of aliens were involved in a potentially bad way.

"At least they have you to save the day," Sarah nodded when Joie finished.

Joie nodded. *AGAIN*. Blushed, even.

Bad habit, but unavoidable with Sarah, it seemed.

"I have to try," Joie said. "If things go exceptionally bad, everything will come apart and US Army studies suggest a mass die-off of Humanity that might be terminal. I don't know what you can do to prepare, but now would be a good time. If nothing stupid happens on the news in the next month, then we probably won."

"But you'll be gone?" Sarah whispered.

Joie nodded, then felt all the emotions she had been bottling inside reach up and overwhelm her. Sarah engulfed her in a hug and just held her. Not a lot of tears, but an almost-impossible amount of shaking until she got control again.

"Will they take immigrants?" Sarah asked. "If they do take all those people away and make them live on another planet?"

"Why would you want to do that?" Joie replied, aghast.

"Because you'll be there, and not here," Sarah smiled. "It won't be as much fun. Plus, all my kids are grown up. They can have their own lives if *Uno* and I decide to go on a long vacation."

Joie hugged her.

Friends.

And all the ones who were there for her were breaking the law to do it.

What did that say about the state of affairs in this country? In the world?

Joie knew, but it felt like a betrayal to tell others how far short of their ideals they had fallen. Not Sarah, though. Nor the *Pedros*. Celeste. Many strangers.

And many friends who had volunteered to march into Hell with her.

She could do this.

Sarah gave her strength.

"Now," Sarah said with a kiss on the cheek. "Go rescue *Dos* and your friend or they will be here all day."

"Yes, Mom," Joie grinned.

She walked over and opened the passenger door. The two men inside abruptly fell silent, like teenage boys being caught at some delinquency.

Not entirely wrong.

*Dos* slid out and she climbed up to take his place after a quick hug.

Stone sobered, but his face broke into a quick grin.

"This is going to be fun," he announced as they both buckled themselves in.

Joie just grinned back. Waved at Sarah as they backed into the alley and started the run east and north.

Things were in motion.

# CHAPTER 49

Taylor sat in his new office and studied things. Once Mitch had the right name and coordinates, he'd been able to find a stupid amount of information about the base, including *as-builts*, but nothing showing recent renovations.

Wasn't a place Taylor had ever visited, but that made perfect sense if it was a genetics research lab. He'd been focused on the cybernetic side of TRC instead.

Old missile silo, so compact and deep. Basically, an office building going down instead of up, with a plug of triply-reinforced concrete over top. Enough to protect against anything short of a direct hit by someone with the right bomb.

Several deep silos down the south side of the hole, all empty after a new round of peace treaties twenty years ago had moved everyone back in the direction of nuclear disarmament. Lots of living space for people once you took out the need to maintain ICBMs, but he had no idea how many people might be there.

Even TRC didn't share certain things with itself, let alone the rest of the government. Once upon a time, Taylor had put that down to good tradecraft, since they were the good guys standing on the shore holding back a rising tide of evil.

Or something equally full of shit.

Now, he could see where it had let Bouchard and a few others start building up their own, personal armies that didn't necessarily answer to anyone else.

And frightened the shit out of some folks who really could do something about it.

How many Senators and Representatives were going to burn if all this came out? Enough?

Or were people so cynical that by the next election it would all be forgotten?

Days like this, Taylor wondered if he should just wallow in the cynicism that came with the job.

A chime at the door, then it opened.

Wasn't Stone. That man was off with Joie borrowing a stolen truck from an unknown chop shop, if Taylor had read the tea leaves correctly. Be back in twelve hours and ready for everyone to make their attack run at Bouchard's castle.

Tanerhald. The Brakhua captain of the other ship. Or something equivalent. Military rank, rather than elected leader of the others Joie and crew had talked about.

Taylor had only met the one. Impressive fellow, for being so small. At least compared to Humans.

"Is now a good time?" Tanerhald asked in a slightly accented English that was probably good enough for radio or the telephone.

"Sure," Taylor nodded, gesturing to the chairs on the other side of his desk. "What can I do for you?"

"I have gotten some of the story from Romana Pham," Tanerhald said simply. "And read reports prepared by Coeurle. Plus, Joie has filled in a few bits when she could."

Taylor nodded. There hadn't been time to cover everything. Not if they wanted to get to Bouchard when they still knew where he was. And could keep it quiet.

There were potential benefits to taking Bouchard's sorry ass right off the Congressional front steps in front of every media organization in the world, but the man hadn't pissed Taylor off that much.

Yet.

"All of you seem convinced that a full-frontal assault against what you yourself have qualified as a hardened military target, was the best way forward," Tanerhald said. "Why is that?"

"Time is short," Taylor explained. "Your patience is not infinite. Plus, Bouchard knows that someone is out there watching. Possibly coming for him. The longer he has time to prepare a response, the more likely it is that Joie fails and you have to resort to extraordinary measures."

"The concept does not seem to fill you with dread, Kehoe," he offered.

Taylor shrugged.

"Nuclear missiles have been a thing for generations," he replied. "Enough firepower to end Earth as an inhabitable planet, if thing got out of hand. For the longest time, that threat has kept trouble to a minimum. Personal things instead of armies clashing, because it could be contained. Joie is exceptional at that. Better than any other agent I've ever worked with, though Bouchard has folks supposedly as good as she is now physically. Not mentally."

"And yet, you simply accept that my kind might have to destroy your homeworld, and possibly eliminate your species, if you fail?" Tanerhald asked. "Not one of you has threatened my person in any way."

"We all woke up one morning and realized we'd been serving evil, Tanerhald," Taylor said. "Humans do that, but the good ones try to get on the right side and make it better. That's Joie and the others. My engagement also contains an element of personal revenge on Bouchard. He was the one who ordered me to burn Joie in the first place. For reasons that didn't make any sense at the time."

"But do now?" the alien asked.

"Carter Faulkener used to be ten percent taller, and proportionally bigger," Taylor explained. "Weighed tremendously more because of the alloy and implants. Joie hasn't changed physically, save for the removal of the breast implants she always hated so much."

He paused and waited for the alien to nod.

"Joie went into La Plata alone," Taylor said. "Took Carter in single combat. She was supposed to kill him. And be so badly broken when it was all done that she died as well, or was medically retired. Something that removed her from the table as an agent, because Bouchard couldn't regrow her arm or other parts, and didn't want her in a position to become his enemy later, if he couldn't suborn her now."

"That sounds like the stories of Humans I have heard," Tanerhald said.

"And it is not wrong," Taylor said. "We're violent, dangerous, and crazy. However, we are also giving and friendly in the right circumstances. Joie is trying to capture everyone so they can be safely removed to live out their days elsewhere, rather than stealing a nuclear bomb, driving it into the middle of that base, and detonating it to get everyone."

"She would do that?" Tanerhald gasped.

"Other than the nuclear bomb part, Carter is something of an expert at using truck bombs to assassinate people," Taylor offered. "I'm sure he could find a way to pull it off if I tasked him with it."

The alien recoiled.

"Instead, Joie is going to try to capture him at great personal risk," Taylor continued. "Taking all her friends. Then tracking down all the folks for you to grab, rather than just shooting them to make sure they are never a threat again. Personally, Joie thinking that way surprises me, because we never trained her for that. My guess is Amy Watanabe is responsible for it."

"Who?"

"After I caused her to be thrown out of the Army, and become *persona non grata*, she had a pension and not much more," Taylor grimaced. "Eventually, she got a job at a coffee shop in DC. Watanabe is the manager of that store. Tiny woman, not much bigger than you. Impressive as hell, too, as I had to sit across a desk from her trying to get Joie to come in from the cold. Pretty sure Watanabe is the one that turned Joie into the person she is now. I owe her a thank-you card for it, too, but can't ever tell her why."

"Interesting," Tanerhald noted. "So you and she would also believe that Humans removed from Earth forever could possibly be shown the error of their ways?"

"A dead man never learns," Taylor replied. "In the old days, sometimes it was just easier to kill them because even the living ones weren't willing to change. Joie thinks that it can be done now. I believe her."

"Thank you," Tanerhald said, standing up. "You have given me much to consider. I had not truly appreciated that saving Humanity was feasible. I was more focused on saving everyone *from* the Humans."

"If Joie can't, nobody can," Taylor said. "Simple as that."

The alien didn't make any comment. Just bowed his head and departed.

Taylor went back to the schematics and wondered if it was really possible that anybody was going to get out of there alive.

# CHAPTER 50

Mitch was getting coffee. Decaf this time, because he wanted to sleep at some point, so he'd be sharp when all hell broke loose later. Not much he could do, but with the sorts of computer access Yormevs had gotten for him, there were a few things he wanted to try.

Everybody else was largely in their rooms or quiet spaces, meditating or however they prepared for shit like this. He was in a back corner just relaxing.

Romana walked in, looked around until she saw him, and started this way.

"No, you don't need to get up," she said as he started to move, so Mitch stayed in the chair.

The space could sit forty or fifty folks when all the tables were out. Coffee robots on one wall that had been expanded and modified to include food for Human, as well as Heecha and Danorak. He'd only seen Bandi, though, as the other two apparently preferred to stay in their rooms.

Bandi had mentioned that both were still young enough to be believers.

Mitch preferred the cynic.

Romana stepped close and kissed him on the top of his head, then moved to the next chair around the small square and sat.

"I talked with Ernesta," Romana said.

Mitch started to say something and she waved him to silence.

"It's all right, Mitch," she said. "I don't think we would have worked out at the time for the same reasons you and Joie wouldn't have. That's fine. I just wanted to say thank you for coming to find me."

"We didn't, though," Mitch countered. "That was all you."

"You were trying," Romana said. "You came aboard with that asshole Kehoe because they were looking for me. Joie never gave up on that, even after you and I gave up on her."

"Joie needed to become somebody else," Mitch observed. "Not the woman she used to be, but someone bigger."

"And I needed that as well," Romana nodded. "They grabbed me out of that barracks because they needed a pure Human that they could recruit as an agent. Not a cybernaut like Joie or Freya. Not one of Bouchard's new advanced people."

"I've seen lists suggesting that you might have been on a short list for that," Mitch said. "Didn't make much sense at the time, but the context of people he could recruit does. Not sure why he didn't."

"I've always had reservations about what they did to Joie," Romana nodded. "How they treated her. How they basically threw her out with yesterday's trash. Pretty sure that Chelsea Vanlaere got the slot that opened when I washed out."

Mitch felt himself blush again. Sure, he knew he was pretty good looking, but Chelsea had used him as a vector to infiltrate Joie's team, using one of the oldest tricks in the book.

Not that he'd minded being her victim at the time.

Romana grinned, like she could maybe read his mind. A woman like that probably could. They'd been that close for a while, both concerned about saving Joie. Then noticing each other.

Mitch shrugged at might-have-beens and focused on this woman.

"So they upgraded you, huh?" he asked.

"They did," Romana nodded. "But I'm not really supposed to talk about it. Nothing compared to what they did to Joie. Just better. And I have a small team of folks. Basically mercenaries I recruited once I could vet a few who wouldn't freak out at who was hiring them. None are at my level, let alone Joie's, or I would suggest taking them as well. They'll stay here and can guard anybody Tanerhald grabs."

"You think he'll be able to kidnap some folks if Stone is successful?" Mitch asked.

"Long shot, I know," Romana said. "Best fallback we've got at this moment. If those shields are down, scanners might work. Might not, considering the hardening down there. My concern is that they might have to get violent. Maybe blow the place up."

"It's more than this one base, Romy," Mitch said. "I'm seeing hints of up to a dozen others, scattered about and doing this kind of research for TRC. Maybe not all of it is genetics like you folks, but some. We'll need Bouchard alive."

"Tanerhald knows that," Romana said. "Joie does, too, but she's operating from a different place. She wants everyone to come out of this one alive. Some of our alien friends aren't so sure."

"What happens if we succeed?" Mitch pressed. "If we nail Bouchard, get him and the others out, and Tanerhald is able to kill all that research by melting databases and removing the minds?"

"Then everybody gets removed from Earth forever." She shrugged exactly like Joie would have. "Human colony on some distant world, hopefully with regular cargo runs home for videos and blue jeans, so that folks remember who they used to be."

"You don't think Tanerhald will reveal himself to Humanity if we succeed?" Mitch asked.

"Not for a while," Romana replied. "I asked him that myself. Most of the alien species age much more slowly than we do, so aren't in the same sorts of hurry as we are about doing things. They often have centuries where we have decades. Maybe in a Human generation, it will be safe to say hello. Or bring in some new, Human agents who have been trained by the aliens. Dunno. I'll be around, after what they did to me. Same as Joie. You might want to ask them for the same treatment, if you're serious about Ernesta. She's got a lot of time alone after you, otherwise."

He'd considered it. Hadn't asked Ernesta that directly, but they'd danced around it. At the end of the day, he'd only known her for a brief time, with half of that being when she was still older than his Mom. Physically. Mentally, she still was, but now she was younger than him.

And might be forever, while he turned into an old man.

Did he want to live forever, too?

"Dunno," he shrugged. "I'll have to leave with the rest of you because I know too much. And, as you said, we'll have time to think about these things standing on an alien world. You four just need to make sure you all come back safely."

He leaned over and kissed her, just because he could. Wasn't anything behind it.

"Four?" she asked when he leaned back.

"Carter has made the greatest strides," Mitch said. "I've read most of his personnel file, dating back thirty years, and any resemblance to the man he was, even three years ago, is entirely accidental. Joie got to him then. And she's done it again since. He's trying to be a better person. After all the shit that generations of TRC folks have put him through, he deserves his bit of happiness."

"Huh," Romy said, blinking at him. "He was always *That Tall Asshole*."

"Agreed," Mitch laughed. "Kehoe heard me call him that after me learning it from you, then took it as a nickname for *Mithras*. But Carter is somebody else. Somebody new. That's Joie. That's what she's trying to do for everybody, Bouchard included."

Romana fell silent and studied his face. Mitch sipped his coffee.

She rose and grinned, but didn't say anything. Just kissed him on the top of the head again and headed out without once looking back. But they'd said everything.

He finished his decaf and made his way back to his cabin, humming a little under his breath as he did.

Opening the hatch, Mitch found Ernesta in his bed. From the pile of clothes on the floor, she wasn't wearing anything. Her lascivious smile confirmed that.

"I talked to Romana," she said.

"So did I," Mitch replied. "Just now."

"She's an amazing woman," Ernesta offered as Mitch closed the hatch and kicked off his shoes.

"I'd like to think I have pretty good taste," he said, moving to sit on the edge of the bed and kiss her.

# CHAPTER 51

Joie counted noses. Habit from the old days. She'd been trained to generally make all the recon sweeps alone, operating solo and looking harmless as she got inside and scouted, before heading up an assault team if that was needed later.

Stone and Freya, dressed like soldiers tasked with delivering an anonymous load to a nowhere outpost. Her, Ernesta, Romana, and Carter in tight, black, tactical gear, entailing plates, armor, and straps holding all manner of whatever a special forces soldier needed in this situation. Not as much ammunition or explosives as in her old life, but she wasn't trying to kill anyone here.

On the contrary, she wanted to do this with zero casualties, if she could. Still, she had a pistol, as did everyone else. It might be necessary.

Sifu insisted on being called Cōng Mǎ now. By everyone. And dressing in a gi and baggy pants, all black with white trim. Perfectly normal for a Wuxia movie. Completely wrong here.

And she would not be moved. Joie had just shrugged and run with it.

Middle-aged, overweight, Cantonese woman? Most soldiers would scratch their heads in confusion.

Briefly.

Tanerhald, Yormevs, and Bandi were behind the control console that would send everyone where they were going.

Mitch and Kehoe were off to one side.

"Comm check," Joie said.

Thumbs up from everyone.

She tapped her chest between her original equipment breasts, just to confirm the plate that would stop most bullets at short range. She wasn't bullet-proof anymore. Others did the same. Old habits were the ones that kept you alive in bad situations.

She'd considered leaving her hair down for this, but that was just asking for trouble, so Ernesta had braided it, then her own. Romana kept her hair high and tight like the Army days. Carter was going for the scruffy lumberjack look.

And Cōng Mǎ was dressed like she was going to teach a class.

Joie shrugged and nodded. She led her team to the platform and turned to look out over everything, wondering if she'd ever see everyone again.

Or anyone.

Yormevs smiled and did something. Light, and they were standing in the back of the truck she and Stone had brought up from California yesterday. Inside a standard shipping container with a few oil stains and a solid wall of boxes at that end suggesting that the whole thing was cases of MRE. Meal, Ready to Eat. Three lies in one, as the old saying went, though nowhere near as bad as the oldtimers liked to bitch about.

They might also be full of shit, but Joie never called them on it. Every generation liked to complain about how soft kids were these days.

The five of them settled in for a two-hour drive from a truckstop in western Kansas.

"Team One, in place," she said simply.

"Team Two, in place," Freya replied a moment later.

The truck started to rumble and vibrate as they rolled. Electric motors on every wheel, with a central generator burning biodiesel to keep them powered and solar skin on the roof. Not quite sufficient to drive coast to coast, but close.

Joie settled in patiently.

Bouchard was down there waiting.

And if she failed today, Humanity probably started dying tomorrow.

# CHAPTER 52

Stone was driving. *Pakhet* didn't have the rating for a beast this size. Granted, not much more complicated than driving a car, but all that mass made his calculations a bit tricksy.

Plus, most of TRC wouldn't recognize him on sight, like the important players might with her.

"How much longer, Stone?" she asked. Then paused. "Do you even have a first name?"

He laughed. Everybody in Kehoe's office had either been officers above him in the food chain or enlistees answering to him, so nobody had addressed him by such a name in…years? Something.

"Does it matter?" he answered.

The only people who probably knew it were the ones who handled payroll. Kehoe and Mitch both knew, but Kehoe hadn't been on first name basis with anybody until recently, and Graydon had his own issues to face.

Three beautiful exes in a single room? Either heaven or hell.

"Nobody ever calls you anything but Stone," she continued. "Occasionally Sergeant Stone. I don't think I've ever heard anything else."

"I would be surprised if you did," Stone laughed some more. "Unless it was *Hey, shithead*. Again, does it matter?"

"Maybe, if you're going to be a grumpy asshole about it," she grinned. "I do outrank you, you know."

"Doesn't matter much if we're all pirates, *Pakhet*," he countered.

"Freya, Stone," she snapped. "Call me Freya."

"Freya," he nodded as he drove. Endless grass horizons, with a threat of mountains in the distance. "I'm Kevin, not that anybody would know it."

"Any reason?" Freya asked.

Stone shrugged. He'd been a paratrooper for as long as that had been a career option. Then a desk jockey once he was too broken to do anything else. Pretty good at filing paperwork. Came of giving accurate map coordinates for some young punk with an artillery battery behind him.

"So why did you go rogue with Kehoe?" Freya asked now. "Back at Hanoi."

"It was that or pretend I didn't know a damned thing about what Joie was doing," Stone replied. "And I'm a lousy liar. Easier to become an outlaw. Especially when I knew the kind of shit I'd get from assholes like Bouchard."

"Personal issues?"

"You know what he's like, Lieutenant," Stone groused. "Three times as bad as Kehoe on his worst day. Roll that up with Joie and Kehoe vanishing and I'd probably be sitting in a concrete room at Fort Leavenworth right now contemplating all the rest of my sins."

"And driving a truck right into their base without any backup?" Freya asked.

He laughed and pointed a thumb aft.

"You think Joie and her friends can't kick his ass?" Stone queried. "You need to get out more."

"I remember when Kehoe first took me to meet her at her old apartment," Freya replied. "She was broken. Then she showed up in La Plata twice and each time she's raised the bar a whole level."

"Yeah," he nodded. "That's Captain Daring. She was even worse in the old days."

Freya fell silent at that point and he watched the road. Morning, but not all that early. Two hours driving from dawn, with one pit stop about twenty minutes back to potty and grab a couple cans of soda for later.

Purchased this time, rather than stolen by aliens out of the back of a truck somewhere.

Now was not the time to discuss ethics with a man holding a gun to your head, however.

"Will we know it when we see it?" Freya asked. "The jammer?"

Again. They'd gone over it a couple of times.

"You've got sixteen discs, Freya," he reminded her. "If we haven't managed to blow it up by then, we're in a lot worse trouble."

She laughed with him at that. The Army liked to reinforce your juvenile delinquency tendencies when it came time to destroy something.

He had an M31A2 *Starbolt* Squad Energy Weapon tucked in beside him. Not enough boom to take out armored vehicles, but sufficient for anything lesser. Freya could take a tank if she got close enough.

Of course, if Bouchard ended up sending heavy armor against them while they were in the base, they were right proper fucked from the get-go.

"Operations, this is Team Two," he said, getting everyone's attention. Hopefully, they'd been ignoring the banter and he wouldn't have people calling him anything but Stone after this, but he'd deal with it when he got there. "I have eyes on the base. Approaching the main gate now. Contact in two minutes."

"What do we do if they recognize us and call Bouchard?" Freya asked.

"Start blowing shit up and hope somebody can rescue our asses," Stone replied. "Anybody ever promise you that you would die in bed, soldier?"

# CHAPTER 53

Joie listened as Stone and Freya jabbered. Nothing important. Just a pair of veterans locked in tight against things about to happen. All of them had been there many, many times. Even Ernesta in her own way.

So Joie focused on her calmness. Borrowing it from Cōng Mǎ, maybe

The truck turned off asphalt and onto gravel from the change in sound and the sudden roughness of the ride. Joie rose and stretched. Considered the pistol by her side, but ignored it for now. People opening the back end to inspect would see several rows deep of pallets of MREs there. If they didn't go ahead and dig all the way to the front of the trailer, they would be none the wiser.

If they did, they already knew what to expect and would be too heavily armed to be surprised.

The others rose as well, taking their cues from her.

Around them, the truck wound down to a stop, air brakes hissing and squeaking.

"What's this?" some soldier asked, picked up on Stone's microphone and transmitted across the open channel.

"Delivery for the CO," Stone groused rudely. "Something about extra mouths to feed so Operations ordered an extra truck of MREs and food for you punks."

"Not that many extra," the soldier replied. "Or were they planning on living here permanently and nobody told us lowly types?"

"They ever tell you anything, Corporal?" Stone laughed.

"Damned straight, Sergeant," the other man said. "Let's check your paperwork."

Joie waited, poised. It should be as good as Kehoe and Mitch could make it, working with exact copies that Stone had acquired. No reason whatsoever to doubt it.

At the same time, she had no idea what new technologies Bouchard might have been able to come up with that would see through this trailer and notice them. Only cyberware to give off electronic signatures was up front with Freya and should be masked by the truck gadgets, and their comm gear used a technology Bouchard shouldn't have ever even heard of.

Paranoia kept you alive.

Joie drew her pistol and confirmed that it had one up the spout before setting the safety and holding it low at her side. The others did the same, like a posse come to arrest a horse thief at the bar.

She wondered if she should add a hat and a badge to her outfit in the future. Not like she'd probably be able to retire, once they got wherever it was that Tanerhald would take them. Joie might end up the sheriff there, at least until everyone got over themselves.

"Looks good, Sergeant," the soldier up front said. "Should I tell the boss?"

"What are your standing orders?" Stone asked in an off-hand way.

"To pretend him and his aides don't even exist when talking to outsiders," the man replied. "Don't figure you count as an outsider, since you were qualified to deliver stuff off-cycle."

"Damned straight, kid," Stone snapped. "So don't even think about him now. We'll get in, drop this crap off as soon as some lazy E-4 can be located to handle the forklift, and then get gone."

"Sounds like a plan, Sarge."

The truck rumbled into motion again.

Joie let go a deep breath and focused on the next stage of things.

She'd never been to this one specific base, but she'd spent time at other, similar places. Secure and private, so you could train without even the eyes of other soldiers around to see what you were doing. Some years, TRC's ammunition budget rivaled the larger Army one. Every week, a lot of bullets fired from a variety of weapons.

At the same time, the Army didn't react to sudden logistical surprises quickly. The odds were that the truck would sit on a loading dock for some time until the right person could be located.

That gave her time.

*Uno* had made some calls for her. The trailer they'd picked up in Arizona had been modified to carry folks back and forth across the border. She moved to the trapdoor that was near the front and unlocked the bolt holding it shut.

Stone spun the beast around and started backing into a loading dock with an expert touch, almost idling backwards until the rear thumped against the rubber, jarring everyone just enough to spill a martini, but not much more.

Joie lifted the trapdoor open and got down to stick her head out the bottom.

They were back under a roof from what she remembered of Mitch's pictures of the base, so all this would have been invisible from a satellite photo, even if the government hadn't threatened everyone doing that to significantly blur certain locations for reasons of national security.

Several truck bays, side-by-side both directions. Artificial lights overhead. Not a lot of noise.

Joie looked up at the others, nodded, and swung her feet out, dropping below the trailer and squatting on the asphalt underneath.

They were inside, sort of. Stone must have backed it farther than she'd expected. No foot traffic.

Joie slipped to the short side, up against the nearby wall, and peeked.

Closed garage doors with a standard door nearby.

The plan called for Freya to stay inside the cab as much as possible, on the assumption that she might be recognized. Stone was just another senior enlisted until you got close and looked at him. That anonymity would work in his favor here.

She watched his legs under the trailer as he walked back to the dock and hopped up, moving around the back and catching sight of her. Just enough shadows that she could remain perfectly still if nobody was looking. Carter might be too white to hide here, but he and the others were ready to move as soon as she gave the signal.

After a few seconds, Stone obviously got impatient, stepping to the side door and pulling it open before vanishing inside. A few moments later, he was running the chain to roll the door up.

Then he walked out and opened the trailer door, stepping inside just enough to speak.

"Move," he said sharply, though quietly. "Nobody in immediate sight. Through the door and left. The one marked storage."

Joie got there as quickly as the other four, vaulting up onto the dock and leading.

She walked normal, even as armed as she was. Someone watching from a distance would only see her shape and style. If she looked nervous, they would become nervous.

If she looked like an officer doing officer things, most enlisted soldiers would hang back, on the wise assumption that the brass might be looking for volunteers to drag into manual labor or something.

Inside, she found the door Stone had mentioned, heading back to surface-level storage. Presumably, elevators and stairwell shafts back there as well, so that things could be moved below easily.

She stepped through.

# CHAPTER 54

Taylor hated this part of any operation. The waiting, while you had troops penetrating somebody's place. Before violence had broken out, but right on that ledge where you just knew it was coming.

"Anything?" he asked, turning to look at Yormevs on his left.

"The truck has been driven into the facility by Stone," he said, monitoring some sort of gyro-stabilized video system that showed the ground in real time.

Not quite good enough to make out faces or license plates, but damned impressive stuff.

"And?" Taylor pressed.

"At present, you know more than I do how to interpret the sounds from the two teams in operation," Yormevs volleyed back.

Taylor grunted.

Yormevs was probably right. Mitch, on his right, was monitoring all manner of emergency channels for notice that the base had woken up, but the place was practically air-gapped itself right now. Probably saved all their email on a local server and didn't send it out until Sunday after midnight.

"What do we expect?" Tanerhald asked, seated next to Yormevs on the far side.

"Captain Daring?" Bandi laughed, beyond Tanerhald. "She will appear as if by magic, with a gun in your ear and in complete control of the situation."

"That's Ernesta," Taylor growled at the man, uncomfortable with that memory.

He'd honestly been expecting her to splatter his brains all over the wall. And she'd mentioned later in passing how close she'd been to killing him that day.

"Ah, but Joie brought Ernesta," Bandi laughed. "And *Mithras*. Plus the other two. Supremely dangerous woman. Women. Plus Carter, but he's not a slouch, most of the time."

Taylor grunted again.

"No news is good news at present," Taylor told the room, aware that he was surrounded by aliens who had no idea how dangerous Humans were in general, let alone those five. Or seven.

Shit, he could overthrow entire civilizations with that team. Best not to say that out loud, though.

Not a thing he wanted to be explaining to the aliens.

"If we hear anything, we will judge accordingly," Taylor continued. "But right now everybody is inside the cloak, so there is precious little we can do. I don't even have backups that I could send, other than Stone and Malik are Joie's backup. If this goes wrong, it is out of my hands."

He said that last part while looking significantly at Tanerhald. He held the trump cards here, however he wanted to play them.

Tanerhald nodded. They all understood each other right now.

All the money on one roll of the dice.

At least he had Captain Daring on the game board again.

If she couldn't do this, nobody Taylor knew could.

# CHAPTER 55

Ernesta didn't have the background in the military that three of her friends did. And Cōng Mǎ had spent a significant amount of time around such people as well.

To Ernesta, this looked more like a picture of Carter's raid in Hanoi where he'd set the warehouse on fire to send a message for that old man. Industrial everything, done in concrete with a dull green paint over that, roughly the color of the old Yanqui uniforms that so many Central American armies had adopted over the years.

Oil stains on the floor spoke to decades of hydraulic leaks and hazardous chemical spills mostly swept up but not treated correctly. The smell in here was old dust, old vegetable oil, old food fried in too much grease, such that it stuck to the walls.

It almost seemed to come out of the concrete like pores of your skin when you had too much garlic on your pizza. If there was such a thing.

Joie led. The rest of them followed, looking, as she had instructed, like a bunch of badass killers who just set the new high score on the range.

Ernesta understood swagger. Back home, the *Federales* had been all about it, but they wouldn't have been able to back it up. Just look at what Joie had done with one arm against four of them that first day.

But this was a Technology Research Command base, hidden on the Colorado plains. Supposedly filled with people in Joie's league. Or at least Carter and Romana's.

Ernesta was of the opinion that nobody was in Joie's league. She was not alone in that belief, either.

Through half-filled racks of wooden and steel boxes and containers, Joie led them past the big freight elevators to a back corner that was invisible from pretty much all sides. They paused there, out of sight on the end of a row with a big, red exit sign over the nearby door.

"Back staircase, if I had to guess," Joie said in a quiet voice. "Carter, were these places pretty standard in design?"

"Utterly, Joie," the man replied. "Once you got your blueprints approved by everyone, nobody wanted to go back and ask for any sort of variance. Careers got ended by the bureaucrats over that shit."

Ernesta nodded. That sounded like most governments.

"Okay, once we go into those stairs, we're committed, and have no idea where we might find him, or how quickly we'll run into someone who recognizes one of us. Romana, you stay at the back and try to use the others as cover as much as you can, since you'll be the one they probably know. At this point, I've been gone so long that I'm probably forgotten. If they do know who I am, the second arm throws them off, or they assume that Bouchard brought me back and they weren't important enough to be told."

"Would he be at the bottom of the shaft?" Ernesta asked her, having seen how the place was laid out. "Or near the top, to make sure he's within the field?"

Everyone turned to Joie. She turned to Romana.

"It it a cloak or a sphere when projected?" Joie asked.

"Little of both," Romana hedged. "Possibly, you could find a way through the entire planet from the back, but that would be so fuzzy as to never work. I like Ernesta's idea that he's as deep as they have quarters, which might be the old base itself, back when this thing had missiles. I'm guessing refurbs meant that they added all the new quarters to the first few floors down, since this place isn't normally a target anymore."

Ernesta nodded with the others. It made sense.

Now, they just had to sneak through an entire enemy base filled with soldiers at a much higher level of competence and alertness than her old *Federales* back home, and kidnap the guy in charge, and drag him out to where Yormevs could grab him.

That, and survive.

# CHAPTER 56

Joie led.

Her team. Her mission. Her responsibility. Cōng Mǎ would stand out, but nobody here should know who she was, so they wouldn't automatically assume a problem. More like one of them who had been teaching. Or something.

You were trained not to ask questions in this business. If you needed to know, someone would be instructed to tell you. Otherwise, you kept your yap shut and your head down.

She went down the stairs like she belonged, rather than taking them three or five at a time in a rapid assault.

Speed was not of the essence. Stealth was.

Surprise.

She did, however, get two stories down quickly, just in case. There were five underground here, so three more.

Any mistake she made would be bad, so she kept going down. Back stairs, mostly an emergency exit and access in the old days for mechanics that needed to service missiles and hardware.

Hopefully unused.

Except that she heard steps coming up towards them. One set.

Heavy tread. Nailing every single step with a rhythm instead of taking them two at a time or moving relaxed.

Joie moved to the inside of the stairs and looked down. Saw a shadow coming up from five. One person only.

She had to gamble.

She moved to the outside and gestured everyone else against the wall before moving down again. When whoever it was came into sight, she could pounce on them at speeds they might not imagine possible.

Hopefully, quietly.

The man coming up met them at the next landing. Total surprise when he saw her boots, then glanced up at her standing there. Shocked eyes. Earbuds blasting some sugary pop number totally at odds with the man's hardass killer look.

He stumbled to a halt. Joie shook her head at the man and scowled.

Looked like someone running up and down these stairs for exercise.

He nodded, glanced at the others, and put his head down.

Bang. Bang. Bang. Up the stairs and turn. Up the next.

Joie moved a little faster going down now. The man might have been a good enough actor to get clear and sound an alarm, but she doubted it. Health nut. Except around here, probably just a paratrooper, defined usually as a guy who runs twenty kilometers, then smokes a cigarette so you don't think he's a sissy or something.

They got to the bottom quickly enough. Joie motioned the others to remain here at the bottom and opened the door as quietly as possible.

Machine shop or something. Maybe that was a spare rocket engine. Or something. Hard to tell and she'd never been a motor pool gearhead.

Still, nobody in sight.

Joie motioned the others to join her, then moved off to a spot back in a nearby corner. Possibly the southwest corner of the base itself, from the way the walls squared off.

"Now what?" Ernesta whispered.

"Now we start hunting," Joie replied. "Everyone spread out a little, but stay close enough to come in if we find someone. Remember, whoever it is needs to be taken down quickly and quietly. Otherwise, we raise alarms and have to fight our way out. I doubt we can bluff it at that point."

She turned to the true outsider here. Considered all those late nights in the dojo. All the mean things Cōng Mǎ had taught her about the ways to trick Humans.

"I want you on point, Sifu," Joie said. "Your costume and haircut will confuse them, as you no doubt expected."

The woman just grinned. Nobody around here had a shaggy mop like hers save Carter. Joie's was long and braided, like Ernesta's. Sometimes, you did that in this game.

"Did you remember to bring a couple of glass bottles filled with tea?" Cōng Mǎ asked.

It took Joie a moment, then she chuckled. Throw a bottle at them like a knife, aiming for the upper chest or face. If it hits, it probably knocks them down.

Then shatters and they are laying in sharp shards as they try to roll over and stand back up.

Beyond rude, which was exactly the thing here, because it wasn't immediately lethal, either.

"I did not, Sifu," Joie bowed her head in mock-penance. "I did one better."

"Oh?"

"I brought my friends."

# CHAPTER 57

Stone had considered just going back up to the cab of the truck once Team One was out of sight. Waiting until the corporal at the gate managed to find someone to send over a forklift to pull stolen MREs out of the back.

But that would be out of character.

No trucker wants to sit and wait on a dead-head. Even when the truck would mostly drive itself. Civilians got paid by the kilometer, not the hour, so they always wanted to be in motion. A soldier would rather get back to his own rack than trust that the *ijits* around here had washed the bedding since the last time someone had been forced to use it.

So he stood for a time. Waited until the clock in his head went off, then stomped over to the office and threw the door open.

Good, three in here, and none of them ranked him.

"Where's my forklift operator?" he snarled at a pitch just below an angry yell.

Grumpy sergeant who has had enough of your shit. Not that he had any experience at that sort of thing. Heavens no.

The two privates turned to the corporal. She got flustered.

"Sergeant?" she asked blankly.

Stone turned to point behind him, using the shoulder that hadn't been rebuilt when he'd had to stop being a paratrooper.

"My truck has a load for you yahoos," he said sternly. "Four pallets. I want somebody to drive their stupid little toy over there and offload it, so I can get home in time for dinner. Simple?"

His scowl must have been working overtime, from the way all three of them blanched.

"Right away, Sergeant," the woman said, reaching for a phone.

Stone nodded and slammed the door angrily behind him as he walked back out to stand next to the open trailer, nodding at Freya's reflection watching him in the side mirror.

Gotta be normal. That means grumpy about all this. *Emergency run for you fuckups and I want to get home, thank you very much.*

He crossed his arms and practiced scowling at the entire warehouse. A skill you should not get out of practice using.

A few minutes passed, but not long. Somebody had gotten a fire lit under his ass, because the forklift came barreling around the corner like a cowboy chasing a calf. Squealed to a halt, but Stone just gestured the private who was driving it right into the trailer. Everything had been loosened by Joie's folks before they left.

Forks lined up, lifted, and the woman driving backed it out.

"Where does it go?" she asked.

Stone considered lines of fire and pointed to a nearby spot that would give him cover if all hell broke loose shortly and somebody started shooting at him. The woman deposited it and went back for more.

She knew her shit, too, because Stone was reasonably confident he couldn't have gotten all four out that quickly. Still, gruffness was called for.

"Good," he yelled as she set the last one down, like teeth across the way.

Or battlements.

Stone closed the back up without looking over his shoulder and locked it, listening to the forklift drive away, mission complete.

Both missions. He'd created confusion. And left somebody a mess to clean up later.

Stone walked around to the front and climbed up in the cab.

Freya was keeping a low profile, but nodded as he closed things up and engaged the drives.

"Now what?" she asked.

"Seen anything we need to blow up?" Stone asked.

That had been her mission, scouting the surface for radio installations that might be helpfully destroyed to open the skies to friendlies. He'd just been driving.

"Got a few interesting targets," Freya said. "Drive forward about one hundred meters and pull over like you need to read the map and I'll point them out."

He nodded and lurched the beast into motion.

Out into the sunlight again. Almost mathematically level terrain around here, but it was all artificial anyway. Dig a great, big, freaking hole in the ground then pour concrete in and build something.

Until some yahoos with fusion weapons come along to blow it all to hell.

Stone had left his window open, so he heard the alarm sirens start up behind him.

Everybody had just run out of time.

# CHAPTER 58

Cōng Mǎ moved with deliberation, though in perfect silence. Training going back to that one place where you had to walk on tissue paper and not leave a tear or make a sound.

When you got good enough, they dampened things first.

Black-on-black cotton fabric. Simple. Flowing. Cuffs and braids in white, as was somewhat traditional, depending on who you asked. Large, heavyset woman walking along the interior of a secret Army base.

As was natural.

She led.

Out of the machine shop. Or whatever it had been. Tools and *stuffff* strewn about as though forgotten.

Cōng Mǎ came to a locked door. Locked from this side. She listened briefly, then unlocked it and cracked it just enough to peek out into a receding hallway, matching doors down both sides.

Missile silos mostly on her left as she crossed the southern face. That suggested bunks on the right, and perhaps offices on the inner portion of her left.

She stood upright, tossed her hair once for effect, and stepped into the hallway.

"Eight paces," she instructed Joie, knowing how quickly she and her friends could move these days when pressed.

Right down the center of the hallway, rather than skulking, though she did pause to look for traps.

In Africa, one tribe of ancients had hunted elephants by digging pits in the center of a trail and covering them with leaves. Nobody else was so arrogant as to stomp proudly in the middle of things, and thus avoided falling to their deaths.

She took the lesson to heart, but the floor appeared stable. Still, elephant hunters.

The rooms on both sides were numbered, but the little slot where you could insert a nametag or something had been left empty. Probably empty and unused, if she was lucky, though that punk Bouchard and his minions might not have been able to bring such things with them.

Carter had the rear position, so she would have to rely on him to keep someone from opening a door behind them and exiting a room.

Her position was to lead.

Ah, that looked promising.

Cōng Mǎ came to a corner and peeked, just because. Door athwart the next hallway, rather than on the side. *Operations Center* in painted letters, faded and chipped by time.

She motioned Joie close and pointed. Joie nodded.

"At a minimum, I would expect alarms," Cōng Mǎ said. "Personal or electronic remain to be seen, but I cannot imagine electronic unless that door is locked and we have to force it. Carter can look at that point."

Joie nodded and watched.

Cōng Mǎ stepped around the corner and approached the door. No camera on this side where someone might unlock it from the interior. No visible alarms. No keyfob sensor, though there was a slot for a metal key in the handle itself.

She rested her hand on the cold brass and gripped it firmly. Turned slowly and carefully enough to assure herself that it was unlocked.

She turned back to Joie to nod.

Once she opened it, a timer would start. She might have minutes. Cōng Mǎ suspected that she would have seconds.

Best make them count.

She turned the knob the rest of the way and leaned into the door.

# CHAPTER 59

Valmy had been reading. A chunk of old Russian literature that someone had left behind at some point. Even the book was thirty years old, but that didn't mean anything. Dostoevsky was timeless, for good or ill.

The Ops Center had been left mostly intact. He was just down here so as to stay out of mind of the troops on higher levels, while he waited for a few Senators and Representatives to work out some details among themselves.

Like who would get the first shot at immortality.

Valmy hadn't wanted to play his trump card for another decade, but he was confident his freedom of action was likely measured in days at this point. He would need the rest of the US government riding in if other aliens had decided to get involved.

It had taken them long enough to notice.

Vanlaere was watching something on a tablet with earbuds in, passing time same as he was. Konicek had run upstairs for something. Probably checking with the messhall to see what lunch would be and how easily it could be delivered to the basement.

None of them wanted to emerge into the sunlight right now. Chile had left them all a little off-balance.

There had been an alien starship available for the stealing for nearly fifty years, and nobody had noticed. Valmy kept wondering what he could have done with such a thing.

Would other aliens have welcomed him, or would he have been an even bigger outlaw once Algom's people realized what had happened?

Water under the bridge.

A door opened in his peripheral vision and Valmy looked up.

Konicek. Smiling, even, when the man was usually more dour and subdued.

"Good news, General," he said as he closed the door behind him and came to rest.

Vanlaere paused her vid and looked up as well.

"Command sent a truck with an additional four pallets of food and such for the base," Koniceck said. "Not that chow hall had been worried, but they've got more options."

"Why would they do that?" Valmy asked, confused.

Konicek paused.

"Somebody told them we were here and needing to be fed?" he asked, voice slowing with each syllable.

"Nobody knows where we are, below the rank of Lieutenant General," Valmy intoned.

He put his book down and rose from his chair. Considered his options.

This had to be a failure of operational security somewhere. But what?

Movement on his left caught his eye. Valmy turned, but didn't recognize the woman standing in the doorway to the barracks where he and the others slept. Where nobody should be. And he knew every face in this base.

The stranger started to charge, but Vanlaere exploded into action, intercepting her. Valmy saw others behind her.

The base had been penetrated. How was that possible? The alien generators were supposed to keep everyone at bay.

Somebody had outsmarted them.

Then Valmy recognized the second person entering the room.

Daring.

How the fuck did she keep doing this?

He leapt sideways and found the alarm switch, lifting the cover and snapping the rocker. Around him, sirens began to wail.

Then Joie Daring was on him.

# CHAPTER 60

ōng Mǎ had an instant to take it all in and formulate a plan of action.

She was back in the Philippines, in that one shack on a nameless beach. Enter the room and take one second to place everything. Then be blindfolded and walk through a small maze to retrieve a single bottle of beer on a small table, without brushing anything or stepping on anything sharp or noisy.

The good old days.

Bouchard was obvious from the man's air of command. Chelsea and Garrison had been with Joie's Hanoi team, and Cōng Mǎ had gotten good descriptions of both.

All three had been augmented by magical technology until they were supposedly better life forms. Comparable to Joie and her team physically.

Cōng Mǎ gestured her student to charge, and led the way.

Chelsea reacted faster than a mere Human could, but Cōng Mǎ was not surprised. That was the nature of the change. Better, stronger, faster, tougher. A healing factor that could close bullet wounds almost in real time, necessitating a bullet to the heart or head to guarantee a takedown.

If you relied on primitive ways.

Chelsea was fast. And well-trained. Probably used to sparring only with her own kind, because she flowed into an attack that a normal Human being would find irresistible.

Cōng Mǎ had a secret. One not generally talked about outside of a small cluster of scholars of the killing arts.

You didn't always have to attack to defeat someone.

Chelsea's punch came high and fast. Cōng Mǎ simply moved out of the way, without bothering to try to counter. Chelsea's timing was thus off, because all of her previous push-hands training assumed attack and counter in a smooth rhythm.

Cōng Mǎ kicked at the woman's ankle instead. Not enough to hurt. Just to focus her mind on the floor.

Bouchard and his two people against Cōng Mǎ and her *four*. All that was necessary was to focus Chelsea into the here and now, so that someone else could either assist, or double up on the two men and overwhelm them quickly.

There were no firearms visible on the Army folks, so this would be settled with hands.

Cōng Mǎ might be the only Human in the room. She was still better than all of them at this sort of thing.

She smiled as Chelsea started a kick.

# CHAPTER 61

Joie saw her Sifu's signal and charged. Someone was in the room and about to do something.

She signaled the others and moved.

Yormevs had done things to her. Reset her to baseline by removing all the cyberware and mechanical parts, then upgraded everything after growing her a new eye, ear, and arm.

Faster. Stronger. Tougher.

Still just as mean as she'd always been. Just as willing to charge into danger.

Captain Daring to the rescue.

She cleared the door and saw Sifu engage with Chelsea. Garrison and Bouchard were there. Joie went after the General.

Not fast enough, though. He got to a console and flipped an alarm switch, then ducked as she threw a punch to drive him back.

The cover snapped into place, but Joie suspected that merely flipping it back wouldn't do any good.

Then Bouchard kicked.

Joie had studied a variety of arts in her time in green. And learned a few new things from Sifu Wěn since. Not many arts focused on side kicks because they tended to be slower than a punch.

Heavier and more dangerous when they connected. Useful against someone at a lower skill level, but evenly matched opponents who knew it was coming could get inside it or back out of range as they chose.

Or you could just punch it really hard to sting the knee.

Bouchard was kicking at her knee with the top of a boot. Savate?

Not an art she knew, but as she bounced just far enough back to make it miss, some rogue voice in her head confirmed that the Frenchman had been an expert at his national martial form.

Kicks and lethal slaps for the most part, because Napoleonic law had considered a closed fist to be a deadly weapon and thus a felony crime. Same with using any sort of belaying pin, resulting in an art that had originated down on the docks among tough, hardy sailors.

Joie shifted back and glanced enough to note Ernesta and Romana entering the room and getting right at Garrison.

Bouchard slapped at her head, possibly going to gouge at an eye or blind her. Maybe just to grab enough hair that he could control her movement.

Joie ducked and swept at his ankle, just to watch him bounce up and over her foot.

Evenly matched. Good. And bad.

Joie had feared that the things Yormevs had done would leave her short of what Bouchard's people had perfected.

Chelsea was probably getting the surprise of her life right now, fighting an unmodified Human who had trained against someone of her skill and speed.

And better.

Nobody ever appreciated Sifu Wěn Cōng Mǎ. The *Clever Horse*.

Bouchard snapped his right arm outward just a little, up and over as if cracking whip. Joie could see the chop coming. Heavy part of the palm to the sensitive spot just behind and below her jaw, where all the nerves clustered.

Great place for a stinger.

Bouchard was also grasping with his left hand, all set to snag her as she tried to elude him again.

Joie rabbit-hopped forward instead, right into his chest. Fist up blocking, she caught the man in the ribs with the point of an elbow as she did, rotating her shoulders down and in and lifting on her thighs.

Sifu had once called it Water Buffalo, though Joie didn't have the knuckles of her fists touching. Still, the crack was audible. She didn't think she'd broken a rib. Just driven the hard parts of two bones together.

Bouchard didn't seem to appreciate it. And was having a little trouble breathing.

Joie flowed into the man, hooking one of his feet with hers as she kept going forward. His arms were around her, so he hugged and pulled her to the ground with him, fighting as they went down to see who remained on top.

She had the leverage, but no space to punch the man. They landed in a heap, but Joie managed to stay on top. A knee would have found his balls, but he twisted and she slammed it into his thigh instead, eliciting a grunt of pain.

Then he had a hand on her braid, dragging her sideways in ways she couldn't resist. Should have gone ahead and chopped it all off like Romana did. No handle for a bad guy to grip.

Joie went over and he rolled with her, punching her once in the face with a bong as her skull rang off the cold, concrete floor.

Joie steeled herself for another punch that never came. She blinked a few times to clear the cobwebs and smiled.

Ernesta, kneeling next to General Bouchard, her gripping him by the short hair on top.

With her pistol in his ear.

"I do wonder if you could regenerate from me splattering your brains all over that wall, General," Ernesta said in a quiet voice still clearly audible over the alarms. "Would you care to find out?"

He did not.

Joie watched Ernesta expertly put the man on his face next to her, never once letting that pistol waver.

Looking around, Garrison was on his butt with his hands over his head and eyes that didn't look like they focused. Plus a double shiner forming, like a raccoon.

She'd always thought he was something of an arrogant—possibly sexist—punk. Probably looked at Romana and Ernesta and discounted them as *girls*. She'd gotten a whiff of that off him a few times in Hanoi.

Chelsea was out cold.

*What the fuck?*

Sifu just grinned. Joie knew she'd have to get the woman drunk on saké to get that whole story. Chelsea was supposed to be among the best that an entire elite fighting force had produced, before Bouchard had upgraded her to a new class.

And the woman was out cold on the concrete. That quickly.

Joie got to her knees.

"How do we turn off the alert, General?" she called to the man, still face down.

"You don't, Daring," he said carefully. "At some point, armed teams will sweep the entire facility, once they have the lockdown secured upstairs. I have no intention of giving you the password to reset the alert."

Joie wanted to growl something at the man. Something rude and abusive.

She'd come this far and done all this so that nobody had to die as a result of her actions.

Her failure would result in enough deaths.

Then light filled the room.

# CHAPTER 62

Stone pulled the Starbolt from next to the door and cleared the safety on a single motion. Too many years of sudden alerts or hiding in strange countries doing things you denied later.

The window was down. The cab was civilian, so it wouldn't stop bullets, once folks started taking potshots at him. He had a whole shit-ton of angry troopers behind him, plus the ones up ahead guarding the gate. Not long until they figured out that they'd been had.

"Out," Freya ordered, no doubt doing the same math he had.

Stone hit the pavement and scampered madly around the front of the truck, having paused just long enough to grab the bag with more fusion disks in magazines.

He watched Freya point her right palm at a nearby radio antenna and blast it.

*Gods, fusion weapons were so much fun.*

Stone located what might be a small radar dome not far from the front gate and lit it up. The crash of exploding electronics was exceptional, but he had no idea if it would do any good.

They both moved to the ditch by the side of the truck. More cover, because the guys at the gate were going to get pissy shortly.

If it looked like a transmitter of any kind, Stone shot it. Then dropped the empty magazine and slammed a new one home, so automatic that he couldn't have told you what other five things he'd just killed.

Freya only had four shots, and had to hand-load disks, so he fell into sniper mode.

"You cover," Stone said. "I can shoot faster."

She nodded and he turned onto his butt, just to see what was behind him on her side.

Bullets started peppering the front of the truck and the ground nearby, but Freya fired a shot back. She didn't have as much barrel to contain the plasma, so it wasn't generally lethal at those sorts of ranges.

Went boom awful pretty, though. Heads ducked and incoming fire slackened. At least for a little while.

Stone killed something. Metal pole in the air. He had no idea what it did, but it was there.

He looked for the flagpole atop the base. Wasn't really a flagpole, as that was over by the front gate. Lightning rod, maybe. Seemed centered. Sounded good.

He took a shot and watched it boom even better than the rest, sparks curling rooster tails every which way and honest-to-freaking-God lightning bolts erupting and grounding.

Damned impressive, even after twenty years in green.

Then shit got weird. Took him a second to place it.

Light.

# CHAPTER 63

Joie was in the room where Yormevs translated folks with the beam. Ernesta was there, as was the rest of her team. None of the others.

"If you could clear the platform, please?" Yormevs asked.

Joie looked at him blankly, still a little woozy.

"Move your ass, Daring," Bandi snapped. "More people in the buffer."

Oh.

Ernesta held out an arm and Joie staggered down the two steps to the main deck, everyone turning and watching as it lit up again to show Stone and Freya, kneeling and grinning.

"That," Stone emphasized as he stood up and flipped his safety on, "was awesome! Too old to do that anymore, but it does bring back memories."

"You're just a juvenile delinquent," Freya said with a grin.

"Guilty!"

"You got it?" Joie asked. "Obviously."

"Flagpole-looking thing, just about dead center," Stone nodded. "Killed it and the explosion was fantastic. Then we're here."

"And you got Bouchard and the others?" Joie asked, turning back to Yormevs, with Tanerhald standing next to him and Bandi grinning beyond that.

"We do," Yormevs assured her. "Unless you need to speak with him immediately, we can leave him in the buffer for a time. Or deposit him in a cell as we did with you that first time."

"I feel as though I have just run a marathon in a blizzard," Joie said. "Can we take a break for food and coffee and then I'll deal with him?"

"That would be lovely," Bandi said. "I'll go wake up the kitchen folks."

He walked out with a jaunty smile utterly at odds with his status as a prisoner, but he didn't have anywhere to go. And might have finally run out of fucks to give at the situation.

Were he Human, the phrase she might have used was *had a coming to Jesus moment*. Something. Faust and von Frankenstein.

Or perhaps he was already taking the idea of rehabilitation seriously enough to become somebody new.

Joie started to walk. Ernesta caught her.

"We need medical first," Carter said. "She has a serious concussion going."

So they ended up in the medbay instead. A technician she'd not met yet scanned her with a handheld device not unlike a salt shaker. Then handed her a nasal spray of something that left a lingering hint of lemon and pine trees when she sniffed it.

Her head cleared almost immediately, which was good.

"Food," she said simply, walking better.

Lunch was comfort food. Taquitos in spicy red sauce that she had taught the messhall folks to make, with fresh ingredients they were acquiring from somewhere. She didn't ask, beyond reminding them that it was more ethical to put on a disguise and buy at a grocery store.

Yormevs and his kind frequently ate a kind of gruel that looked like oatmeal gone rancid and smelled like ripe sewer water.

Coffee. Because coffee. Water of life.

In the back of her mind, she was pretty certain Ponce de Leon would have been better served looking for coffee beans.

"So, you have been successful," Tanerhald said as she finished eating. "You have captured Bouchard and the other two. Will that be sufficient?"

"Not even sort of," Joie said. "Too many people know about how it was done. How to do it. We only found Bouchard because he'd reached out to certain politicians in Washington, DC, about the project."

"Why would he do that suddenly, after all the secrecy?" the Brakhua asked.

"Guessing he'd been backed into a corner," Bandi spoke up. "Needed to bring in friends with the only coin he really had left at that point."

Joie turned to the man. Carefree. That was what he was.

Caught finally, he was willing to tell everyone everything.

"I concur," Joie said as he grinned at her. "Bouchard was probably about to offer the treatment to some of those men, and possibly women, because he needed his army now."

"How many people do you expect we will have to capture and remove?" Tanerhald asked.

"I believe the minimum number is four hundred and twenty-seven," Mitch suddenly spoke up. "Possibly as high as nine hundred, depending."

All eyes turned to him. Mitch's grin was almost as big as Bandi's.

"He might have hidden everything just fine," Mitch said. "Air-gapped and top-notch security around all his operations. Good for him. Payroll is handled on an entirely different platform. I have a list of names of folks assigned to various places where Bouchard blacked out their role and assignment, even in those computers. Once I had that clue, finding everyone was pretty easy."

Joie laughed. How many times had she captured the accountant in order to bleed an organization?

"Is that too many?" Joie asked Tanerhald, including Yormevs in the look, as they were seated together.

"Not at all," Tanerhald nodded. "At Romana's insistence, I had brought a larger vessel this time. You and your friends have been contained on this deck alone, mostly for your own safety. The vessel is enormous."

The way he said it suggested thousands or even tens of thousands of crew. Maybe a small city in space.

She turned her confusion to Tanerhald.

"Humans do not truly understand scale, Joie," he smiled. "The biggest problem will be depositing them on a colony somewhere and supervising them while they build it out, lest they starve or suffer permanent psychological damage."

"Food will be a problem, yes," Joie agreed. "I doubt that the latter, assuming you intend to offer them the chance to gather up families as well. Mitch can get you those names, I'm certain."

"Already got it," he said. "That's the low number with immediate family."

"Four hundred isn't enough people to survive as a colony," Carter, of all people, spoke up. She would have expected the science fiction nerd Ernesta to say it. "You'll need something much larger. Are you willing to recruit folks to go elsewhere openly?"

Joie caught the surprised glance that Yormevs and Tanerhald shared. They'd been dealing with this as a law enforcement issue. Obviously, but it was so much more, particularly now.

How many people would happily depart Earth, possibly forever, for the chance to live in a wider, galactic community?

"I am not authorized to open diplomatic relations with Earth," Tanerhald said in a firm voice.

"Well, they were planning to come in a few centuries," Ernesta reminded them. "Maybe you should contact your superiors about moving that date up significantly. As the big goofball says, four to eight hundred isn't sufficient to survive, but you also don't have to make any final decisions for a few years. Capture the ones you need now, then come back later to say hello?"

"I disagree," Kehoe said. He'd been quietly absorbing the conversation from the far corner of the table.

Everyone turned to look at him expectantly.

"Removing Bouchard from the middle of a secured military facility is going to cause any number of people on the inside to panic," he continued. "They will start to look much more closely at what the General was doing. They will want to take advantage of that science while they can. It is not enough to grab the folks doing it currently, because others will press ahead with the research. If the wider galactic community intends to talk to Earth, they need to do it right now. Not even a year from today."

Joie stewed over his logic, but couldn't fault it. The US Army was paranoia writ large. If Bouchard was bringing in Senators, they would be able to cow bureaucrats and civilian researchers reliant on such funding.

"What about other countries?" Ernesta asked next, blowing the conversation even wider. "Do we know what the Chinese or Nigerians are up to?"

Joie found that she did not. Looking around, nobody else did, either.

"I agree with Kehoe," she said. "You need to do this immediately. Otherwise, they might make as many more as they can, expecting to fight some guerrilla war like a bad alien invasion movie."

Ernesta snorted at that. Humans always managed to win a war against aliens who came down to invade with sketchily-explained motives. If you could travel among the stars, monkeys with machine guns shouldn't be a threat.

And Tanerhald only had to blow up a number of key satellites, while preventing their replacement, to do a lot of damage. More if he took out a few, specific nodes of the global communications network. It was far more fragile than anybody on the outside ever understood. Whole nations could be blacked out in the blink of an eye.

"All or nothing, Joie?" Tanerhald asked now, glancing around at the others.

"I would need to see more of Mitch's research," she hedged. "And go deep on Kehoe's logic. At the same time, they are among the best I know at that sort of thing, so I think we can take it at face value. The war isn't over, for all we've managed to win a couple of key battles against Bouchard. Losing a queen in chess isn't terminal, if a good player can recover. And there are a lot of smart folks on the other side. Plus, if they know any element of the truth, they might get desperate, for all the reasons Kehoe mentioned."

That sort of killed the conversation. They'd danced around the topic, but never really confronted it directly.

What would it take to neutralize Humanity as a threat to the Brakhua and everyone else?

Secrecy was no longer a guarantee of success. If anything, it was more a promise of failure.

Things you didn't know meant you made what would be seen as bad choices in retrospect.

"If they decided to get stupid, could you survive a nuclear detonation?" Carter asked.

"Our shields are sufficient for anything in anyone's current arsenal," Tanerhald replied dryly.

"Which suggests that there were things that could be done, if Humans decided to get even more stupid," Joie pointed out. "And they might, if threatened. All the more reason to move now and force the bad guys in this situation to give way."

"Define bad guys," Kehoe said firmly.

"The entire United States Government might qualify," she replied coldly. "Considering what I, Romana, Freya, and Carter have been doing for however long. Mitch could probably get you a fairly accurate body count of the number of people we've collectively killed. At the time, in the line of duty, but how many of those terrorist organizations were the result of US meddling in somebody else's affairs? Or over-throwing popularly elected governments we didn't like? It's not like this is a new thing either. How popular is the Marine Corps in Central America, even today?"

"Throw in the Russians, the Chinese, and however many else," Ernesta spoke up, in her role as the sole true civilian present. Even Sifu spent too much time around soldiers. "How much of the current mess of things are the big players getting pissy and not letting everyone else decide how to live their lives?"

The soldiers all grimaced, almost perfectly in unison. *For God and Country* broke down if you started thinking about how you would feel to be on the receiving end. Terrorist is just a freedom fighter for the other side.

Didn't that describe at least the entire twenty-first century in international relations? And however much longer, if you wanted to talk about British Empires before the American one? Or Russian Empires, to say nothing of European colonialism?

"Would it work?" Tanerhald asked. "To just leave everyone alone?"

"It has never been tried," Mitch laughed. "So it could not make things any worse than they are now. Personally, if you folks did come down and start explaining that there were big, bad aliens out there, at least half the governments in the world would probably collapse overnight. And not the good half. Not sure where the US falls on that spectrum. I suppose it depends on how much of what I've learned over the last few months you wanted to put on a front-page somewhere."

"Sunlight cures many ailments," Kehoe said. "I can tell you how many I've been involved with. The rest of you are nowhere near as guilty as me, that's for damned sure. I like the thought of a painful year now. The casualties are likely to be in the thousands as people freak out, but it offers them something entirely new in the twenty-second century."

"What's that?" Joie asked.

He turned to her and smiled.

"Hope."

Joie nodded. She had learned the power of such a thing the hard way.

# CHAPTER 64

Valmy was in a room.

He had already explored the limits of it. Transparent walls that had resisted any blow he could unleash with his hands or feet. His pockets had been emptied at some point, stripping him of all potential weapons.

He was still not sure how he had gotten here.

One moment, he had been face down on the cold concrete, having been surprised by Daring and her friends. The next, he had been standing here, with only a flash of intense, white light separating the two.

It had to be the aliens.

He knew they existed. Had met at least three in his time. What were the limits of their technology?

Or their power?

Valmy did not know. He did know that they had hidden a starship. Had made it vanish off tracking radars specifically intended to see such things.

There had been a second ship. It had captured the first. Then vanished again.

Except capture was the wrong word. Daring had been on that ship.

And had somehow found him in Colorado, penetrating a secure base and capturing him.

Valmy would have said that was impossible, but Captain Daring was the best in the world at such a thing. Even against her own kind.

So he was in an invisible room.

A door appeared now. Outlines lighting up in the wall and something disappeared.

Daring was standing on the other side, along with the woman he recognized as Wěn Cōng Mǎ, the martial artist who had been training her. Dangerous woman.

More dangerous than Daring? Possibly. Two of them meant that they wished to control the situation. For him to understand that physicality was a second choice, presumably after talking.

Two others followed. A tall man and…

Yes, that was an alien. No way about it. Short. Tiny, but it gave the impression of control. A leader.

Light purple skin. Almost leathery. No hair. Eyes the wrong size and shape.

Humanoid, but that was about it.

Daring and the Cantonese woman took up positions in front of the two others. Guarding.

"We have a problem, General," Daring spoke first.

Valmy did not roll up onto his toes to attack. Considered it and discarded the notion as quickly as it had come.

He had been radically upgraded by his scientists. Daring had, as well. Perhaps more. Wěn just made it obvious that he could not expect to win a physical confrontation.

Ergo, talk.

"Go on," he replied.

"There are people out there watching Earth," Daring said. "They are freaking completely out at what you have started doing. Project Herakles was a combination of cyberware and genetics, so they didn't pay as close attention as they probably should have then. Project Cybernaut was purely electronic. What you've done to yourself, Chelsea, Garrison, and however many others, threatens galactic society."

"They weren't supposed to notice," Valmy retorted. If she knew that much, she probably knew more than he did.

Not many openings left he could exploit.

"Bandi was pretty good at hiding things," Daring smiled. "He's had a change of heart and told Tanerhald here everything."

That would be the small, purple alien. The one in charge, obviously, from the way the other three deferred to him. Bandi had been the one in charge in La Plata.

Bandi Algom. Alien agent. Working for some alien Party intent on overthrowing things out there with the help of humans.

Little had he known. Or had Algom come to realize that he'd lost control of the situation and decided to save the rest of the galaxy before Valmy and his army could escape Earth? That made the most sense.

If so, he was also smarter than he had appeared.

None of which did Valmy one bit of good.

"Now what?" Valmy asked.

"They scanned you when the beam grabbed you, General," Daring said. "So we know that you and the others are not fertile. That had been their greatest fear. Those of us who were upgraded to stop you are also unable to have children, so we only represent a threat to the present."

"The present?" Valmy asked, confused.

"You will live some three hundred years, General," she said with a smile. "At least according to scientists who have been trying to understand how dangerous humans are. If you could have borne advanced children, that's a new species on top of everything else. That, they will not allow."

"What will they allow?" he asked.

"Exile, Human," the purple one spoke now. Authority. Unbending command of the situation. Commanding General sort of voice. "You will be permanently removed from Earth. Others of your kind as well, plus those with the knowledge to make more. We will cause the remaining information to become corrupted, and will monitor your world to make sure that nobody else picks it up later."

Valmy could not hide his grimace. At the same time, he had laid out all those options at the beginning and calculated his chances.

Not every gamble wins.

"Just like that?" he asked, turning back to Daring.

"The alternative was a Carrington Event as only angry aliens could manage it, Bouchard," she growled at him. "I'm trying to save our entire species from extinction."

Carrington Event. 1859 CE. A solar flare so powerful that it induced magnetic fields in telegraph lines on the ground, causing some to catch fire. Northern lights visible as far south as Mexico.

Today, it would be utterly devastating. Yes, that might threaten the species, if they did it right.

Valmy felt defeat grip him by the back of the neck. It was one thing to gamble his own life and that of his soldiers, all of them volunteers.

It was something else to kill his world with his arrogance.

Because that's what it was.

Joie Daring had just turned out to be better than he had ever imagined.

"Why are you telling me these things?" he asked, concerned.

Were they going to just execute him anyway?

"We need to kidnap and remove several hundred Americans, General," Daring replied. "Scientists and their families. People who know enough to be a threat. My friends would like to you contact the key players in DC, both in Congress and the Pentagon, and explain to them that all such research will be permanently curtailed. And why. What did you call the operation, anyway?"

"Project Carpenter," Valmy said automatically. "You're taking everyone away? Just like that?"

"There has been conversation about offering a similar exile to other Humans," Daring smiled. "Enough to make it a small slice of home. Humantown, as it were, instead of Chinatown or Little Saigon like we have in so many American cities."

Valmy was shocked to hear such an option. Take everyone away and put them on a reservation somewhere?

Would it work?

Could he foment more revolution from the inside, or would they be watching him so closely that he just ended up getting himself killed later?

With three hundred or more years, how much could he see out there?

"Why aren't they demanding anything harsher?" he asked Daring.

"I convinced them that just removing the bad players was enough," she said. "That continuing to remove anyone who decided to try again would be sufficient threat to keep people honest. Personally, I think that we are less than a year from a starship appearing in the skies over DC and other places to introduce themselves and explain to everyone that the time has come to behave. I'm looking forward to it, even though I won't be there."

"You won't?" he asked.

"*Everyone* who has been modified must leave forever, Bouchard," Daring explained. "Everyone who knows how it is done joins them. Anyone trying later gets the same punishment. It was much better than the alternative. And that will hang out there like the Sword of Damocles until such time as Humanity is developed enough, polite enough, to be admitted to that greater civilization without us being a threat to everyone. Like you intended."

"So they will watch me like a hawk?" Valmy demanded.

"You especially," the purple alien stated. "Joie has asked for leniency in your case, and that of a few others who would normally be executed for your crimes. We have honored that. For now."

"He means you have a pardon for past behavior, Bouchard," Daring continued. "Anything you do after today likely gets that revoked and they put you in the ground. I don't think you deserve that sanction, but it was a close discussion with a lot of people. Don't make me regret going to bat for you."

Valmy nodded, surprised.

He'd seen Daring as his enemy. Set her up that way years ago when he ordered Kehoe to send her after *Mithras*, then burn her when she'd succeeded. Or when he'd ordered Kehoe to reactivate the woman, adding her as another game piece to a complicated board, just to see who else might show up.

He had not been expecting the rest of the aliens. Not this early.

And he wouldn't have given her the same benefit of the doubt.

Something more he needed to meditate on, when he got wherever it was he was going.

How had he screwed up this badly?

"And now?" he asked.

It felt like endgame here. Time to roll the credits and call it a day.

"And now, you will assist us in contacting everyone who needs to emerge from inside those shields Bandi gave you," Daring said. "That way, we can get them all with a minimum of fuss. Plus, we probably need to kidnap a few Senators, if we were able to understand some of your recent conversations. Since that's going to cause a shitstorm, we need to brief the President. And others. Or rather, I do, so I would appreciate you telling me everything I need to know to keep a lid on things."

"We can't do this in secrecy?" he asked.

"There will be no more secrecy, Human," the man thundered. Tanerhald, though he wasn't sure if that was first name, last, or species. "Joie is going to save Humanity from what you've done. Or not. That decision is yours."

Valmy gulped. As Good Cop/Bad Cop games went, he'd hardly ever seen better.

What made it worse was that neither of them was bluffing. He could tell that.

Anything he did now risked everything he had spent a lifetime in service of. And everything else.

"Okay," he said, letting go of a heavy breath. "This debriefing will take a while."

# CHAPTER 65

Joie sat quietly in the mess hall with a mug of hot chocolate of unknown provenance. Just like all the rest of the food. Maybe she could point them at a few of the uglier crime cartels to steal suitcases of money from? Two birds, one stone, as the narcotics trade had always been a thing of cash on the barrel. LOTS of cash.

She grinned. The door opened.

Ernesta.

"That look is pure evil," the woman said, stepping close and grinning back.

Joie shrugged.

"Thinking about people we could rob," she offered. "Folks who deserve it, so that Yormevs has real money to spend on buying supplies. Easier, I suppose, than just selling off gold bars here and there. Or printing their own."

"Ha," Ernesta laughed and sat across from her. "That might be fun. Not that I've *ever* done anything like that in my career. Pinky swear."

Joie supposed that she had. Ernesta had been on the wrong side of the law her whole life, born and raised in a criminal syndicate family politely at war with an incompetent Mexican government.

At the same time, both them and the US government were probably entirely wrong here. Ethically wrong. Legal just meant whatever laws you could get passed, including slavery, which Mexico had done away with long before the US.

Hell, the entire point of Texas was white settlers rebelling against the Mexican government because they wanted to keep their slaves. A lot of people had died over wanting to do something that was legal, and wrong.

"Now you're sad," Ernesta said, watching.

"Exhausted," Joie said. "And angry. I've spent twenty years serving my country, one way or the other. Doing everything I was told without question. That got me a job in a coffee franchise in DC, no friends, no life, and no hope."

"We're going to make it right," Ernesta said.

"I know," Joie said. "But a lot of people will get hurt in the process, because they will adamantly refuse to admit that they might have been wrong in the first place, regardless of the evidence put before them."

"At least we know enough now to start them on the road to recovery," Ernesta said. "Your President is known to be a pretty smart guy. Mexico probably collapses for a while. Hopefully, there isn't another Pancho Villa out there, just itching to cross the border to get back at Americans."

"Same," Joie agreed. "That would just be the frosting on the cake."

"Personally, I think Costa Rica has the right idea," Ernesta continued. "They don't have an army. And they have a government that has always been focused on social justice, rather than the oligarchies of their neighbors. All of their neighbors."

"Part of me wishes I could be here to see what happens when the Brakhua and others do come down," Joie snickered. "Just to watch the entire economy flip-flop as everyone in power is suddenly junior varsity again. And can't just buy their way into power again."

"A few will want to go to the stars, just to see what's out there," Ernesta nodded. "That South African guy who started the car company and then got into rockets almost a century ago. That was always his dream. Pity he died before he could see this. But there will be others."

"That's my hope," Joie sighed. "That we can coexist with the

Brakhua, the Heecha, the Danorak, and whoever else. That we can learn to live in peace, even with ourselves. Long road."

"A very long road," Ernesta agreed. "But we have started. And we will be able to talk to the right people as we go. Hopefully, they will listen."

Joie nodded.

Hopefully.

# CHAPTER 66

Joie wasn't used to civilian clothing. Even something Ernesta had picked out and had custom tailored by one of Yormevs's machines. Stylish and utterly elegant, at least according to Ernesta, who really knew these things.

Carter's wolf whistle when he saw her probably spoke louder.

Straight-leg slacks. Slate gray with razor-thin pinstripes that probably made her look eight feet tall. Matching blazer, cut low for two buttons. Soft green button-up shirt without a tie. Hair in a complicated braid Ernesta had done.

She materialized in a room. Larger than an office. And not the oval office, because his advisors had recommended someplace they thought a little easier to contain. As if the rumors of this meeting would be kept in a single space.

Four marines. Combat troops rather than slick, pretty boys. Armed, but nobody was pointing a pistol at her right now. Just holding it down on their thigh.

The President of the United States of America always tended to be tall when men were elected. Something about height suggesting strength, even though that was pure Madison Avenue.

Late fifties, at the point where his hair had been still half-brown six years ago when he was first elected, and now was almost completely white. The weight of the office did that to every President, it seemed. Strong face, in a style she might have called aquiline. Pure Anglo, even though that hadn't always been the case in the twenty-first century. Yale Law. Harvard undergrad. Pretty tie.

He sat at the far end of the room, at the head of a long, oval table. Joie recognized the Secretary of Defense on the man's right, and the Chairman of the Joint Chiefs—her nominal boss, except that she was technically Unlawfully Absent from Duty—on the President's left.

National Security Advisor and several of her ilk at the table, plus a few technical experts, at least one of which Joie recognized as being near the top of TRC.

She took a breath, smiled, and nodded to the man at the far end of the room.

"Good morning, Mister President," she said. "Thank you for taking this meeting."

"Wouldn't have missed it for the world," he said in that breezy way that resonated so well with Midwest voters. "I'm given to understand that most people call you *Captain Daring*?"

"My friends simply call me Joie, sir," she said.

He smiled.

"I think for today you can get away with calling me Ed then, Joie," the President of the United States said.

"Ed," she nodded, moving with great care to the chair at this end, several empty seats removed from everybody else, and sat.

"That was one hell of an entrance, Joie!" Ed exclaimed.

"I currently represent folks that wanted to make sure you understood the newly evolved circumstances," she said. "That there will be changes. Unfortunately, at the end of a gun, but my friends and I were able to prevent them from taking more drastic measures. This is an outcome that will satisfy them, at least for now, as long as you, your successors, and several other leaders around the world abide by their rules."

Ed turned to his SecDef. Smiled at the man.

"Why wasn't I told any of this before?" he asked in a polite voice. And a razor is a polite blade.

That man had the decency to look chagrined.

"Ed, one of your predecessors, almost a century ago, was so bad at keeping secrets that the military actually found it necessary to create a type of security clearance that excludes certain folks," Joie stepped in to save the man.

Around her, she felt the four marines start to relax, but they stayed vigilant, and made sure they were on all sides of her, so that she could not maneuver. That would help everybody's nerves.

"Not tell the Commander-in-Chief?" Ed asked with exasperated disdain.

But then, he'd been a Senator once. Chairman of the Armed Services committee and something of an expert on the topic.

"It stayed on the books," Joie said. "I can show you the various orders by previous Chairs of the Joint Chiefs of Staff. My technical experts have the ability to penetrate any computer system in the world. And have. Technology Research Command managed to maneuver itself into being covered by those statutes, so that most of what they were doing only got reported to you or the Senate in broad, mostly vague terms that hid more than they revealed."

"Such as?" Ed asked, focusing those sharp, blue eyes on her again. The man was magnetic that way.

"Did you bring the thermometer?" she asked.

One of the aides reached under the table, presumably into a briefcase, and put one on the table.

"What's my current temperature?" Joie asked.

The man pointed the thing at her and clicked it. Then banged on it and cursed under his breath.

"Fucker's broken," he said.

"Probably not," Joie said. "What was the reading?"

"Forty-one centigrade," he said. "But you wouldn't be functional at that temperature."

"Correct," Joie said. "If I was still Human."

The whole room fell to deathly silence.

"Joie, did I understand you correctly?" Ed asked in that *aw, shucks* way he did. "Not Human?"

"That is correct, Ed," she nodded. "In order to fight what General Bouchard had done with Project Carpenter, my alien friends upgraded me."

"I seem to recall from earlier reports that you were missing an arm, an ear, and an eye, as recently as six months ago," Ed said.

"They removed everything cybernetic," Joie replied. "Then used existing parts to model new ones. Then upgraded me significantly."

"How significantly?" Ed asked.

The rest of the room was still catching up. But Ed was in charge.

"About twice as strong as your strongest soldiers," Joie said, nodding to one of the marines close by. "Comparable to professional weight-lifters, without the mass. And faster than Olympic sprinters, or ultramarathoners. And I could heal from a bullet wound almost in real time, at least theoretically. Fortunately, nobody has gotten shot in all these adventures and shenanigans to test that."

Ed nodded.

"And Bouchard did the same to himself?" he asked.

"And fourteen others," Joie agreed. "All of them will be removed from Earth to permanent exile on an alien world. All of the scientists who know enough about the process will go with them. Families will be given the option, but it will be a permanent choice if they leave. I am still working with my various alien superiors to open a test program for Human emigration in controlled numbers. They have not yet gotten buyoff from their own leaders that we can be allowed off this rock."

"I feel like I'm missing important parts, Joie," Ed interjected. "How about you start at the top, so I have a solid grasp of what decisions I need to make."

Joie nodded. She'd booked the man for the entire afternoon. And possibly longer, as this was potentially the single most important decision in the history of the office itself. Maybe the world.

Certainly the civilization.

The Vice President was somewhere in California today, prepared to take power if something happened.

Looked like it wouldn't. That would be good.

"It all really starts in 1928, when an alien man named Bandi Algom comes to Earth and starts working with a small, German, fringe group of scientists to push Human technology forward…" Joie began.

# CHAPTER 67

Mitch had been surprised by the summons, but came. Yormevs and Tanerhald were in the main mess hall that seemed to be where everybody had important meetings these days. Especially when there were so many folks around.

He did note that not everyone was here. Bouchard and the others were still technically prisoners, so they had been transferred to Tanerhald's ship.

But the core group, as he liked to think of it, was here. Kehoe, Stone, Freya, representing the active duty folks. Him, too, he supposed that he should be in that group. Joie, Romana, Ernesta, and Carter. Cōng Mǎ and Bandi.

"We have just gotten confirmation from the White House," Tanerhald announced as they all got settled, coffee or cocoa as they preferred. "Joie's embassy was successful, and they are going to make all the people on Mitch's list available, after briefing them. Some will no doubt cause trouble, but we believe that most will look on this as an adventure. Plus, as biological researchers, they will be confronted with many new alien species to study, in addition to becoming the primary medical experts on Humanity for everyone else."

Cheers around the table. Mugs clinked together. Looking back,

Mitch could not imagine that it would have all come down to this. Especially after the way Joie just showed up on his doorstep one afternoon, in the middle of freaking nowhere.

"Also, I have extra good news, and wanted to share with all of you immediately," Yormevs continued, causing everyone to slide to the edge of their seats. "I have been in negotiations with Tanerhald and his superiors. They have allowed me to make this offer to you. It must be done in complete secrecy, now and forever, because of the implications, but they are willing to allow all of you to remain on Earth, in recognition of the immense service you have done for everyone involved."

"I thought they wouldn't allow any advanced or modified Humans to remain behind," Kehoe spoke up. "That was the issue going in. They could be upgraded, and then had to depart forever, even if they were successful."

"That was indeed the deal we offered," Yormevs nodded. "Tanerhald is a most stubborn negotiator. However, I do have an out. We can reverse the process on the four of you."

Mitch thought his heart had stopped. Certainly, the ringing in his ears was suddenly much louder. There weren't enough people in here for true bedlam to break out, but the sound was trying.

Finally Ernesta put her fingers in her mouth and whistled. That got everyone quiet.

"How?" Joie asked.

"We had to baseline each of you," Yormevs grinned. "Then reset you to a youthful age that made you even more formidable. It was only from there that we pushed your design as far as we could. Because we still have those baselines, we could reset you to being merely Human, aged twenty-five, and no longer a threat to the future of the galaxy."

"You specifically told me you couldn't do that," Joie pointed out harshly.

"I lied," Yormevs said with a smile. "I needed you committed. Willing to give your life to this mission. It was the only way I thought you would see it through. Tanerhald is willing to bend his rules if you are returned to a factory-default setting, as it were. None of you know enough about our technology to be a threat, nor about the modification process. There is no reason you should have to leave Earth forever, especially if you would be forced to live among other Humans who would rightly resent you. They will be forever isolated from Earth, so no one remaining would know the truth."

"Why can't you undo Bouchard, then?" Carter asked.

"We do not have his baseline, Carter," Yormevs replied with a nod. "Not like we could do with you when we put you into the machine to remove you hardware. Thus, we could not establish what would be normal for him."

"Plus," Bandi interjected, "he's an asshole who deserves a long life of exile as punishment for the shit he's caused. The others volunteered, so they get punished as well. You shouldn't have to. I argued for Yormevs on this one."

Mitch turned to Ernesta. Saw a light come on in her eyes. She probably didn't want more kids, since she had grandkids already, but they'd talked about going away forever. What they might do, out there among the stars.

Could they stay in Seattle or Guadalajara? Or anywhere else on Earth? Or would they still want to join Tanerhald and the rest on the grand adventure?

Her smile spoke volumes, all of it good. They would find time to talk more later.

For now, he turned his analytical mind to Yormevs and the others.

"People will figure it out," Mitch said. "Everyone here exists as a person. If they return, they will show up on various radars of potentially inimical folks who will want to know what happened. And how they might test any of those four to see if there were secrets they could steal, not caring initially that they end up going to live with Bouchard as a result."

Bandi laughed out loud like a braying mule.

"You people trust computers," he said. "Dumb idea. Anything in a computer can be changed. And records of the change removed if you do it right. Poof. All that gone. Hell, with the kinds of access Yormevs has, he could transfer a couple million dollars into your bank account and have everyone agree it was legitimate, because they would look at the computer records with all the right everything and assume it was copacetic. Dumb. Just another mark of your primitive nature."

Mitch wanted to scowl at the man, but Bandi was grinning ear to ear as he spoke.

"Is that true?" he asked Yormevs.

"Functionally," the man agreed. "We can manipulate the records in the right places to create most of you as entirely new people. Necessary, in any case, as both Carter and Ernesta look nothing like their most recent passport photos in addition to being wanted criminals. Plus, we will not be leaving you alone, though nobody will outwardly interfere until Tanerhald talks to his ultimate superiors for guidance. We can continue to adjust computerized records as necessary to protect you. This assumes that you wish to remain. Romana has taken service with my crew after spending some time here, as have several of her people who were not upgraded. They also have the option to stay or go."

Mitch shut his mouth at that point. Too many variables, but if they thought they could adjust things, he was willing to assume that they were right. And he needed to talk to Ernesta, because everything had just changed.

He looked at Joie instead. Saw the pensiveness in her eyes.

She'd assumed that she would be going away when it was all done. Losing everything she'd just regained. All the friends she'd found that she'd talked about, utterly surprised.

"If we stay, could we leave again later?" she asked Tanerhald, rather than Yormevs.

He would be the decision maker.

"Yes," Tanerhald replied. "In your specific cases, I am not sure that you wouldn't be required to travel back and forth, as an ambassador perhaps. At least later, after we have formally ruined everybody's lunch."

They all laughed at that. Tanerhald was learning some impressive idioms in both English and Spanish. And some excellent dirty jokes.

"I cannot decide now," Joie said, looking around the table and getting nods.

Yormevs and Tanerhald both nodded as well.

"We have several weeks rounding up all our stray calves," Yormevs said. "A few might even consider running, though it will not do them any good. We know where all of Bouchard's shields were placed, and the President assures me that he will send in troops if necessary to recover people on the list."

Mitch nodded. A few days would see everyone comfortable with whatever decision they needed to make.

He and Ernesta shared a smile. Whatever it was, it would be good.

# CHAPTER 68

Joie was driving. She'd rented the car. Or rather, she'd had Mitch tickle a system to get it all lined up and paid for, using a little bit of financial chicanery that they would eventually make right.

She hoped.

There were a lot of changes coming. Perhaps as long as a year of calm before the storm. It would leak, but too many conspiracy theories would obscure the honest truth of aliens coming down to chat.

She was Human again. Whole. Reborn. Somewhere, a system would be paying her a monthly retirement as a one hundred percent disabled veteran with twenty years' service as a retired captain, so there would be money. And both Yormevs and Tanerhald had assured her that there would be more, for everything she had done.

It was good.

So she was driving. Everyone else had fallen silent as they made their final approach. Carter was next to her, with Ernesta and Romana in back of the cute, blue, four-door hatchback.

Joie turned into the parking lot and found a spot right next to the front door. She pulled in and put it in park.

She looked over at Carter.

"Can I admit to being a little frightened?" he asked.

"You can," Joie grinned. "But I don't honestly think Amy will really throw you out. Or kick your ass. You will have a lot of explaining to do, but she likes the lumberjack look."

And he had it going, with the beard finally full and his hair long and roughly slicked back. Handsome, now that he was more properly scaled. Just not her type at all.

"And you won't come in and run interference?" Carter asked, almost plaintively, eliciting a round of laughs from all the women in the car.

"You're a big boy, Carter," Ernesta teased. "You should be able to handle it."

"She made me nervous when I weighed three times as much and could shotput a motorcycle," he admitted.

"All the more reason to be polite, tough guy," Romana laughed now. "Go, get yourself some coffee. We'll be there in a bit."

Joie caught the false note in her voice, but didn't say anything.

Carter grumbled, but got out. Walked in the door of the coffee shop where Joie had once worked, and didn't immediately run back out with an angry manager chasing him.

Joie knew she was working today. Had confirmed it, and then seen Amy inside when she pulled up.

But Carter needed to do this himself.

She unbuckled her seat belt and turned to look in back.

Romana had a pained face.

"You're not staying, are you?" Joie asked.

"No," Romana shook her head. "There's too much out there to see. At least as a normal Human again, I can return later, but Yormevs made me one hell of an offer, and I intend to take him up on it. I just wanted to see if Carter had the balls to actually walk in there, after what you've told me about previous times."

"He's a dork, but he stood up when he needed to," Joie said. "Like so many others."

Romana had a sad smile.

"Thank you for coming for me," Romana said. "I've said it before, but now I truly understand everything all of you went through, when you thought something bad had happened to me."

"That's what friends do," Ernesta said, even before Joie could.

It was.

"And if you need us, any of us, do not hesitate to call," Joie said. "I will always be there when you need me. Whenever. Wherever."

They hugged, but it was awkward, sitting like this. Romana opened her door, so they all got out and hugged in the parking lot. Tears flowed, but it was good.

Kehoe had showed up on her doorstep because Bouchard had ordered it, lost as to what could have possibly happened to one of his top agents, vanished right out of the middle of a base in the middle of the night.

Nobody could have possibly predicted that outcome, except Romana and Yormevs. And they hadn't been willing to talk at that point.

So much had changed.

"Anywhere," Romana said, stepping back and sniffling at both of them. "I will hold you to that."

"Anywhere," Joie agreed.

A column of light engulfed her friend and Romana Pham disappeared.

Joie sighed. Ernesta stepped close and put an arm around her waist. She let the woman hold her weight for a bit, but Carter was still inside, so hopefully that was going well.

She suddenly didn't have the energy to deal with explaining to everyone she had worked with. Those that remained, with transfers and new hires. Amy was Carter's problem.

"Now what?" Ernesta asked after a minute.

"Right now?" Joie asked. "There's a nice place where we can get some good half-smoke and mambo sauce not far from here."

"Then what?" Ernesta asked, turning her to look Joie in the eyes.

"Then I think I'll come visit you and Mitch and Celeste out in Seattle sometime," Joie said. "Or Guadalajara. Or wherever."

"But?" Ernesta asked.

"But I lived without hope for two years," Joie said. "And the last year has been a mad dash to save the world from our own stupidities. I think I'd like to just wander around for a bit, and absorb some of what it really means to be Human. I haven't been for more than a decade. Not really. Project Cybernaut turned me into a cybernetic killing machine secret agent. I haven't stopped to have time for myself in…decades."

"You'll do fine," Ernesta assured her.

Joie shrugged.

From everything to nothing to everything again. And now a special kind of nothing, where nobody was relying on her for much of anything.

She chirped the locks closed on the rental and Ernesta hooked elbows with her, like they were back in La Plata that first time, before all hell had broken loose. Two tourists out for a jaunt. A saunter.

Some half-smoke and mambo sauce, with fries on the side.

A taste of home, whatever that was. Wherever.

"What about Carter?" Ernesta asked as they left the parking lot and turned left.

"He has my number," Joie laughed. "If Amy's not interested, we can find him some other babes. He deserves to be happy."

"We all do, Joie," Ernesta said.

Joie nodded. They all did.

She was looking forward to finding it, but she had something better.

Friends.

# READ MORE

# ABOUT THE AUTHOR

Blaze Ward writes science fiction in the Alexandria Station universe (Jessica Keller, The Science Officer, The Story Road, etc.) as well as several other science fiction universes, such as Star Dragon, the Dominion, and more. He also writes odd bits of high fantasy with swords and orcs. In addition, he is the Editor and Publisher of *Boundary Shock Quarterly Magazine*. You can find out more at his website www.blazeward.com, as well as Facebook, Goodreads, and other places.

Blaze's works are available as ebooks, paper, and audio, and can be found at a variety of online vendors. His newsletter comes out regularly, and you can also follow his blog on his website. He really enjoys interacting with fans, and looks forward to any and all questions—even ones about his books!

**Never miss a release!**
If you'd like to be notified of new releases, sign up for my newsletter.

http://www.blazeward.com/newsletter/

**Buy More!**
Did you know that you can buy directly from my website?

https://www.blazeward.com/shop/

**Connect with Blaze!**

Web: www.blazeward.com

Boundary Shock Quarterly (BSQ):
https://www.boundaryshockquarterly.com/

# ABOUT KNOTTED ROAD
# PRESS

Knotted Road Press fiction specializes in dynamic writing set in mysterious, exotic locations.

Knotted Road Press non–fiction publishes autobiographies, business books, cookbooks, and how–to books with unique voices.

Knotted Road Press creates DRM–free ebooks as well as high–quality print books for readers around the world.

With authors in a variety of genres including literary, poetry, mystery, fantasy, and science fiction, Knotted Road Press has something for everyone.

Knotted Road Press
www.KnottedRoadPress.com